THE FIRES OF SHALSHA

Novels by John Michael Greer

The Weird of Hali:

I – *Innsmouth*

II – *Kingsport*

III – *Chorazin*

IV – *Dreamlands*

V – *Providence*

VI – *Red Hook*

VII – *Arkham*

Others:

The Fires of Shalsha

Star's Reach

Twilight's Last Gleaming

Retrotopia

The Shoggoth Concerto

The Nyogtha Variations

A Voyage to Hyperborea

The Seal of Yueh Lao

Journey Star

The Witch of Criswell

The Book of Haatan

The Hall of Homeless Gods

THE FIRES OF SHALSHA

John Michael Greer

Published in 2024 by
Sphinx Books
London

British Library Cataloguing in Publication Data

A C.I.P. for this book is available from the British Library

ISBN-13: 978-1-91595-216-5

Typeset by Medlar Publishing Solutions Pvt Ltd, India

www.aeonbooks.co.uk/sphinx

THE SIX LAWS

One: No hierarchy of superiors demanding obedience from inferiors, nor any organization claiming the right to interfere in the affairs of communities except in defense of the six laws here established, shall exist on Eridan. Deliberate violation of this law shall be punished by death.

Two: No permanent community of more than ten thousand persons, nor any community located less than ten kilometers from any other community, shall exist on Eridan. Deliberate violation of this law shall be punished by death.

Three: No act or threat of violence by members of one community against members or property of any other community, except in defense of the six laws here established, shall occur on Eridan. Deliberate violation of this law shall be punished by death.

Four: No weapon of mass destruction, nor any armed or armored vehicle, nor any weapon having an effective range of more than one kilometer, shall exist on Eridan. Deliberate violation of this law shall be punished by death.

Five: No contact with machines or remains of machines made by or under the former Planetary Directorate, beyond that required to repel or destroy them, shall occur on Eridan. Deliberate violation of this law shall be punished by death.

Six: No action that causes significant damage to planetary or regional ecologies shall occur on Eridan. Deliberate violation of this law shall be punished by death.

CHAPTER 1

THE SHADOW IN THE FOREST

1

The air around him stank of blood.

Stefan Jatanni considered the wreckage before him; his right hand hovered a few centimeters from the grip of his gun. Mist drifting through the clearing made pale shadows of trees and the dozen or so corpses within sight. Further off, dim blues and violets of the forest blurred into featureless gray. Patches of color—tents, or what was left of them, and the clothing of the dead—were muted in the ashen light. Nothing moved but the mist.

Nothing in sight, Stefan amended, cautioning himself. He walked out into the middle of the clearing, stepping around the nearer corpses, scanning the surrounding forest left, right, ahead. Behind, two others in the black close-fitting garments of the Halka stood motionless. A few meters further back, some two dozen Shelter folk whispered among themselves, watched Stefan or the dead. Like the corpses, they wore looser clothing of many colors, browns and forest hues, and the only weapons they carried were brush knives and long antique rifles. They had come this far in the first place only against the advice of Stefan and his colleagues.

A first trace of wind stirred the mist as Stefan reached the clearing's center. Vague swirls of movement formed and faded between nearby trees, and more distant shapes came into sight. Subtle awareness, intangible as the mist, whispered *there is no enemy* in his mind. He sighed and let combat mode fall away. "We're too late," he said aloud: to himself, the forest, the dead. "They'll have left hours ago."

The two in black behind him glanced at each other. One walked out to where he stood.

"Stefan."

"Amery." He turned around, considered her: brown hair tied loosely back, serious brown eyes: a student of his, not so long ago. "What do you think of this?"

"I'm not yet sure." Amery looked at the nearby corpses. "Outrunners. That, or a battle-drone. I would much prefer outrunners."

Stefan allowed a smile. "Granted."

"I'll search the perimeter, if you like."

"I would. And Toren?"

"Will stay here." A slight motion of her head indicated the others. "They need one of us. They're frightened— understandably."

"They chose to come."

"Still." When his frown did not break: "It's our burden, Stefan. *Halka na.*"

Unwillingly, he nodded. "*Halka na.*"

Minutes later, when Amery had vanished into the remnants of the fog and Stefan himself knelt beside one of the corpses, the words still remained in his ears. *We are Halka*, they meant: the black garments and the gun at his hip given voice, perhaps. He muttered the phrase once, then brought his mind back wholly to the task at hand. Subtle awareness had already searched for signs of life among the sprawled bodies, and found none. By Halka tradition his next duty was to determine what had happened, and why.

This first one, now: a young man of perhaps seventeen, shot three times in the back. From the tracks leading to the corpse and the way the meadowmoss lay crushed beneath it, he had been running, running hard, when the bullets struck him. Stefan glanced at the wounds, and frowned. Outrunners had guns, he'd fought some who had, but those were mostly long rifles cobbled together by anyone with a trace of technician's skills, wildly inaccurate at anything over fifteen or twenty meters. They had to be reloaded by hand after each shot, and yet since any one of the wounds would have dropped the man all three must have hit within a few seconds.

He stood up, followed the young man's trail to the far side of the clearing. Tracks in the meadowmoss, faint but clear to subtle awareness, told him something of the last few minutes of that one's life. He'd been there beside the meria tree, gathering newly ripe seeds for planting closer to the Shelter, when he saw or heard something further up the slope. He stood facing it without moving long enough to crush the mossflowers, then turned, dropped his bag of seeds—there it lay, atop a broken cluster of bone-white fungoids—and ran until the bullets hit him. More bodies lay sprawled in one or another of the graceless postures of sudden death near the meria tree, some shot while running, others cut down as they stood. There, for instance: an old woman who had been kneeling to gather seeds already on the ground. She had risen to her feet, took a few uncertain steps in the direction of whatever it was, and then took bullets in the throat and one leg, fell backwards, died. Three tents, Stefan counted, and maybe twenty bodies. No one who ran had time to run far. It had happened very fast, then.

Beyond the clearing, tall thildas loomed up into the last of the mist. The reek of blood was stronger among them. Stefan walked on, noting the way the corpses lay, the telltale marks in the litter of dead summer-leaves. The events of the massacre took on a ghostly solidity in his mind as he walked further on into the forest, and the corpses and footprints added up. The killer or killers came downslope in something close to a straight line. Those people further upslope, closer to whatever it had been, ran first, and most of them died first.

Those further down had little time to react between the firing of the first shots, which would have given the alarm, and their own deaths—a matter of a few minutes, probably—and yet in that time the attackers had fired more than a hundred shots in the area Stefan had seen. Each trail he saw ended in an intact corpse; none of the bodies had been stripped, or had meat cut from them for protein, and no footprints but those of the dead marked the meadowmoss.

Not outrunners, then. Stefan stopped among the knotted roots of a thilda, stood there with his arms folded for a long moment. Around him, pale shafts of sunlight began to break through the forest canopy, setting drifting spore-dust to sparkle and lighting patches of meadowmoss. He glanced at one of these last, and remembered a test that might make all other clues unnecessary.

The hand lens counted as one of the lesser Halka tools, but it had an ancient place in the traditions of the order. Through Stefan's, the gray-violet fur of meadowmoss became a mass of featherlike shapes mixed with long fungoidal threads and the buds of mossflowers. The tips of the feathers ... yes, they curled back as though scorched, and the few uncurled tips had gone pale. Halka used that trace during the Insurgency, when the battle-drones they hunted were not battered remnants washed out of old mudslides and river sands but the pride and chief strength of a dying civilization; the fighters against Shalsha learned to read the subtlest of clues, or died themselves. That degree of skill saw little use in these more peaceful times, to be sure, but the Halka preserved the old lore, and not alone in books. Stefan moved the lens to two other places on the patch of meadowmoss. Both showed the telltale marks of lifter-field burn, and since lifter fields were among the banned technologies that meant, had to mean, a battle-drone.

As he returned the hand lens to his pocket, a whisper of sound to his left and a prickle of subtle awareness announced Amery's presence. Without looking up, Stefan said, "Not outrunners."

"I know."

He glanced up at her then. "What did you find?"

"Tracks in arrowgrass north of here."

Stefan nodded. "A battle-drone?"

"Six of them."

"Six?" He got to his feet. "You're certain?"

"As certain as I can be, yes." She motioned up the gentle slope. "This way."

Maybe a hundred meters to the north the long rise crested, and the ground fell away among weathered gray rocks. At the foot of the slope an arrowgrass plain began, nearly a kilometer of chest-high grass between the place where the two sen Halka stood and the line of deep blue where forest rose up again. In the grass lines too straight to be natural showed faintly.

"Linear tracks a meter and a half wide," said Amery, "with the grass broken off and scorched a meter above the ground. About two hundred meters out, they fan out from a single line going further north. I'm guessing that the drones came in along that track, spread out, came over the edge at six different points all at once. There's another trail, a single one, that starts about sixty meters from here." She gestured to the west. "I assume they left that way."

"Northwards also?"

Amery nodded. "If you wish to see …"

"Thank you, no. There's no need."

"There are no other tracks into or out of the area, barring those more than twenty-four hours old." She glanced at him. "Stefan, is all this as unusual as I think?"

He considered that. "In my experience? Yes."

They went back through the wood to the clearing where the people from Talin Shelter waited. Unspoken questions all but cried out in the silence. Stefan glanced at Amery with a fractional change of expression, as if to say, *this is yours if you wish it*; she replied with a glance, a minute shake of her head, the silent innerspeech of the Halka: *you are senior among us here, Stefan. This is your place.*

"As far as I can tell, there's no one left alive," he said aloud. "A group of six battle-drones came here from the north, attacked the camp, left the way they came."

The middle-aged woman who had led the accompanying party looked at him with round eyes. "There were more than a hundred people here, sen Halka. No one escaped?"

Stefan met her gaze, then lowered his. "I can't say for certain. We haven't searched the whole camp area. I think, though, that if anyone survived the attack they probably died during the night. The drones were very thorough."

She stared at him for a moment longer, then turned and forced her way blindly through the surrounding people toward the clearing and the dead. "She'll have her child to mourn," one of the others said quietly. "Sen Halka, we've sent runners back to the Shelter with the news. I hope that was well done."

"It was," said Stefan. "Thank you for seeing to that."

"Will more sen Halka be coming?" another asked, a young man cradling a rifle easily three times his own age.

"They'll be here in force shortly," Stefan said, "with all the weapons they can carry. You'll have the help you need."

"Good." Then, with visible nervousness: "Do you expect the drones to return here?"

That cut off what little talking had begun among the Shelter folk. "I don't know," said Stefan. "It would be sensible to keep watch."

The young man nodded, turned, went upslope. The tight knot of people around the three sen Halka came unraveled. As the last few moved away, the third sen Halka faced the others. "Someone needs to follow those things. Six of them, Stefan? Forgive me, but are you certain?"

Stefan glanced at Amery, who answered, "There are six separate trails in arrowgrass. You'll want to see them, Toren."

"I will indeed." Then, to Stefan, and in a more diffident tone: "One of us needs to stay and prepare a judgment, and you're senior here."

"I know." He considered both of them. "I'll see to it."

Toren nodded, and took a map from inside his coat. Amery caught Stefan's gaze and in the Halka innerspeech said, *I know you would rather hunt the drones. If you ask it I will stay in your place.*

Stefan shook his head minutely. *My thanks, but no. This hunt is yours and Toren's.*

She nodded, and said aloud, "I haven't hunted drones before. What do I need to know?"

"If you don't know already it's too late." He permitted a smile. "Stay out of range, record the drones' path and actions, and don't engage them directly if you can possibly avoid it. If you must fight, unless you're sure of your target, use grenades." He unclipped four short metal cylinders from his belt, handed two to Amery and two to Toren. "You may need these."

"Thank you," Toren said. "I'm not certain how far we should follow the drones."

"Two days?" Amery suggested. "Three, perhaps. If we haven't returned in six, don't expect us."

"I won't. *Halka na.*" He held out his hand at shoulder level, palm down; they placed theirs atop it, repeating the phrase, one momentarily with Halka since Mariel's time. Toren and Amery turned away, and without another word set out across the clearing at a lope. Stefan watched them until the trees hid them from sight.

He sighed then, and went more slowly up the slope. Vital as it was, the work ahead of him held little appeal. It would be his task to put together the story of what had happened, in the same way that he might report on a quarrel between Shelters or an accusation involving one of the six Laws. Tradition, and the experience of generations of Halka, made his initial judgment a thing of great importance. Stefan knew already the framework on which he'd build that judgment, but he needed a more precise sense of the flow of events during the handful of minutes it took for the slaughter to begin and end. Above all, he knew, he needed to work out the movements of the drones, and from that and the old lore try to guess at the programming the machines followed. That was the crucial point; the dead were dead, but if the drones could be anticipated they might be ambushed and destroyed before any more lives were lost.

Disciplines honed by years of practice cleared his mind as he came to the far side of the clearing and started into the thilda grove. A thin dusting of silvery spores, set drifting by the breeze, had settled already over the corpses in the wood. Footprints left by the Shelter folk lay over the fading marks made the evening before, but not enough of them to hide the signs he needed to find. Now and then, as he walked from place to place in the few hundred meters between the clearing and the arrowgrass plain, he came across one or another of the people from Talin Shelter in the company of a dead friend, sibling, parent, child. Others, without such ties to the dead, kept watch in case the drones returned or simply wandered through the forest much as Stefan did, blind with horror or with tears, seeing little where he saw much. Some of these stared at the sen Halka as he examined the mud on the soles of a dead woman's boots or used his hand lens to check for lifter-field burn on the meadowmoss atop a log storm-felled a dozen winters before. For his part, Stefan barely noticed them as awareness caught at the details he sought, fit them into a first sketch of the pattern he needed to find.

Finally, Stefan paused on a low hillock not far from the clearing and folded his arms, thinking. Jewelflies, long and bright-colored, flitted back and forth across the clearing. Behind him, he knew, one of the drones had come howling out from behind a meria thicket with guns blazing, and cut down thirty-eight people in a few seconds. The dead lay in two loose clusters a few meters away to his left, where two women from the Shelter now knelt, crying. That was clear enough—but subtle awareness stirred, warned of something not yet noticed. He frowned, cleared away his thoughts and heard the whisper of the inner-mind: *movement*.

Combat mode was on him in a fraction of a second, and his hand hovered over the grip of his gun just as fast. The drones? Subtle awareness denied it, and the strident whine of lifter fields would have been audible over the fitful wind for half a kilometer or more. The hush of the forest around him lay unbroken; nothing moved visibly but jewelflies, drifting spores, and the two women among the dead; his awareness shot outwards in all directions, searching, and then caught on a still figure huddled between a thilda trunk and a gray boulder about ten meters away. He stared, and then ran toward it.

The body was a young man's, maybe twenty years old, his haggard face half buried in the bloodstained cloth of a loose robe. Wide empty eyes stared blindly at the ground near his feet. Dead, Stefan thought, dead for certain—but corpses do not breathe, and as the sen Halka skidded to a halt on the litter of dead leaves the faint sense of motion resolved itself into the rising and falling, faint but regular, of the folds of the robe over the young man's chest.

Stefan dropped to one knee beside him, pressed three fingers against the man's neck. The flesh felt cool to the touch, but the carotid artery still pulsed feebly against Stefan's fingertips. Glancing over him, Stefan realized that he had no visible wounds at all; blood caked his robe, yes, but none of it seemed to be his own. Still, if not dead, he was in shock so deep he might well not survive it. Stefan's presence did not register at all in those empty eyes.

"Sen Halka?"

Stefan looked back over his shoulder. The two women who had been among the dead stood a short distance away. The elder went on: "He is ..." She could not finish.

"The drones missed one," Stefan said. "Yes. He's alive."

"Oh bright Earth," the old woman said, and burst into tears. The younger asked, "What can we do, sen Halka?"

"He'll need blankets and warmth," Stefan said. "Find some of the others, if you will. Tell them there's a survivor. Ask their help."

She nodded, turned, ran. Stefan took off his coat and spread it over the survivor for warmth, then turned to gather dry sticks for kindling as the first sounds of voices and running feet came from the near distance.

2

Some eighteen hours later, Stefan set another sheet of paper on the low table in front of him, searched for the loose end of a sentence, wrote:

> said that they had heard unusual sounds from the direction of the camp that evening. Since none of those expected at the Shelter that evening had arrived and no message had been sent, the three sen Halka then at Talin prepared to investigate.
>
> An armed search party from the Shelter insisted on coming with us, against our advice. A radio message was sent out to nearby Shelters, and we and the search party left Talin Shelter at first light, arriving at the camp just before noon.

He stopped writing, ran one hand back through thinning gray hair. Enough, he decided. Tradition required that Halka sitting in judgment explain how they came to be involved in the matter, but did not insist on any great length in the explanation. Next, though, would come the recounting of the events under judgment, and that would call for most of the half dozen sheets of paper he had with him.

> One hundred sixteen people had been at the camp. Of those, one hundred fifteen were dead when we arrived. All the dead had been shot, most more than once, with large-caliber weapons. Clear lifter-field burn could be seen on meadowmoss in the area, and tracks in arrowgrass

north of the camp indicate that six battle-drones acting in concert were involved.

He paused, and then spent the rest of that sheet and most of three others listing the details he had noted and the conclusions he had drawn. On yet another page he diagrammed the camp, sketching topography and the movements of the drones, marking and numbering the location of each trace his judgment described. Finishing, he spread all he had written so far on the table and considered it for several minutes, frowning. The formal style appropriate to judgments barred certain nuances of the event, required overtones of emotion and subtle awareness to be set aside so that others inside or outside the Halka order could judge the judgment in their turn. Familiar enough, the traditional strictures seemed to block out more than usual of the reality of this particular event. He read through the finished sections once more, put them back in order and set them on one side of the table.

Next came a summary of his actions at the camp. Here again he could be brief, as nothing he had done would be of any great importance to those who would read the judgment. Again, the words could only communicate a fraction of what he had seen and done that morning, but perhaps it was better that way. He described the arrival of the Halka, the decision to follow the drones, his search of the camp and the finding of the one survivor, then wrote:

> At this time the survivor, Jerre Amadan, is still unconscious, though the Shelter doctor expects him to wake within a day or two. His testimony, if he is able to provide any, is crucial to a clear assessment of the situation. Until he can be questioned in detail this judgment must be considered tentative.

The rest of the events of that day, the arrival of help from Talin and Weir Shelters and the long mournful journey home with the dead, took no more than a few lines. Finishing this, Stefan paused, pressed the back of the pen against his chin. The formalities required that he end his judgment with whatever action he felt the Halka needed to take, and it was by this more than anything else that the validity of his judgment would be measured. What needed to be done was clear enough, but he paused for some minutes before going on:

> That these events call for immediate Halka action is clear. The presence of six functioning drones beyond the edge of settlement in the north country, programmed to operate together as a single force, poses an extreme threat to the Shelters and Shelter folk in this area. I propose that Halka strength in the north country be increased at once, that Shelters be urged to prepare themselves for defense, and that heavy weapons be brought up from Zara and Halleth as soon as possible. I further urge that sen Halka without urgent commitments elsewhere come north to take part in the defense of the Shelters or the hunt for the battle-drones.

He read the whole of it over again, signed it with his full name, and then folded the judgment in half and sealed it with a circle of adhesive from the drawer under the table. On one side of the packet, he wrote in block letters:

Stefan Jatanni s. H., Talin 2821

And beneath that:

Linda Meridun s. H., Kerriol 1108
judgment—open distribution
URGENCY CODING

Enough, he told himself, and capped the pen. Kerriol was well down in the southern plains, far enough that the judgment would pass through eight or nine Shelters before it arrived and be read by at least as many sen Halka on the way.

Kerriol Shelter itself was a center of the Halka message network; once there the judgment would be copied and reviewed, sent out in all directions, summarized over the radio net; word would spread, and the Halka would begin the gathering of strength.

He pocketed the letter and stood, the loose black robe he had for Shelter wear settling around him. Joints crackled as he stretched. The room's one small window showed a first shading of light in the sky. Dawn, then, he thought, and wondered why it surprised him. He had closed off all but the deepest parts of his awareness to the need for sleep, and after momentary review left the barrier in place. Too much still needed to be done. He pushed the writing table over to the nearest wall with one foot, kicked the seat-cushion after it, went to the door.

Outside was a larger room, octagonal, with doors in each wall and two electric lamps in handblown glass globes hanging from the ceiling. Dark lines inlaid into the pale wood of the floor traced out stark geometries, a triangle within a circle, the Halka seal. These rooms were set aside for Halka use by the Shelter folk; behind one of the doors, a reinforced vault held enough ammunition and grenades for two years of normal use; beyond another, a short hallway opened onto the core facilities of the Shelter. Just past the end of that hallway was a door with the word RADIO painted beside it in neat white letters.

This was Stefan's destination. As he slid the door open, static growled at him from a loudspeaker on the wall. The radio operator looked up, nodded in greeting, and turned back to a dimly lit console. The sen Halka nodded absently in reply, found a square arrowgrass basket marked MAIL beneath a mostly empty bulletin board and put his judgment inside atop two other waiting letters. Turning, he found the message logbook on a table next to the main transmitter, and leafed through the log for several minutes, noting the messages sent and received since the killings. His own message at nightfall, describing what had happened and warning nearby Shelters of the danger, had been noted down; the time was indicated to the minute, all necessary details set out in clear script despite water stains on the paper that could only have been made by tears. Below that on the page, he found replies from some twenty Shelters acknowledging the message and the warning, and below these a long list of messages sent and received with no notation but the word *personal* after the times and the Shelter names and numbers. Stefan nodded, placing Shelters on a mental map of the north country. Word of the killings had already spread far. When his judgment reached Kerriol, it would not come unannounced.

He closed the logbook. The radio room had no windows, but a clock near one of the receivers marked the slipping away of the last minutes of the night. In less than half an hour the machineries around Stefan would wake as Shelters across Eridan's one inhabited continent sent out their first messages of the day. Time, he decided, or past it, and went to where the radio operator was sitting.

The operator, a man close to Stefan's age with weary eyes and sparse graying hair, looked up at the whisper of footsteps. "Sen Halka."

"I need a message left for the morning staff."

Tired eyes met his, and the man reached for pen and paper. "Of course. And the message?"

"Have them keep a watch on radio traffic across the north. If anything comes in about drones or more killings, send for me at once, and relay the message south under Halka urgency coding. If anything comes for me personally I should be sent for."

The operator's pen scratched across paper for a minute or so. "I'll be sure they get this."

"My thanks," said Stefan, and left the room.

Closing the door of his own room, he felt the weariness he had been suppressing all night, measured his need for sleep against the other needs that might arise. Part of his mind clamored for him to raise the barriers higher, go back to the radio room and monitor the morning's communications himself, but that would court exhaustion at a time when he might need all his resources without warning. A time and a place for each thing, he told himself, and here and now is for sleep. He bent, unfolded the sleeping mat, began to arrange blankets atop it.

Crimson fire caught at his vision then, and he turned, looking out the window. Above the distant line of the forest, searing through mist, the upper edge of the sun's disk burned like a distant beacon. Stefan paused to watch it, though it dazzled his eyes. The deep levels of the innermind mirrored it in a rush of subtle awareness, shaped it anew into images: darkness, fire flashing into being at its heart, a whisper of sound, a shadow spreading like wings. Within these images and through them moved a sense of threat, distant, almost abstract, but potent.

He blinked, and the images vanished.

Startled and, for the moment, wholly awake, he tried to recover them and could not. Neither subtle awareness nor the accessible levels of the innermind offered any trace. He frowned, turning over the images in his mind, and the frown deepened as nothing rose in response from any of the levels of himself where echoes might be expected to linger.

At length, puzzled, he gave up the search. Understanding would have to come in its own time, he decided. He pulled curtains across the window and turned back to the sleeping mat.

3

A tap on the door of his room woke him three hours later: a messenger from the Shelter doctor, with half-expected news.

"He awoke an hour ago," said the doctor, as she and Stefan walked down a gray Shelter corridor and stopped at a closed door. She turned to face Stefan. "If that's the right word. His pupils respond to light, and I can't find anything physically wrong with him."

"But he doesn't respond?"

"No more than a stone." She pulled open the door. "But you'll want to make your own assessment, I think."

Stefan, remembering the survivor's empty gray eyes, nodded and followed the doctor through the doorway. Inside was a little room four meters on a side, with two small windows letting in pale morning sun, an electric lamp, a sleeping mat with blankets. In the middle of the floor was a single white cushion, and on the cushion sat the young man Stefan had found in the forest. The dead pallor of shock had gone, replaced by a healthier color, but the haggard look and the utter emptiness of the eyes had not changed. The Shelter folk had dressed him in soft robes, white and warm brown, and his dark unruly hair had been combed. Still, something like wilderness seemed to move in him or through him: wind off the northern barrens, deep wave of the sea: something less than human or, just possibly, more.

"May I examine him?" Stefan asked.

"Please."

The sen Halka knelt, sat back on his heels in *ten ielindat*, the posture-of-awareness. The same mode of subtle awareness that allowed him to sense which way bullets would come in combat, the same openness to potential and intent, reached out and wrapped around the still figure in front of him. Subtle awareness opened up in response to the triggering phrase he whispered in his mind, and as motes of subliminal detail settled into place he found himself searching an emptiness that went deeper than he had anticipated.

"He's very far away," he said finally, shaking himself out of trance. "Or absent altogether. I'm not sure which."

The doctor nodded slowly. "Sen Halka, I'll be frank. I'm completely out of my depth. We normally have little call for mindhealing here, and what we need, the Halvedna handle. But now ..." She gestured helplessness, palms up. "I've sent for their help, but it will be days at least; they have more urgent work. I hoped you might be able to offer some help."

Stefan glanced up. "I fear we have little skill at healing."

"But more than a little knowledge of the mind's deep places—if what they say about the dwimmerwine is true."

When this brought no response, she went on. "Again, if what they say is true, you have—powers—in those places, sen Halka. I beg you to use them."

He regarded her in silence for a long moment, then nodded once. "I can try to search his mind. Did you know him? Anything you can tell me might give me a key."

"I knew him only slightly," said the doctor. "If I remember, he came here last autumn from further south, traveling from Shelter to Shelter as the young do. Some people claimed he was from a technician family—" A slight shrug, dismissing. "But I've never seen any point to the old prejudice. According to my records he had no illnesses worth mentioning. I treated him for a sprained ankle once after he fell doing Shelter work, but that was all."

"What was he doing?"

"Helping to repair a broken wind turbine." A sudden smile, edged with memory. "He was very disappointed. He loved to dance sama, but he had to sit out two or three dances while the ankle healed."

"Did he have friends or a lover?"

"If he did they were probably with him at the camp."

Stefan considered that, nodded. "I'll need complete silence for a time."

He turned back to the survivor, repeated the triggering phrase that took him into the first of the three levels of trance, opened the channels of subtle awareness until the senses stretched and fused into something beyond them. The second level of trance followed, and then the third. One small part of himself went to monitoring his own breathing and vital functions; the rest of his awareness moved to the deeps where self and other blended in the innermind's unity.

He was silent for a long time, long enough for the square patch of sunlight on the floor beside him to creep halfway to the nearest wall. Then, finally, he drew in a ragged breath, turned to face the doctor. "I cannot find him at all," he said. "I saw…"

At that moment the survivor's lips trembled, and he whispered four unintelligible words.

Stefan was facing the survivor again before the young man's lips had finished moving. Subtle awareness reached out; once again, emptiness reached back to the edge of his perception, but this time he sensed a disturbance in the void, like turbulence left by a bubble rising through dark waters. The inward track turned insubstantial when he tried to follow it. Further out, though, echoes of the words still lingered in the speech centers, and when Stefan found these he used a Halka technique of subtle prompting that forced unspoken thoughts out into speech.

Again the survivor's lips trembled. When he spoke, his voice was louder and the words more distinct: *shcha lyu ang chwem.*

The doctor looked from one of them to the other. "Cha lu … I wonder what that means."

"*Shcha lyu ang chwem,*" repeated Stefan. "That's unsettling."

"Do you know the words?"

"No." Stiffness in his knees hampering him, he got to his feet. "Nor why he said them. Maybe I brushed the place where he's hidden himself. I can't be sure."

Frowning, he stared at the survivor, wondering what had driven him so deep into himself, what the blank eyes had seen before they stopped seeing anything at all. An idea he did not want to think about had begun to take shape around the four words, drawing on Halka lore and tales from the time of the Insurgency. Since Shalsha's destruction, only a few scholars recalled the languages of Earth, and this one showed no signs of scholars' memory training. Yet the four words weren't just gibberish, he was sure of it.

That left just one possibility. Around it, subtle awareness flared into incandescence.

Command language.

The implications chilled him. If the four words were command language, someone must have been with the drones, directing them, when they attacked the camp. That meant nothing less than the supreme nightmare of the Halka come suddenly to life. On the abandonment of Shalsha's killing machines and the rigid limitation of weapons technology to a personal scale, two centuries of relative peace had depended, and for that reason nothing had a higher priority to the Halka of an earlier time than obliterating every trace of the artificial language the weapons of the Directorate obeyed.

That priority had not weakened over the years, Stefan knew. If the facts even hinted at a rediscovery of command language, his actions came under the sway of ancient imperatives. Halka tradition required a judgment circle to consider the case before one of the emergency codes could be invoked, but calling together a circle would take time, and all Stefan's instincts told him that time was crucial here. One other option remained, and though he knew the consequences he faced he knew also that the situation would allow no other response.

It would have to be Orange Sky, then.

He turned to the doctor. "I fear there's little else I can do at this point. If a sen Halvedna comes, send for me."

"I'll do that."

"My thanks." Stefan nodded once, went to the door. Somewhere above, a high, electric note cut through the low noises of Shelter machinery: a kyrenna being tuned for sama music. A second note followed, and then a momentary screech of amplifier feedback. They would be dancing sama tonight, he realized, dancing for the dead. A flicker of old regret stirred; sama music intoxicated the unawakened mind, brought oneness and healing, but the Halka stood forever outside that door.

"Sen Halka?"

He turned, considered the doctor.

"You said—before he spoke, you said you saw something. Would it be proper to ask what that was?"

"A stray fragment of his memory," said Stefan. "Only one. Most minds are cluttered with them, which is why I thought it worth the comment." When the question in her eyes did not go away: "A jewelfly, nothing more."

She nodded, then, and he did the same, turned, left the room.

4

"One moment." The radio operator at Annun Shelter looked up at the monitor on the shelf above him, twisted the receiver dial. "There's something else." The loudspeaker crackled.

"... Talin Shelter. This is Talin Shelter. I have a general message under Halka urgency coding ..."

In the radio room at Sat Island Shelter, a young woman on her second day of training turned toward the loudspeaker and reached for paper and a pen.

"... Urgency coding from Stefan Jatanni sen Halka at Talin. All Shelters copy and relay. The message runs as follows ..."

"Go find the sen Halka." The operator at Eltanna Shelter pushed hair back from her eyes. "He'll need to know at once." Her assistant nodded, hurried from the room.

"... Runs as follows. I have received new information about the attack by battle-drones near Talin Shelter two days ago. This information raises the possibility that the drones were acting ..."

A woman in Halka black stepped into the Ilun Shelter radio room, a half-dozen Shelter folk at her heels. The radio operator motioned at the loudspeaker with his head and kept writing.

"... Acting not on old programming but under human direction. I am therefore declaring Orange Sky. End of message."

The young man who sat all alone in the radio room at Keldevan Shelter stared at the loudspeaker with round eyes. The copy of the message scrawled on the paper before him ended with the last letter of *declaring*.

"... Orange Sky. End of message."

A small crowd had gathered around Seredin Shelter's radio equipment. As the loudspeaker fell silent, two sen Halka near the edge of the group glanced at each other and left.

"... Orange Sky. End of message."

Just behind the Talin Shelter radio operator and her assistant, shadow among shadows in the dim light of a single hooded lamp, Stefan waited, his face still and expressionless. As the operator set down her microphone and the hiss of static gave way to voices acknowledging the message, he stepped back, said, "My thanks."

The operator turned as if to speak, looked at him, and said nothing. Stefan nodded and left the room.

In the corridor outside the low noises of the Shelter machinery whispered at him; the air from the ceiling vents tasted of rain. The door to the Halka quarters and rest stood a few paces away, but he was not ready to take that path, not yet. Images burnt in the night of his inner eye: darkness, fire, sound, shadow. Around them others gathered just below the level of awareness, murmuring with the voice of the Shelter machineries, and that murmur blurred and twisted into the sound of four incomprehensible words. He squeezed his eyes shut, and his hands drew up into fists at his sides.

It was done, then, and there could be no turning back. The regional alert set in motion by Orange Sky would spread across the north as quickly as the radio net could carry it. Halka tradition made the invocation of any of the high emergency codes irrevocable, but set consequences for that act that could not and would not be set aside. That his own death might be among these Stefan knew, but that changed nothing. He cleared his mind as best he could and started for the Halka quarters.

5

The hallow room was completely empty, except for a single cushion at its center and the one who sat there, and the only light in it came through a single round window in the southern wall.

Complex angles of wall and ceiling gave it a sense of open space startling in a room only six meters across. In the polished stone of the floor, an intricate circular diagram was inlaid in pale metal, its dim symbols and symmetries invisible except where a long oval of sunlight turned gray stone into silver and dull alloy into fire. Beyond the window and the brown roofs of the Shelter, meadowmoss reached away past a band of gray metal to the forest's edge, wind scattered fragments of last summer's leaves, thin wisps of cloud hurried across the sky. Inside, nothing broke the stillness.

At the center of the room, legs folded in *ten sedayat*, the Halka posture-of-contemplation, Stefan waited. He had been waiting already for something like eighteen hours, since the last members of the judgment circle arrived by helicopter the afternoon before. The interval was little more than an abstraction to him. He had withdrawn most of himself into the timeless place at the center of awareness, leaving only enough behind to be sure that his heart did not at some point forget to beat. His gaze rested on the symbol at the center of the pool of light on the floor: *kel eshonat nen*, ninth glyph of the Sequence, the image of Stability.

As he watched, a shadow crossed the sunlight and blotted out the glyph for a moment.

Time, then. He brought himself up out of trance, back to the current moment, considered and then decided against rising to meet the one they would send for him. Stability, he reminded himself. The afterimage of the glyph hovered before his eyes. It would not be long now, one way or another.

The door behind him opened with a breath of sound.

"Stefan," said a voice he recognized. "They're ready."

He unfolded his legs, rose, turned. In the doorway stood a slim woman in Halka black, iron-gray hair pulled loosely back around her face, her expression neutral. Stefan met her gaze, said, "Then I'm ready. My thanks, Carla," and came to the door.

She did not move. "I must ask you to surrender your gun."

"Of course." He drew it, handed it to her. She accepted it, and without a word turned and led him from the room. She did not look back to be sure that he was following, but Stefan could sense subtle awareness flowing back around him, monitoring his movements. The penalty Halka tradition ordained for evading judgment was immediate death, and though Carla Dubrenden was one of Stefan's closest friends among Halka, he knew better than to think her shot would miss if he tried to run.

A walk across a roof terrace and a short flight of stairs brought them to a sunken courtyard surrounded by walls and tall windows. At its center, rising from an opening in the stone pavement, a single tree of unfamiliar shape held out straggling limbs to the sunlight and the scattered clouds. Its leaves, long green needles set in clusters along branches covered with rough brown skin, looked uncanny to eyes raised among the soft purples and blues of Eridan's forests: a product of an alien biology, able to grow even in this sheltered place only given chemically altered soil and unremitting care. Stefan, who had seen maybe two dozen like it in his years of traveling, looked up at it for a moment.

On any other morning in spring, the courtyard with the tree from Earth would have been full of children, Shelter folk with no work that day, couples young and no longer young. This morning, the only ones present wore Halka black.

He took his place in the circle as it formed, knelt and sat back in *ten ielindat*. Those around him did the same. For a brief time no one spoke. Finally an elderly woman across from him looked up.

"Stefan Jatanni sen Halka."

He made himself answer. "Julian Mereval sen Halka."

"I've been named Speaker for the circle. Is this acceptable to you?"

"It is."

"The traditions of our order instruct us that a sen Halka who kills or injures another person, who is accused of an offense against our traditions, who reports a violation of one of the Six Laws or who declares one of the high emergency codes without a judgment circle's approval shall submit to judgment. It is my understanding that you authorized a message over the Talin Shelter radio three days ago declaring Orange Sky. It this your understanding as well?"

"It is, yes."

"Knowing the alternatives, do you accept the judgment of this circle?"

The alternatives: one of them stood on the pavement at the side of the thin young sen Halka to his left, a cylinder of black shockproof plastic and metal fitted with a shoulder strap and a heavy combination lock. The other rested in the holster at the side of each sen Halka in the circle except himself. The gun and the dwimmerwine between them defined the foundations of the Halka path; either, circumstances being different, might be better than a judgment that might include one or the other. Neither a quick death nor the mind-shattering ordeal of dwimmertrance held any attraction for Stefan at that point, though. "I accept the judgment," he said.

"Even so." Julian Mereval considered him for a moment. "Tell us, then. Why did you declare Orange Sky?"

As Stefan paused, considering his words, he could feel the others in the circle bringing subtle awareness to bear on him. What precisely he said would be of secondary importance, he knew. What would decide the judgment would be the fit between his actions and the imperatives of Halka tradition. Still, for his own reasons, he hoped to show the validity of his decision, and so several minutes passed before he spoke.

"You'll have heard of the attack on one of Talin Shelter's foraging camps on the third day of this month. One hundred fifteen people died there. I was one of three sen Halka in the group that reached the camp first. This is what I found." He described the scene from memory, pausing now and again to be certain of his facts. As he spoke, the others in the judgment circle watched him and said no word, the rapport among them nearly tangible in the quiet air. When he had finished his account of the camp, he went on without pausing to the one survivor, the emptiness in his mind and the words that had come from that emptiness.

At last, when he had finished his account and was silent, Julian spoke. "These are the facts as you know them?"

"They are."

"What then is the interpretation you give them? The facts alone, as you've presented them, don't justify Orange Sky." She leaned forward slightly. "Tell us. You've set half the north country into motion over this. Why?"

Once again Stefan paused for a few moments before answering. "To my mind there are two interpretations for the attack, given the facts as I know them. The first is chance, the second design. If the first is correct, the drones represent nothing we have not faced before, relics of the Directorate following commands two hundred years out of date, and the words Jerre Amadan spoke were the gibberish of a broken mind.

"If the second interpretation is correct, those words were not gibberish but command language."

"I see." Julian's expression had not changed, but Stefan sensed her sudden shift of attitude as the implications registered. "Go on."

"If the second interpretation is correct, the attack on the camp was carried out at the will of someone now living." Stefan's voice here became quiet, meditative. "Someone who was with the six drones, perhaps riding one, as Directorate infantry did during the Insurgency. The question then becomes who, and why. One of the renegade technicians we usually find violating the Fifth Law? Unlikely; they survive only so long as they remain hidden from us, and would have nothing to gain from such an act. Outrunners? Also unlikely; the dead were untouched except by bullets.

"Not outrunners, then, and not technicians, or if it was one of those, they were seeking a goal none of these have sought in the past. The attack on the camp was an act of war. I can interpret it in no other way. If the drones were not just blindly following old commands—fighting a war two hundred years lost—then I am forced to think they were carrying out the first act of a war not yet fought."

"A war." Julian's voice and the mood of the circle were both sharp with surprise. "Toward what end?"

"I can think of only one possibility," said Stefan. "Our oldest nightmare. Restoration."

"Of Shalsha?"

"Or something like it."

The circle considered this for a time. "Two alternatives," Julian noted. "In your estimation, what is the likelihood of each?"

"I cannot judge that," Stefan replied.

Her eyebrows rose perceptibly. "Cannot? Please explain."

The words came only with difficulty. "I'm unable to judge clearly in this matter. I know that both alternatives are possible. I know that the second is wildly unlikely, but ..." He stopped, gestured helplessness and frustration. "The innermind will only see it one way. I can't think of the situation at all without calling up images of war."

Julian regarded him for a long moment. "I think," she said at last, "that you're carrying a vision, Stefan."

He paused, and his eyes widened. "I hadn't even considered that. You may be right. You may indeed be right."

"You spoke of images." She watched him intently now. "Show them to us."

"I'll attempt it," he said, and closed his eyes.

Around him the others in the judgment circle slipped into shallow trance. He whispered a triggering phrase and fell deep into the hidden places of his mind. Far down, moving through the innermind like the great armored fish that swam through Eridan's ocean, the potentialities that haunted him could be found, caught, brought up still alive to the levels of conscious awareness. So, out of darkness, images:

Battle-drones, thirty or forty of them, hurtling across an arrowgrass plain in close formation, the sky above them an angry crimson streaked with black;

A long line of refugees with their belongings on their backs, trudging up a muddy trail through the forest in the rain, the smell of smoke heavy in the air about them, their faces drawn, weary, hopeless;

A broad uneven plain where masses of weathered concrete broke through a carpet of pale windflowers, low irregular mounds stood dark against distant mountains, and a figure robed in green stood, arms folded, surveying the marks of an ancient cataclysm;

Sen Halka on a rocky slope, firing at something unseen, pressed backwards step by step;

The clearing north of Talin Shelter on the edge of the destroyed camp at sunset, with a cold wind howling down out of the north, darkness gathering beneath the trees, the huddled shapes sprawled on the meadowmoss blotted out as the shadow in the forest swallowed them;

Darkness;

A burst of intense blue-white radiance, an opening blossom of flame, a sound so loud it was no sound at all, a dim looming mantle of smoke rising high above the fires;

Darkness again, lit from within as by dying coals.

Stefan wrenched his eyes open. The members of the judgment circle were watching him, the elder among them with the formal reserve proper to sen Halka in judgment, the younger in something not far from shock.

"How long have these images been present?" Julian asked him, once the rapport of the circle reestablished itself.

"All of them? Three days."

"They didn't arise at a single point of time?"

"No." he blinked, tried to clear echoes of the vision from behind his eyes. "At first there was only the fire. The others came gradually. I think that there may be more still to come, but I do not know. I cannot know."

Yes, he was thinking, of course, a vision, and wondered why he had not thought of that earlier. One spoke of carrying a vision in the same sense as carrying an unborn child, and certainly his own vision had grown in the womb of his mind from the simple sense of unease and foreboding into a complex web of patterns, intuitions, logic that filled him with a certainty of evil to come. The mere possession of the word gave him a certain comfort, as if to say *it is a vision, I am a visionary* were somehow to contain the driving forces of the innermind and give them a shape he could touch.

"The final image," Julian said then. "The fire of Shalsha. That was the seed of it?"

"It was, yes."

Julian nodded slowly. "Even so." She glanced at each of the members of the judgment circle in turn, and then said, "We have no further questions. Is there anything more you wish to say before we finish?"

"No."

"Then we'll decide upon a judgment." She closed her eyes, bowed her head, retreated behind a mental screen that sealed her off from Stefan's perceptions. The others in the circle did the same. In the silence that followed, every small sound from the rustle of the alien leaves of the tree above him to the rhythm of his own pulse came clearly to Stefan. High wisps of cloud alternately hid and revealed the sun. Nearly as alone as he might be on the great northern barrens, hundreds of kilometers from the nearest Shelter, Stefan cleared his mind and let the sounds and shifting light occupy him as he waited.

At length Julian blinked and raised her head. By ones and twos, the others did the same. "Our judgment," she said, again glancing around the circle, "finds your actions within the limits set by tradition." She nodded to Carla Dubrenden, who handed Stefan's gun back to him.

The hard knot of tension in his belly came undone as he slipped the weapon back into its place. He drew in a deep breath. "And Orange Sky?"

"We've agreed that there may be a chance your second possibility is correct. We cannot yet confirm that, and change the code to confirmed status, to Orange Sun. The alert stands, and we'll authorize full defensive preparations at once." She paused, began almost unwillingly: "However."

He raised his eyes to meet hers, knowing what would come next.

"You know the traditions concerning visionaries, Stefan. It may be our great good fortune that you've seen what you have seen. We cannot know, and the Halka have been endangered more often by visionaries, and more seriously, than by all the drones we've faced since Mariel's time. You'll therefore take no part in the preparations or in the hunt for the drones. Until your vision has been proved one way or the other you are barred from active involvement in this matter except in emergencies."

"I accept the limitation," said Stefan, knowing he could do nothing else.

Julian nodded in acknowledgement. "Within those limitations, there's something I would ask you to do. The survivor will have to be treated by a mindhealer if we're to find out what he saw. The sen Halvedna here advise that we take him to a specialist elsewhere, and I'd like to ask you to accompany the survivor and supervise his treatment."

Stefan considered her. "I know a specialist I can recommend."

Whisper of a smile on Julian's face: "I imagine you do. Tamar Alhaden's at Mirien Shelter, as I recall; that's far enough south to be out of danger if the drones return."

"I'll do it, of course."

"My thanks. I would also like to send Amery Lundra …"

"Amery? She's returned?"

"While you were in seclusion last night." Julian met his gaze squarely. "Wounded. If she's willing, I would send her with you to Mirien to set up a center for the message net there."

"And Toren Dall?" Stefan asked.

Silence answered him.

He looked at Julian in dismay a moment longer, then bowed his head. "Toren," he whispered, and then in a more normal voice asked, "How did it happen?"

6

"We walked into an ambush." Amery gestured northward with her good arm. The other hung useless in a sling, white plaster of a cast showing at hand and upper arm. "On our second day out, on the far side of an arrowgrass plain. The drones ran compass-straight for more than forty kilometers, and we were both off our guard, I admit. We saw and sensed nothing until the first bullets came at us."

"The drones anticipated pursuit?" Stefan was frowning.

She nodded. "So I suspect. One drone stayed behind to deal with us while the rest went on. It hid in a meria thicket, and waited until Toren and I had begun to search the wood before it attacked. I was ..." Her expression twisted. "Lucky, I suppose. I took one bullet above the wrist. Toren was hit in the belly and legs, and had time to throw two grenades from the ground before he bled to death. One of them landed on top of the drone and wrecked its main sensor housing, which is why I'm alive just now.

"I tried to shoot out the drone's cooling unit, failed, and then managed to take shelter in a clump of glacial boulders and see to my arm while the drone blundered around trying to find me with its peripheral sensors. After we'd played catch-me-catch-you for half an hour, I finally hit a cooling vent. As soon as the core overheated and burnt out I blew the drone to scrap metal with three grenades. After that I saw to Toren and came back as quickly as I could."

"And the rest of the drones?"

"Nowhere to be found. No trace of them in the wood, or the arrowgrass beyond it. My guess is that they split up and took evasive courses from there on." She paused. "Julian told me about your Orange Sky message last night. The more I hear about all this, the more I think you may be right. I can't claim to be an expert on drones, but this isn't like the old strategies."

"Not at all," Stefan said. "Expert or not, though, you faced a drone and survived the encounter. That was well done, Amery."

She gave him the faintest trace of a smile. "When the drone came at us I was certain I was dead."

Stefan's gesture meant *I have been in the same place.* "Have you begun your judgment?"

"Not yet." The smile turned rueful. "Julian asked me to have it ready before I leave for Mirien, but I've done little but sleep since I reached here." She shifted, leaned back against the wall. "Julian told me some strange things about the survivor you found. I hope I have a chance to see him sometime soon."

"You'll have the chance. He'll be coming to Mirien as well."

Her eyebrows went up, and then she shook her head, laughed. "I should have guessed. Who else would they have chosen?" Then, after a moment: "Well."

Stefan nodded, but said nothing. The air in the little room was thick with questions Amery wanted to ask but could not; to require of a sen Halka just come from judgment the details of the circle's decision would have been ill-mannered even for ordinary Shelter folk; that Stefan had been allowed to leave the judgment circle alive made the heart of that decision plain. Doubtless one of the members of the circle would tell her the details soon enough.

He rose to his feet. "Apparently the helicopter will be ready by first light, so I won't risk Julian's wrath by delaying you longer. Do you have everything you need for your judgment?"

"I think so, yes. Thank you." Then, as he turned to go: "Stefan?"

He looked back at her.

In the innerspeech: *I'm glad you're still alive.*

Stefan moved his head slightly, acknowledging. *I'm glad you're alive yourself.* Though he did not allow himself to express it, a pang of gratitude for the gesture went through him. After a moment, he went on: *I must go now. They'll be waiting.*

The door closed behind him noiselessly. Inwardly his mind was racing ahead, fitting Amery's words into the fabric of his vision. The drones had followed a precise plan, that much was obvious, and the ambush was part of the plan from the beginning: thus the arrow-straight tracks to and from the place of the killings, a bait too tempting to ignore. That tactic had little in common with the ways of Directorate forces during the Insurgency, and that implied that whoever was controlling the drones had enough wisdom or cunning to learn from ancient mistakes. The Halka had of necessity learned every detail of coping with the massive frontal attacks on central positions that had been the Directorate's tactic of choice, but how well would the standard responses work against an enemy who used other methods?

Hold back, he said to himself, hold back. The steps his mind wanted to take led straight into mist and confusion, and he knew it. He cleared his mind and crossed the Halka common space to his own room.

CHAPTER 2

THE WINDS OF MEMORY

1

Thirty meters down, the forest canopy slid past, an unruly carpet of indigos and purples.

"Keldevan Shelter," the pilot said, pitching her voice to be heard over the pounding of the rotor blades overhead. "We're ten minutes from Mirien."

Stefan looked through the streaked glass of the window next to him. Off to the left trees gave way to meadowmoss, a protective circle of metal, and within that the concrete and glass of the Shelter. Six turbines atop widely spaced towers turned in a wind he could not feel. In windows on the near side of the complex, mirrored for an instant along with the broken clouds that filled the sky, the helicopter's angular shape appeared briefly and was gone.

Amery, who sat next to the pilot, turned toward her. "You've flown this way before."

"Twice last summer." A sudden gust of wind buffeted the craft, and the pilot spent several minutes fighting with the controls before turning back to Amery. "Your pardon, sen Halka. This wind would blow us from here to the barrens if it had its way."

"So I gather. I trust you'll be able to get back to Talin safely."

The pilot looked past her to the southwest sky. "So long as the wind is no worse than this, there'll be no trouble. It'll be helping me, not fighting me, on the way home. I'll have to leave as soon as you're on the ground, though."

"Bad weather coming?"

"No, Shelter council worrying about our only helicopter. If there's a single cloud in the sky all they can think about is two years' worth of trade credit in a heap on the forest floor. They insisted I get back by nightfall."

Another gust hit the helicopter, and the pilot turned back to her controls. Stefan watched Keldevan Shelter slip into distance behind them. Mountains marched across the eastern horizon, white peaks incandescent in the afternoon light. Closer, breaks in the forest marked the positions of other Shelters, widely spaced as the Second Law demanded.

He leaned forward. "I've been keeping count of the hills and valleys we haven't had to cross on foot," he said to the pilot. "You'll have to give our thanks to the council, sen Kerril."

"I'll do that. They already have mine. Ever since—what happened—the helicopter has been grounded, and I didn't expect to have the chance to fly again until the emergency is over. This was a welcome surprise."

"You remind me of my brother," Amery said then. "He flew one of Dallan Shelter's helicopters for two years. He was forever trying to talk the Shelter council into sending him somewhere for whatever reason."

The pilot glanced at her. "Dallan? We may have met, then. I took three loads of lumber there the summer before last and met most of the Shelter pilots. What's his name?"

"Tam Lundra." Amery's voice could barely be heard over the noise of the rotors. "But you won't have met him. Tam was killed by outrunners in the mountains five years ago."

"I—" The pilot looked away. "I heard of that," she said. "I'm sorry, sen Halka. I don't mean to stir up old griefs."

"No harm," Amery told her, but neither one of them spoke again until another clearing came into sight, full ahead, and the pilot said, "Mirien."

A moment later the forest fell away and the Shelter stood in full view, glass and concrete catching the sunlight below, wind turbines churning the air above. The pilot brought the helicopter around in a broad turn and circled the shelter once. Then, slowing, she took the craft in between two of the wind turbines and descended. Walls rose up around the helicopter, blotting out the surrounding forest. As the jolt of landing shook the cabin, metal doors began to slide shut overhead.

Stefan pulled himself out of his seat and stumbled back into the cargo space. Reaching the main door, he threw it open, letting in a blast of noise and wind that came close to breaking his uncertain balance. He turned, then, and made for the cot on the far wall of the cargo space, as other sounds joined the pounding of the rotor blades and the rush of air: voices and the clattering of feet on the metal of the cabin floor.

Jerre Amadan, asleep or apparently so, lay on the cot. Stefan threw back the blanket covering him and pulled him to a sitting position. On the other side of the cargo space Amery directed a knot of Shelter folk as these handed down baggage and gear to others below. Two of the Shelter folk, seeing Stefan, came to assist.

"He can't walk," Stefan shouted, trying to be heard over the noise. His two helpers, seemingly more used to the din than he was, nodded and took hold of the survivor. With little trouble they carried Jerre across the cargo space and passed him down to waiting arms outside. Stefan let subtle awareness search the cargo space for anything forgotten, then jumped down.

The shock of landing sent spikes of pain through his bones. Behind him, someone slammed the helicopter door shut. All around him Shelter folk pressed, drawing him away from the craft, welcoming, giving news, shouting directions to the ones who carried the baggage. Children gathered to watch. A few meters away Amery spoke with an elderly man who seemed to be directing things, no doubt a member of Mirien's council, but Stefan could not hear one single word. He moved with the crowd toward the side of the landing bay as the doors above slid open again and the helicopter lurched and rose into the air.

The children and some of the adults waved. The pilot, dimly visible through glass, waved back. The helicopter climbed, turned, retraced its path to the north country.

"Sen Halka." One of the Shelter people had come up to him. "I've sent someone to the radio room to let Talin know you've arrived."

As Stefan thanked him another, a young woman with startling red hair, came from behind him. "We've sent for the doctor, sen Halka. Does the person you brought have injuries?"

"No. He needs only to be carried, and kept warm."

"That we can do." A quick smile, and then she forced her way out through the crowd.

A moment later Amery was with him. "Tamar's here," she told him. "Over by the wall with our passenger."

Stefan glanced at her. "Examining him, I assume?"

"I think so."

He nodded, and followed Amery. The crowd gave back around them.

Jerre Amadan had been left sitting against one wall of the landing bay to wait for the Shelter doctor, a blanket around him for warmth. Empty eyes still stared through the concrete floor into nothingness, and the lines of his face still showed no trace of emotion or awareness. Facing him, her back to the two sen Halka, a plump gray-haired woman in the many-colored robe of the Halvedna knelt; around her, unmistakable to the inner senses, gathered an aura of focused attention subtly different from the Halka mode. After a moment she got to her feet. "This is uncanny," she said. "Is the sen Halka—"

"Here." Stefan had come up beside her, screening his presence from her perceptions, and stood next to her with half a smile on his face. Startled, she turned, then broke into a broad grin.

"Stefan! I hadn't thought to see you until winter at the earliest. A pleasant surprise."

"The message from Talin didn't mention me?"

"Not at all—only a new patient."

"I hope that wasn't an imposition."

"Not at all. He needs my help." Then, laughing: "It's been four years since you brought me Amery, and that's longer than your usual interval. But this one is welcome and so are you." She looked past him, then, and gestured with her head. "And here's the Shelter doctor. If you and Amery would like to sit and have some tebbe, my room isn't far."

Stefan turned to where Amery had been standing, but found himself facing Shelter folk. "Gone," said Tamar. "She'll bring me greetings in her own time, I suspect."

Stefan allowed a wry smile. "My guess is she wanted to be sure our baggage went to the right place. But I'll accept your invitation, gladly."

She motioned toward a nearby door. "I have a new room now, closer in to the center, and something in it I want you to see." She stepped past him. Stefan followed.

2

"Next to the window," Tamar told him, "and in the opposite corner."

He looked. Two globes in stands of dark daula wood and brass rose out of disorder, giving some small trace of symmetry to the cluttered room. The one in shadow, in the far corner, showed the two continents and innumerable islands of Eridan in grays and purples on a ground of deep green, the northern continent marked with the names of mountains and rivers in flowing script, the southern continent and the islands almost wholly bare. Marks just perceptible across the room traced out currents in an ocean broken by so little land that Eridan's inhabitants had never divided it into separate seas or even given it a name. Three white crystals in the northern continent marked the Gatherings at Werelin, Halleth, Amris. Another crystal, red, glowered between the two northern Gatherings, a shadow out of the unforgotten past.

The globe in sunlight, in the near corner, glowed green, brown, blue, polar white. The lines of seas and continents on it looked forced, unnatural. Names written in antique script across land and sea named cities and nations long since passed into legend. An extension of the stand held a smaller sphere the color of ashes and ghosts, mottled with dark irregular blotches, marked with the names of the handful of cities built there before the time of Journey Star and her sisters. Stefan, staring with wide eyes at the image of Earth—he had seen only three or four like it in his life—found himself wondering what it would have been like to stand on the surface of the homeworld, with its huge dead moon dominating the sky, before the poisons of human industry condemned it to its own slow death. The leap proved too great; he fell back to the present moment with a jolt, holding only to an image of Earth's moon, low in the sky, staring at him blindly with the empty eyes of a skull.

"What do you think?" she asked him.

"They're beautiful," Stefan said, still looking at the globe of Earth. "How did you come by them?"

"I had a patient last year, an arbiter for one of the trade networks." She knelt and began to clear away some of the clutter, moving books and periodicals, boxes and cushions out to the edges of the room, revealing the bright handwoven rug beneath. "He gave me them as a gift after his treatment was finished. I know I shouldn't be so attached to material things, but I love them dearly." Then, looking up at him: "Oh, sit down, Stefan. You look as worn as the last week of winter. Sit down."

He found a cushion and sat. Tamar went to the kitchen-unit set into the floor near the globe of Eridan. After a minute or so of clattering and the hiss of hot water she came back with two bowls of pale bluish liquid. "Our own blend," she told him, handing him one. "Nearly up to hill country standards, I'm told."

Stefan sniffed at the vapor. "I've never been able to stop thinking of tebbe as one of the minor medicines."

That won him a smile. "Outer circle lore, after this long?" Then: "Of course it is, but it has other virtues."

Stefan nodded, sipped the hot tebbe, considered her. Her hair, worn long in the Halvedna style, had more gray than he recalled from four years ago, and the face it framed was heavier, the roll beneath the chin a little deeper, wrinkles gathering at the corners of her eyes. The loose many-colored robe of the Halvedna made all of her besides head and hands an abstract form.

She glanced up from her bowl. "Four years, now. Where did you go?"

"After training Amery? East to play catch-me-catch-you with outrunners in the forests on the other side of Wind Gap. After that was done, north to the edge of settled country, going from Shelter to Shelter and waiting for something to happen. Nothing much did." He sipped tebbe. "Until the killings at Talin."

"And you met Amery again?"

"Just last autumn, and by chance. I'd settled in at Talin for the winter, and a week later she arrived on the way north from the hill country. The first snows kept her from going any further. I cannot say I was sorry for that. I welcomed her company."

She gave him a questioning look, and he laughed. "Tamar, she's thirty years my junior, and a student of mine besides. No." The laugh went away. "And some things don't change."

Tamar sipped her own tebbe and looked at him; he could feel her weighing the words. After a time: "And so you've brought me another patient."

"What do you think of him?"

"A strange one." She paused, considering. "I'll need induction probes to be sure, but he's almost certainly in reactive withdrawal."

"I'd suspected that."

"I don't know of anything else that would account for the symptoms. Do you recall the structure of reactive withdrawal?" Stefan gestured noncommittally, and she went on. "The mind freezes on a single image, unable to accept it, unable to put it aside. You'll recall the woman I was treating when you brought Amery here, the one who lost her child in the spring floods? She could see or hear nothing but her daughter's face and cry as the river pulled her under. Until we could get that out of her mind, nothing helped, and I had to use a catamnetic."

He nodded. "You removed the memory chemically."

"And every other memory she had. Dalla built her entire inner life around her child—every other thought led her back to the core image—so I gave her complete amnesia and helped her reestablish a stable identity. It was either that or leave her in withdrawal until she died."

Stefan frowned. "Is there a way to break withdrawal without erasing the memory of the event that caused it?"

"Not to my knowledge. Why?"

"We need to know what Jerre Amadan saw. It's of the highest importance."

She gave him a long thoughtful look. "I assume that's your reason for coming here."

"My main reason, yes."

"You must have searched his mind first. Didn't that answer your question? Normally the image at the core of the withdrawal is just below the surface level."

"I probed his mind down to the autonomic levels," Stefan said. "Level by level, as far as I could. He had no trace of mental activity at all."

"None?"

"None."

"That's astonishing."

"There's more. Just after I finished the probe, he spoke four words aloud."

"He emerged from withdrawal?"

"No. He said the words apparently without leaving withdrawal at all."

Tamar stared at him. "That's unheard of." Then: "What were the words?"

"Nonsense, seemingly. *Shcha lyu ang chwem.*"

She repeated the words. "You think they mean something."

"I think they might be command language."

Tamar began to speak, stopped, and then said slowly, "That implies that someone was with the drones when they attacked."

"Exactly."

She stared at him again. "Bright Earth. That would be an unspeakable evil."

"And a supreme danger."

"That also." She paused. "That might explain a case of reactive withdrawal all by itself. But how likely do you think that is—that the words were command language?"

Stefan looked troubled. "It's a possibility. It's also possible that the words mean nothing and the drones were following old orders. Thus our need to find out exactly what Jerre Amadan saw and heard. Until the drones attack again his memory is the only evidence we have."

Tamar nodded. "And so you need the memory at the center of his withdrawal intact, and you also need it taken away. A pretty puzzle." She fell silent for a time, hand to chin, thinking. "There might be a way. It has risks, but I believe it can be done."

"What do you have in mind?"

"I'll need to examine him thoroughly first. I might be able to find some other way to reach through the barriers. If not, with your permission I'll give him a strong temporary catamnetic, and after he's reestablished a stable identity, try to break through the induced amnesia. If it works he'll regain most of his memories intact."

"And the risks?"

She frowned. "First, the amnesia might not break. If that happens, what's lost is lost, and there won't be anything anyone can do about it. Second, the returning memories might be too much for him to bear, and he may return to withdrawal. If that happens I'll have no choice but to use a permanent catamnetic; anything else would risk permanent damage to his mind."

Stefan pondered that. "How long will it take?"

"A month or a little more. It depends on how fast he reestablishes a stable identity."

"And the chance of success?"

She met his gaze squarely. "Maybe sixty per cent. I'll try to find another way, as I said, but we may have to choose between that sixty per cent and no chance at all." She drank the last of her tebbe. "I wish there were a more reliable way but I know of none."

Stefan nodded once. "How soon should the process start?"

"As soon as possible—tomorrow, if you're willing. The longer the withdrawal lasts, the worse the odds of breaking it. I'll review the literature and carry out a basic examination tonight, use neural probes tomorrow morning to make sure it's reactive withdrawal, and proceed with catamnesis at once if that's indicated."

"I'll send word to Talin, then. They'll need to know."

She looked at him. "The command circle is at Talin?"

"For now, yes."

"Then you'll be returning there soon?"

"No. I'll be here at Mirien for at least a month, probably longer." He had not meant to speak of his vision, had intended to tell Tamar of it later, when he'd had time to make more sense of the images. Still, the words came out. "Since shortly after the killings I've been—haunted, I suppose—by a series of images I cannot drive from my mind. The judgment circle ruled that it's a vision, and as a visionary I'm barred from taking part in the response or remaining in a potential combat area."

"A vision." Tamar was watching him with a look somewhere between surprise and concern. "What do you see? What are the images?"

"Specifically? Battle-drones. Refugees. More corpses than I care to think about. The ruins of Shalsha and the fire that destroyed it. If I interpret the vision correctly it predicts something like war." He swallowed. "A war for the restoration of Shalsha, or something like it, involving hundreds or even thousands of drones. And I have yet to see an image of victory."

Tamar nodded after a moment. "And you first saw this after the killings."

"The first image came about a day later. The others followed over the next week or so. I feel that there are more to come." He scowled. "Unfortunately. I would happily be rid of it."

"You find it that problematic?" she asked, genuinely surprised.

"Yes. One other time in my life I followed what I suppose would be called a vision. I doubt you've forgotten that."

Tamar nodded, said nothing.

"Beyond that, this thing has made me give up any role in the Halka response. I'd hoped to help coordinate Shelter defenses in the north country. It's something I've had experience doing, and needs to be done quickly and capably. Instead I'll be here indefinitely, with nothing to do but watch you work on Jerre Amadan's mind, because Halka tradition quite rightly bars visionaries from putting themselves in a place where their ravings could harm anyone but themselves." He allowed a brief bitter laugh. "There speaks my sense of self-importance, of course. They'll doubtless be able to organize a creditable defense without me. Still, I'd rather be part of the response, and I don't trust the things I'm seeing. I don't trust them at all."

"Tell me this," Tamar asked him. "If you had to choose irrevocably between standing with your vision and rejecting it wholly, which would you do?"

Stefan opened his mouth, intending to say he would abandon it at once, and found that the words would not come. He'd spoken before of the power of his vision, but failed to grasp just how literally true the words were. Now, caught between vision and intellect, he struggled with both for a time before forcing out, "I would stand with it. I wish I could say otherwise."

"Perhaps it's a Halvedna habit," Tamar said then, "but I cannot help thinking of a vision as a help, not a threat."

"Your visionaries," Stefan pointed out, "don't carry guns."

She considered that. "True. We can also use the Root to test the nature of our visions. I don't imagine that can be done with the Wine."

"Not with more than a five per cent survival rate, no. It's been tried."

"I thought as much. And of course the Halka have no chapter houses where a visionary can be kept safely." Her voice went very quiet. "What do the Halka usually do with their visionaries, Stefan?"

"If they obey the traditions and ordinances of the Order, they remain sen Halka like any other. If they violate those, like any other sen Halka they're tried and shot." He looked away. "Most are eventually shot. Visionary states have a momentum of their own and don't pay much attention to Halka regulations, or anyone else's."

Tamar gave him a long dismayed look, then picked up her bowl. "I'll want more tebbe, I think," she said. "And you?"

"Please."

She took both bowls and moved over to the kitchen-unit.

3

Stefan settled onto the cushion. Above him, visible through a skylight and the last traces of mist, morning deepened into full day in a streaming glory of sunlight.

"Please be comfortable," said Tamar. "This will take an hour even if all goes well."

She stood by a tall cabinet, considering an array of hand-sized devices of glass and polished metal. To either side shelves of massive clothbound books reached from floor to ceiling. Except for a stack of cushions in the corner, the rest of the room was bare and unfurnished, left free for its many uses. In its stark simplicity, Tamar's workroom, clinic, and place of meditation warred in the mind with the wild clutter of the room on the other side of the door behind Stefan. Still, he recognized in it the unmistakable stamp of her personality.

"Here." Tamar selected three of the instruments and closed the cabinet. "Now we'll see." She went to a bright orange cushion near the center of the room and sat. Near her, Jerre Amadan stared through the floor, lost in whatever private nightmare still held him. A short distance away Stefan and Amery watched, and near them another, a gaunt wild-haired sen Halvedna with a ring of twisted bark-cord around his neck. Tamar had introduced him as Daval, and told the two sen Halka his presence would be necessary. He himself had not spoken a word. His eyes, their pupils enormous, stared unblinking at Jerre Amadan with unnerving intensity.

Tamar turned from her patient to Stefan. "I saw Jerre for nearly an hour last night and did the basic tests."

"What do you think?"

"His nervous system's intact, and the deep structures of his consciousness still respond. Beyond that ..." She shrugged. "We'll see in a moment."

The room dimmed as a torn fragment of cloud fled across the sun. Stefan looked from Tamar to Jerre and back.

Tamar herself watched the survivor in thoughtful silence. At length, unhurriedly, she picked up one of the instruments, held it in front of Jerre's forehead, and pressed a small button on the side with her thumb.

To the outer senses, the device produced nothing but a soft humming sound, but subtle awareness scanned it and drew sharply back, overloaded. A faint tingling played in the peripheral nerves on the front of Stefan's body. He turned to Jerre and slipped into a shallow rapport, aware that Amery had done the same. In the deeper emptiness behind the survivor's empty eyes, a ghost of consciousness flickered and moved, shifting like smoke in the wind as Tamar moved the instrument up, left, right.

"Neural induction probes?" Amery asked.

Tamar gave her a surprised look. "Yes. I didn't think you would remember that."

Amery nodded, but her gaze faltered. "I remember … more than I thought. The way the probe touches his mind brings back a great deal."

"I suppose it would. If this will be difficult for you—"

"No." Amery was looking at the survivor now. "Thank you, Tamar, but no. I'll stay."

After a moment, Tamar turned back to her patient. "Then we'll begin in earnest."

In the end, it took just short of an hour and a half to finish. Tamar held one probe or another over nearly every square centimeter of Jerre's scalp, watching him intently, turning now and then to Daval and being answered, if at all, by some Halvedna variant of innerspeech. Toward the end of the examination, Tamar's expression grew more and more troubled. When she finally set the last of the probes on the floor, she turned to the others.

"Deep?" Stefan asked.

"Extremely so," she replied, shaking herself out of deep rapport. "And you were quite correct. His awareness is closed down so thoroughly that I got no response to the probes or to mindscanning. I've never seen withdrawal so deep." She paused. "I wonder. Could he have some form of mindtraining?"

"No one at Talin mentioned it," said Stefan. "Why?"

"If he'd placed a strong shield around his thoughts and then hidden within it, that might explain what I saw."

"Did you find any other signs of mindtraining?"

"None." She shrugged. "It was just a passing thought." She turned to the other sen Halvedna. "Daval?"

"He will not emerge on his own." Daval's voice, no more than a whisper, had overtones that made Stefan give him a startled glance. "Your alternatives fade. I see only the one."

Tamar nodded. "And I."

"By Halka tradition," said Stefan then, "I hold responsibility for Jerre Amadan's welfare until he's cured or returns to Talin Shelter. I must ask you to affirm in my presence that the treatment you intend to use is in your judgment the best option available to you for his cure." He spoke quietly and with no particular emphasis, but his tone had abruptly become that of a sen Halka in judgment.

"I affirm that," Tamar replied, "to the best of my knowledge."

"Thank you. You may proceed."

Tamar returned the probes to their cabinet, opened and shut a drawer lower down. She returned with a slim hypodermic. "I'll need a certain amount of assistance."

"What needs to be done?" said Amery, beginning to rise.

Tamar gave her a smile. "Something requiring two hands, I'm afraid. Stefan?"

"Of course." He moved to Jerre's side.

"His arm needs to be held, so." She gestured, indicating.

Stefan pulled back the sleeve of the survivor's robe, held the arm extended and still. "Exactly," said Tamar. "Don't allow him to move." She cleaned the skin over one vein with an alcohol swab and then used the hypodermic. Before the arm in his hands could jerk back, Stefan blocked the nerve impulse with a quick jab of one thumb on a pressure point.

"Thank you," said Tamar. "That's all."

Stefan went back to his place and turned eyes and inner senses alike toward Jerre, waiting for the first effects of the drug. The young man sat motionless as always, the minute movements and responses that marked the presence of ordinary human consciousness still wholly absent. Somewhere, Stefan thought, somewhere in that one's mind, a human being huddled in on himself, conscious of nothing except a single terrible memory. What would he feel when the catamnetic reached his brain and even that slipped away?

A moment later the drug began to take hold. The image that remained longest in Stefan's mind was that of winter snowfall: soft, silent, wrapping forms of forest, stone, and Shelter alike in featureless white. The channels of subtle awareness linking his mind to Jerre's drew him inward, so that for an instant he felt the catamnetic flooding into his own brain, felt past and future falling away as a lifetime of memories dissolved. A sudden burst of terror—Jerre's, or his own? He could not tell—leapt out like a scream, and then was gently silenced.

Stefan shook himself free, closing down the linkages, clenching his eyes shut. The blurring in his mind faded. He felt Amery's awareness brush against him, insubstantial as mist. A second mental touch from Tamar, so light he was not sure for a moment that he'd sensed it and not simply imagined it, brought reassurance. He drew in a breath and opened his eyes.

Jerre Amadan was looking directly at him. The young man's face was transfigured, stripped of tensions and barriers. The haggard look had vanished utterly. The eyes that met Stefan's were those of a child, or perhaps a madman, but unquestionably they saw him, moved as he moved, responded to his tentative probe. The mind he touched, empty of thought and memory, was equally free of the walls of withdrawal.

"It will be six to eight hours before the drug clears his system," Tamar said then. She was standing by her cabinet, arms folded, watching Jerre. "Until then nothing we say or do will remain in his mind for more than a fraction of a second. After that, the real effort begins; he'll have much to relearn."

Daval rose to his feet in a sudden surge of motion. "True," he whispered. "Do not teach him, Tamar. Let him remain in silence. Let him die."

Tamar turned on him, horrified. "What are you saying?"

"It would be better if he died at this moment."

"Daval! The Affirmation!"

With painful deliberation: "He will loose the fires of Shalsha on us all. Let him die." He took one step toward the survivor.

Before he could take a second Stefan was on his feet facing him, in that moment wholly Halka: the image of the gun. "If you attempt to harm him I'll intervene. I'm required to tell you your life is at risk."

Daval faced him, and drew in a breath sharp with surprise. Wide eyes widened further. "You have seen the fires!" He looked to Amery, to Tamar, back to Stefan. "Let him die."

Tamar came toward him. "Daval—"

"No!" He turned and bolted for the door. As he reached it, Stefan and Amery exchanged glances and a burst of the innerspeech, and before Daval was through Amery was on her feet and halfway to the door, following. His pace, uneven, and hers, measured, faded slowly.

Stefan sat on his cushion again in silence. After a moment, Tamar did the same. She stared at the floor in front of her in something like shock. Neither spoke again until Amery returned some ten minutes later.

"He's gone," she announced, closing the door. "Straight through the Shelter to the main southern doors, and out. The Shelter folk are wondering what in Earth's name happened. I took the liberty of telling them you'd explain shortly, Tamar."

Tamar nodded, but said nothing.

Amery found her cushion, settled. "May I ask something? I don't know much of the Halvedna, and I know even less of what spoke in that one's mind. I sensed—I'm not sure what."

It was Stefan, though, who answered. "Daval is a sen davannat, one of the sen Halvedna who seek the innermind through the unrefined dwimmerroot. He'll have used the root daily for years. The sen davannat aren't sane by ordinary standards, but they aren't insane either, and they see things that even the most perfected awareness can't." Something too ambivalent to be called a smile touched his expression. "I saw myself as one of them, once." Then, setting aside the memory: "I'd guess that Tamar wanted his help in searching Jerre's mind."

Tamar looked up. "I hoped to have the assistance of his clear vision. We've worked together more than once in the past, with good results. What can I say? I'm deeply ashamed that he spoke as he did—that he advocated violence and urged me to betray a patient's trust. I'll send a message south to the sen Halvedna there warning them, and I apologize for myself and for my order." She shook her head. "The fires of Shalsha. I wish he hadn't said that."

"The sen davannat speak truth," said Stefan, "sometimes. They also speak a great deal of the most improbable folly."

"True. I wish he hadn't said it, nonetheless."

4

Afterward, the one thing he remembered was the light.

Before that and around it, gray emptiness reached away into distance, with ghosts of forgotten images haunting it like unremembered dreams. Dim motes of sensation flickered into his awareness and back out again, but none of these left more than a shadow of itself behind. Transient and nameless, each touched him in passing and vanished utterly.

The light remained.

The light, yellow-white and warm, came from somewhere above him and to his right. What missed him traced three sides of a rectangle and part of a fourth on the floor in front of him. He noticed these things and then forgot them immediately, noticed them again, forgot them again, noticed. The light remained, and so after a time did his awareness of it.

Later, other things moved toward continuity. Pressure and texture scattered in many directions fused into the sensation of a soft robe wrapped loosely around him. Voice-fragments became voices, talking quietly, though what they said still eluded him. A dull intermittent pressure inside him took on location, found a rhythm, drew together into the beating of his heart. Around him, the world began to settle into place.

He looked up. A dark figure he couldn't quite see clearly stood in front of him, watching him. Two others sat further away. One of these, seeing the movement, rose and stood beside the dark figure. The two of them spoke, their words never quite making sense , and then watched him. Their shapes gradually took on definition against a background that every moment made less random sensation and more a place, a middle-sized room with plastered walls and a wooden floor, skylights and bookshelves and a stack of brightly colored cushions in one corner.

The one closest to him knelt and said something. To him? He could not tell. He strained to hear it, and the figure repeated it. This time he formed the word in his mind, and unbidden, his lips moved, repeating it: "Jerre."

"Yes," the one speaking to him said. "Jerre. You are Jerre. Your name is Jerre."

Not without effort, sound and meaning came together. "Jerre."

"You are Jerre."

"You," he began, and stopped, sensing the mistake. More effort brought the words he wanted up out of darkness. Tentatively: "I am Jerre."

"Yes."

With more certainty: "I am Jerre."

"Yes. Your name is Jerre."

"Yes." The last fragments of the world settled into place with a whisper only his mind could hear. The whole of his memories

presented themselves to him: a few minutes of slowly clearing awareness, no more. At their farthest border was a blurred
image of light. Beyond that lay emptiness, its nearer reaches
littered with the husks of sensations he had not been able to
keep, its more distant spaces barren not only of those but of
any trace of his own existence.

Out of the emptiness, then, came a new thing, breaking over
him like a wave.

Fear.

In the instant before it struck he was certain it would destroy
him. After that he had no space for thought, only blackness
and a roaring in his ears like rushing waters. In time, though,
the terror drained away, the trembling stopped, the pounding
of his heart slowed and gentled. He drew in a breath, uneven
and ragged, and then another, smoother.

The one who had spoken to him had not moved. A woman
past middle age, he saw now, plump and gray-haired, wrapped
in a robe that danced with bright colors. She watched him with
an expression for which he had no name. The last of the fear
trickled away, and in its place, vague and unformed at first, came
questions. After a time one of these found words. "You are ..."

She smiled, and he realized with a start that much of the
smile was relief. "My name is Tamar," she said. "Jerre, I need
to tell you several things. Please listen carefully."

He listened, and with an effort found meanings for the
words.

"You were in an accident, a terrible accident. Many people
died. You survived it, but you lost your memory. Do you
understand?"

He stared at her, eyes going wide, and nodded.

"Your full name is Jerre Amadan, and before the accident
you lived at Talin Shelter, north of here at the edge of settled
country. You're at Mirien Shelter now."

He nodded again, with less hesitation. Though the emptiness
still remained, it had a name and a reason, and that alone took

away half its vastness and most of its power. He himself had a name and, yes, a reason of sorts, and these gave him something to limit the emptiness and begin to trace its shape. One other question demanded asking, though, and he wrestled words for it from the shadows at the far edge of memory. "What was it? The accident. What happened?"

"Later," said Tamar. "It's not safe for you to talk about it this soon." She glanced back over her shoulder, nodded to the man in black who stood behind her. He smiled wanly, went to a cushion nearby and sat. "Later."

5

The young man with the headphones stared intently at nothing for a moment, then reached for the black notebook on the desk beside him.

"Anything?" Stefan asked quickly.

"Weir Shelter, sen Halka." The operator paused again, listening. "Nothing new to report. No sign of drones." He opened the notebook, wrote a few words and the time inside it, closed it. "Tenth hour is their time to contact the rest of the message net."

Stefan gestured at the notebook. "May I?"

"Of course."

The sen Halka opened it, scanned the notations inside. Two messages written down the night before announced the first shipment of heavy weapons and ammunition from the south, due at Mirien sometime in the next twenty-four hours. Other than these, the only entries noted routine contacts twice daily from the Shelters in the message net. He glanced at the top of the page; the headings on the columns—date, time, source, message—were in Amery's almost-scrawl, of course, along with the instructions taped on the notebook's inside cover. Stefan read these last, then closed the book and handed it back to the operator. For someone who had never set up a message net, he thought, Amery had done an impressive job. Everything necessary had been put in place, the emergency instructions and the list of operators in two-hour shifts pinned up on a nearby wall, the map of the north country above them. As for the Shelter folk, he knew only what he'd seen, but those who staffed the message center during his visits to the radio room knew their business.

He crossed the radio room to the main receiver and the record book for ordinary messages, read the latest two pages. The operator there glanced at him briefly, then returned to her work. Nothing, again and as always: Stefan shook his head, forced a wan smile. Six days had passed since he'd seen the light of awareness return to Jerre Amadan's eyes. He had haunted the message center, watched Tamar at work with her new patient, wrapped himself in the deepest levels of trance he could reach and stayed there for hours on end, hoping to coax new fragments of his vision to the surface, and the end result of all of it had been precisely nothing.

Six days, he thought, and the smile failed. And if it turned out to be six weeks, or six months, or six years?

"Sen Halka?"

He turned, too quickly. "Yes?"

"A message from Talin Shelter." The message center operator was writing in the black notebook, and not merely the few words marking a routine contact. "For you."

Stefan had crossed the room before the young man had finished speaking. "What is it?"

"The command circle at Talin plans to send a patrol north along the drones' track as soon as heavy weapons arrive." He wrote two more words in the notebook. "The message is from Julian Mereval sen Halka."

"Anything more?"

"No, sen Halka."

Stefan nodded his thanks and turned away. Again nothing, he thought, and found himself remembering the old Journey

Star meditations from the Halvedna outer circle: infinite silence and space, the vastness of the sky opening up between Earth and Eridan, the slow shifting of the nearer stars as the colony ship passed from world to world.

Abruptly a different image forced its way into his thoughts: battle-drones, a hundred or more of them, hurtling across the blue windswept barrens of the far north. Emptiness? The image denied that flatly, spun outward into a pattern of meaning centered on the fires of Shalsha. More images burst into being around it, images of combat, destruction, death, the constant themes of his vision. Drawn into these, his mind leapt to the patrol about to set out from Talin, leapt again to the certainty that it would be ambushed as Amery and Toren had been. How many drones? How many more deaths?

A moment later he realized the danger within the images, and reflexes forced his mind clear at once. The vision demanded belief, but until the facts could be known belief opened the door only to madness and his death. That much he knew with cold clarity. At length, shaking his head again, he turned to the door.

As he reached it, he thought: and if the patrol finds nothing, if it scours the north from here to the barrens to no avail, what then? How long can I remain suspended between ground and sky?

As if in answer, the too-familiar images burst into being in the space behind his eyes: darkness, light, fire, sound, and then again darkness: present, and then gone again in less than a heartbeat. Stefan drew in a breath and left the radio room.

6

Amery came out of the Shelter's main stair, stood uncertain for a moment, went down the corridor. In a common space to one side, a circle of children played the Sequence game, laughing or groaning with the turn of each card; they noticed her and fell silent, staring with round eyes at the black garments and the gun. She nodded to them and went past, counted doors down the corridor, stopped at the twelfth and tapped on it.

"Please come in," a voice she didn't recognize said from within.

She pulled open the door, stepped inside. The clutter of Tamar's room met her eyes. In its center, in a cleared space, Jerre Amadan sat with an open book and a collection of flat black objects in front of him. He had half turned to face the door; recognizing her, or perhaps simply her garments, he nodded uncertainly in greeting, said, "Sen Halka."

It had been his voice, then. "Sen Amadan," she replied, and managed a smile. "Do you know where Tamar is now?"

"Amery! A moment, please." The room's other door slid open. The sen Halvedna came in a moment after, dust on her hair and sleeves and the top of the wooden box she carried. "Might you clear that table for me? The books can go anywhere. Thank you." She set the box down, brushed at the dust on her robe. "I must look like a ghost come from its grave. Your arm's healed now? Good. How may I help?"

"I'd like to speak to you, in private." Amery looked troubled. "It's about Stefan."

"Something's wrong?"

"I wish I knew."

Tamar nodded. "Let me make sure Jerre has enough to do while we talk."

Amery gestured acceptance, turned toward the survivor again. The flat black shapes, she saw, were triangles of various sizes, and the book showed silhouettes of shapes that could, with some difficulty, be made from them. "Logic problems?"

"Yes." Tamar's attention was fixed on her patient, who just then picked up one of the triangles, examined it, set it down. "One learns most about oneself when facing a challenge."

"I remember."

"Of course." Tamar glanced at her, turned back to her patient.

Jerre took up another of the triangles, turned it over, and then set it down. Without hesitation he began setting other pieces around it, and a perfect five-pointed star took shape. Finishing, he looked up at Tamar, who said, "Very good. How long do you expect the rest of the book will take you?"

He thought about it. "An hour. Maybe more."

"Amery and I will be in the next room. We shouldn't be disturbed unless it's an emergency. If anyone comes to speak to me, you may as well tell them that."

"I'll do that." He waited a moment for more to be said, then turned back to the book and the triangles. Tamar motioned to Amery, and the two of them went through the far door into the sen Halvedna's study.

"I'm inpressed," said Amery, sitting on a convenient cushion. "With Jerre, I mean. I didn't expect him to come so far so quickly."

Tamar smiled. "He's an exceptional student. I've caught myself taking time from my other duties to keep him working up to capacity. He can care for himself completely—he has his own room now—and he's been assigned Shelter work, helping in the maintenance shop down on fourth level. I understand he has a talent for machines; there's been some speculation that he might be from a technician family, though of course no one's rude enough to mention that. His inner rebuilding? I have no idea; I haven't searched his mind except at the most superficial levels, of course."

"Of course."

Tamar gave her a rueful look. "Amery, I'm sorry. All of this must be painfully familiar to you. I'm surprised you chose to stay through his treatment. It can't have been easy."

"Less difficult than I'd expected." She did not meet the sen Halvedna's gaze at once. "I have the dwimmerwine to thank for that, I suppose; my treatment was one of the things I relived during baya." She looked up then, and suddenly smiled. "In fact, it's been a lesson in the difference between reality and memory. Was I that serious after the catamnetic?"

"Not really," said Tamar. "You were quick to laugh or weep, like a child. I would be happier if Jerre moved further in that direction. I don't believe he's smiled once since he came here, and that worries me."

Neither of them spoke for a moment. Finally the sen Halvedna said, "But you came to speak of something more important than the doings of my favorite patient."

Amery still smiled, but the smile grew strained. "I don't mind. I'd almost rather we talked about Jerre."

"What has Stefan been doing?"

"Nothing. That's just precisely the problem."

Tamar paused. "I haven't seen him in several days."

"No. He spends most of his time in his room. When he goes out it's either to the Shelter library or the radio room. I've seen him only once myself in the last four days."

"He's always been solitary."

"Not this solitary. Not in the time I've known him." Then, after a moment, and in a different tone: "It's his vision."

"Ah." Tamar folded her fingers in a knot in her lap. "I'd suspected as much."

"I came to you," said Amery, "because I need knowledge, Tamar. The Halka lore about visions is practical and legal: how to recognize them in myself or someone else, what limits bind a Halka visionary, what use may be made of visions in a legal case. I need more than that. I need to understand what's happening to Stefan, and that's Halvedna lore, isn't it?"

"Visionary experience is one of the core tools of the Halvedna path. What precisely do you need to know? I'll tell you whatever I can."

Amery paused a moment, phrased her questions. "I need to know where his vision comes from, how it's likely to affect him—and what it means."

"Halka traditions say nothing about that?"

"Only that visions are a product of the innermind's own processes, and that they're sometimes true, sometimes false, most often a mix of the two."

Tamar waited a moment for her to go on, then frowned. "No wonder the Halka end up shooting so many of their visionaries. That isn't even a first step toward understanding."

"That's why I'm here," Amery reminded her.

"True. How to begin? You Halka have something you call 'subtle awareness,' a way of scanning perceptions with the innermind so that things that the conscious mind misses don't slip past. We have a practice like it, of course. It's a useful skill, but it doesn't begin to tap the full powers of the innermind. You're aware of that?"

"Yes."

"Good. Now we have a series of meditative trances that go progressively deeper into the innermind. I imagine the Halka have something similar."

"There are three levels of trance for heightening awareness," Amery said. "I've heard that some of the southern lineages have a few other techniques."

"Exactly. Those improve on our primary scanning or your subtle awareness the way those improve on ordinary conscious perception, but even so they don't tap into the innermind's deeper powers."

"Understood."

"What limits them is that they use the innermind only as a way of expanding perception and memory—but the innermind can also expand reasoning. Just as it's better at perceiving and remembering than the conscious mind, it's better at fitting many factors together, sensing patterns and projecting from the known into the unknown. The one problem is that it doesn't think in the same way as the conscious mind, and the chance of misunderstanding isn't small.

"Nearly half my books—" She motioned at the tall shelves. "—are about understanding and analyzing the way the innermind thinks: predicate thinking is the technical term. The conscious mind thinks in words, images, perceptions, but the innermind thinks in patterns, symbols, lattices of meaning. Do sen Halka dream?"

"Not after the dwimmerwine. Do sen Halvedna?"

"It varies," Tamar replied. "I don't. If you remember any of the dreams you had before baya, though, you'll know the sort of thinking I mean. Most often, the innermind reasons about the ordinary content of consciousness. Rarely, for reasons no one understands fully, the full resources of the innermind turn to one subject, and present the conscious mind with a cluster of images and intuitions of what is or what will be."

"A vision."

"Exactly."

"And is there any way to tell if the innermind's reasoning is correct?"

Tamar folded her hands. "In a sense, every vision is true. In another sense, every vision is false. They're true because if they're understood correctly, they mirror reality more precisely than any construct of the conscious levels of the mind, and they're false because it's fearfully easy to misinterpret them."

"So Stefan's vision ..."

"Expresses truth, but may not mean what it seems to mean." Then: "And of course there's the difference between our orders. The dwimmerroot wears away the barriers between the conscious self and the innermind, so each becomes transparent to the other. The wine breaks through the barriers completely and brings the two into direct contact. What difference that makes in visionary states is anyone's guess. The legal barriers between the orders haven't exactly made research easy."

"So we can't know whether this war Stefan foresees is reality or symbol."

"Exactly."

"I trust he's aware of this."

"I hope so." Tamar frowned. "There's a thing called visionary psychosis. It happens in visionaries who can't reconcile their visions with the reality of the world around them, and choose to believe the vision rather than the world. The results aren't pleasant: a swift descent into paranoia and madness that usually can't be stopped."

Amery gave her a long troubled look. "Could that happen to Stefan?"

"I don't know. I think he's experienced enough and canny enough to avoid it—but I don't know."

"Is there anything we can do?"

Tamar considered that, shook her head. "We'd do more harm than good by trying. Our teachings say that the visionary state is a space of supreme paradox. There are maybe two dozen sen Halvedna who are qualified to guide other sen Halvedna through visionary states. I'm not one of them, and if I were I'd be out of my depth with Stefan, because he's Halka. The differences between our paths are just too great."

Amery said nothing for a time. Tamar watched her in silence. Finally the young sen Halka shook her head and said, "Then there's nothing."

"Essentially. He'll have to find his way through this himself."

Another silence came into the room, remained while clouds drifted past the skylight overhead. Amery considered the floor, and Tamar considered her. Traces of conflicting emotion so subtle even Tamar's trained awareness could barely detect them touched the sen Halka's face. Finally, without looking up, she spoke. "I suppose it makes sense that there's nothing I can do for him. I've been able to give him little enough otherwise."

"Ah." Tamar smiled, just perceptibly. "So that's the heart of it."

Amery said nothing.

Gently, the older woman asked, "How long have you loved him?"

The sen Halka shut her eyes. "Tamar, of all the people on Eridan you're the last I want to burden with that."

Tamar's laugh was soft as rain. "Because I have the same bad habit?"

Amery looked up at that, met the older woman's gaze, then looked away. "Because you're a friend—and because I know what's between you goes back a long time."

"Since before you were born, yes. But I don't fault you for following your own heart." Tamar laughed again, but this time a rueful note touched the sound. "Amery, what's between Stefan and me is a long story, but not a very exciting one. Some things don't change—that's how he put it, and of course he's right."

Amery nodded, after a moment.

"Be sure he's aware of your feelings. That's doubtless why he's accepted so little from you. He's too honest to promise something he cannot give."

The sen Halka nodded again. "That's some consolation. Thank you, Tamar." She rose to her feet.

Tamar stood also. "Of course you're welcome." Then: "But there's something else I should tell you—not about Stefan, and I'm not sure he should hear about it. Word arrived from Setneva Shelter earlier today. Daval came there yesterday, spent the night, and left on the main path southward this morning."

"The sen davannat?"

"Yes. A friend of mine at Setneva spoke with him. He told her, and anyone else who would listen, that a disaster was approaching the north country, and only those who fled south at once would survive."

"A disaster. Did he say anything else about it?"

"Not a word." Tamar shrugged. "He may simply be delusional. I thought you should know, though."

7

Lightning danced overhead, branching, random energy flung across the sky. The thunder following rattled the skylights of Tamar's workroom and drowned out every other sound. Two pairs of eyes turned upward, waiting.

"The clouds are aching with rain," Tamar said after a moment, when nothing more had happened. "Can you feel it?"

Stefan nodded absently, watching the sky. Dim outlines of clouds the color of cold iron hinted at shapes he recognized: battle-drones, flames, a looming shape of smoke. The images had taken on a familiarity that reminded him of creases and rounded corners, of things carried in pockets for months at a time. With a moment's thought, he could set the whole of his vision out in its proper order, contemplate it as a unity, almost see it as something unconnected from himself. Almost: the word turned in his mind. The connection remained, a constant presence, pressure, threat.

Another bolt of lightning seared the clouds, closer. The thunder came a heartbeat behind it, bursting in a dozen uneven claps that shook him with an almost tangible force. Tamar looked upward again, but said nothing.

Tension whispered in the air around Stefan; the clouds and the room alike bristled with it. When Tamar came to him the day before to tell him that Jerre was ready for the attempt to restore his memory, heat lightning flickered over the mountains to the east. During the night, as Stefan wrestled with the possible outcomes and went over his vision again and again in the darkness, the dim muttering of distant thunder whispered through the Shelter ventilation system, a shadow of foreboding over the silent images of the innermind. Now, in the gray light of an uncertain morning, bright energies of the sky danced above the roofs of Mirien Shelter, promising rains they had, so far, withheld. What air came in through the vents was dry as old bones.

"I wish I knew what was keeping him," the sen Halvedna said suddenly.

Stefan glanced at her, startled by the show of impatience. "You're worried?"

"Deeply. This is probably the most dangerous procedure I know, Stefan. If anything goes wrong we may have to choose between his memory and his reason." Thunder rolled again, and she waited for stillness before going on. "If it comes to that, you know which one I'll have to choose."

"If I even asked you to consider the other," Stefan said calmly, "the command circle at Talin would have me shot within a week, and I'd deserve it."

She looked at him, nodded after a moment. "If we were talking about anyone but you, I'd find that reassuring."

More thunder shook the room, drowning out whatever else Tamar might have said. By the time the last rumblings had died away, she had wrapped herself in a thoughtful silence, looking up into the roiling sky. Stefan did the same, and frowned as the innermind reshaped vague lines and shadows into the elements of his vision, stretched the faint sounds that came through the air vents into shouting, screams, the rattle of gunfire. That anything could so cloud his awareness annoyed him, stood in constant conflict with everything the Halka path taught: *tessat-ni-Halka shol ielindat*, the path of the Halka is clarity of awareness, was one of the first maxims in Halka tradition and one of the first lessons to be mastered during training. He muttered a triggering phrase under his breath, let reflexes decades old bring his mind back to the present moment. The vision subsided.

And if it's all true, he thought then, if Jerre saw battle-drones under human control and the peace we've struggled to keep intact for two hundred years is about to break into open war, what then?

After a moment, and more slowly: and if it's not?

He shook his head, repeated the triggering phrase. Either Jerre's memory would answer the question or it wouldn't, he told himself. Either way there was no point in brooding over it.

Another roll of thunder broke in on his thoughts. Again the rush of sound blurred and twisted along the paths of his vision, and this time he could not force his perceptions back into their ordinary channels. He looked up again, eyes going wide, as a darkness that seemed as real as the sky spread over the clouds, hiding them, and at its heart a deeper shadow took shape: the shadow of a threat he could sense but not quite see.

Light burst over him, blue-white, blinding.

The sound that followed broke over him with the force of a blow.

He blinked, and only then realized that the flash had been lightning, the sound thunder, both of them reality and not prophecy. He rubbed his eyes, opened them again in time to see the first drops of rain splash on the skylight above him.

All Eridan seemed silent. More raindrops fell. After them the rain slackened briefly, but a flurry of heavy drops followed, splattering against the glass. More followed. The rain became a drumming on the roof, a visible flow and darkness across the glass, blotting out the clouds. Air came through the vents in wet, clean gusts. Minutes passed, and the rain fell harder and still harder, until the roof rang with it, the sky could not be seen at all through the rush and splash of water on the skylight, wind scrubbed clean by the downpour came through the vents and cleansed the room's still air.

Tamar rose and went to stand under the skylight. "It's beautiful," she said after a moment. "I only hope the procedure with Jerre ends as well."

Stefan smiled also, fractionally. "We'll see."

A short time later, when the rain had settled to a steady drumming on the roof, the door to the corridor opened and Amery came in. "He'll be here in a few minutes," she said, and sat on a cushion near Stefan.

"What happened?" Tamar asked.

"Repairs on the hydroponics pumps, again. Jerre was in the pump room helping the technician for more than an hour." Amery shook her head. "Covered with grease and babbling in mechanic's jargon. I had no idea he'd learned so much so quickly."

"The mind forgets but the hands remember," Tamar said, "and even the mind remembers if it's prompted enough. He probably regained most of his skill with machinery the first time he had any reason to call on it." She took a folded sheet of paper from a pocket of her robe, handed it to Amery. "You'll want to read this carefully."

"The procedure?"

"Yes. I've translated it out of Kendeval symbols for you and Stefan."

Amery nodded, and read through the paper twice. "This seems remarkably simple."

"There's little room for subtlety in a frontal attack." Tamar's smile had vanished. "Unfortunately no one's found a better way to break through chemical catamnesis."

"You don't have drugs for that?"

"Only the dwimmerroot. Once the catamnetic's out of the bloodstream, there's no chemical barrier to memory. All that's needed is concentration and the right—"

Someone tapped on the door.

Amery glanced over her shoulder, handed the sheet of paper back to the sen Halvedna. Tamar gestured her thanks, put it back in her pocket, called out, "Please come in."

The door opened and Jerre entered. He had evidently washed and changed, for the grease was nowhere to be seen, and his gray robe was cut far too loose to be practical inside a pump room. He nodded greetings to Tamar and the sen Halka, stood by the door without speaking.

"Please be seated, Jerre." Tamar gestured at a cushion. "I hope you won't mind if we begin at once."

"I'd prefer that." He went to the cushion, considered the three who waited for him, drew in a breath and sat. Tension and uncertainty showed through his surface calm in a hundred subtle ways. "What must I do?"

"Nothing so terrible," said Tamar. "We'll give you certain things that were yours before you lost your memory, and ask you some questions. That's all."

Stefan stirred. "There's one thing more, sen Amadan. This entire business is of interest to the Halka, and because of that I'm responsible for your well-being while you're in treatment here. For that reason I must ask you to affirm that you know what's to be done here, and accept it freely."

"Tamar's going to try to help me regain my memory." Jerre's voice was little more than a whisper. "And yes, I've accepted that freely."

"And you're aware that there are dangers."

"Tamar's spoken of them."

"Sufficient." Stefan sat back. "Thank you."

Jerre acknowledged this with an uncertain nod.

"Then we'll begin," said Tamar. She got to her feet and went into her other room, returned a moment later with a packet wrapped in coarse brown barkcloth, which she handed to Jerre. "This came from Talin Shelter two weeks ago. As you see, I haven't opened it. The sen Halvedna at Talin said that everything they're sure is yours is here."

"Open it," Stefan told him, "and tell me of any images or memories that come to mind."

Jerre stared at the package with a look compounded of more emotions than Stefan could count, then tore off the adhesive seals. In a few moments the bark fell away. Inside was a bundle of cloth that proved to be three robes, two green, one gray; some other clothing; and a smaller packet in the same brown barkcloth. He glanced at the clothing, reached for the packet.

"Wait," Tamar said. "Please look at the others first. One at a time, and closely."

He glanced at her, nodded, picked up one of the robes. The soft meria-fiber cloth rustled at the edge of hearing as he shook the folds out and held it up, turning it one way and another. No trace of remembrance touched his face. Stefan, noting this, frowned.

Jerre set the first robe aside, picked up another. For a moment he stared at it without recognition, but then his eyes widened.

"What do you see?" Tamar asked.

"A young woman," Jerre said slowly. "Crying, I think. I'm wearing this robe, and I'm with her." He closed his eyes, paused. "It's dark, and we're somewhere outside."

"Think of her." The sen Halvedna leaned forward, intent. Subtle awareness brought Stefan whispers of a half-familiar movement of mind, some Halvedna trick of prompting. "See her, search for her. What's her name?"

"Shennan," Jerre said after a moment. "Shennan."

"What else do you remember about her?"

Time passed as he stared at nothing, eyes closed. "That's all. I'm sorry, Tamar."

"Don't be. That was more than I expected, and sooner." She gestured at the rest of the clothing. "Please go on."

He nodded, and picked up the last robe. That brought no memories with it, nor did the rest of the clothing until he came to a plaited barkcloth belt. He looked puzzled, said, "This one ... there's something. I don't know."

"Look for images," said Tamar.

Jerre stared at the belt. Tentatively: "Crowds. Noise." Then: "There was an old man behind a table, and dozens of these."

"What was nearby?"

"People, many of them." He put the belt down. "That's all."

The last of the clothing brought back no images. Jerre finished with it, turned to the packet and opened it. Inside were three pens, an oddly shaped stone, and a notebook with a plain green cover.

Jerre picked up the stone first. "This was from the seashore," he said slowly, turning it over. "If you wet it, it turns the most luminous blue." He set it down, looked at the pens in turn and put them aside. Then it was the notebook's turn. Jerre opened it to the first page, and drew in a sharp breath.

"What is it?" Tamar asked quickly.

"Drawings." He set the notebook on the floor, open, so the others could see. On one page, a beach below a rocky headland reached away into almost tangible distance. On the facing page, the cast-off shell of a sea-scuttler lay on the sand. Both had been drawn with remarkable skill. "This was the beach where I found the stone. I remember it, Tamar. I remember it!"

He turned to the next page, which had studies of driftwood and another beach landscape on it, and then to the next. There a dark-haired young woman looked out from a Shelter window with sad eyes.

"Who is she?" Tamar asked.

"Shennan." He stared at the drawing for a time, went on. The pages that followed were full of the same young woman, here sitting on a stone against a forest background, there nude and asleep amid a tangle of bedding. A final portrait, done in meticulous detail, showed her standing in a meadow beneath a sky full of autumn clouds. After it came more landscape, a quick expressive sketch of a fireflower, a view of a Shelter from a distant height.

As Jerre turned still another page, Stefan looked to Tamar, who nodded fractionally. He turned back to Jerre. "Sen Amadan?"

Jerre glanced up.

"What do the words *shcha lyu ang chwem* mean to you?"

Before Stefan had finished the fourth word Jerre had gone as white and rigid as a dead man, and for one terrible moment the emptiness of withdrawal showed again in his eyes. Tamar gave Stefan an alarmed look, but the sen Halka did not see it. He faced Jerre with an absolute concentration that shut out all else, subtle awareness tracing every nuance of Jerre's path as the young man came to the edge of the precipice, stood there unsteadily, and at length drew back.

A low moan broke through the silence, and Jerre, shuddering, lowered his face into his hands. Stefan waited. Finally the trembling stopped, the clenched lines of tension in the survivor's shoulders faded somewhat.

"What did you see?" Stefan asked.

Jerre drew his hands down from a face gone white with horror. "Are they all dead?" he whispered. "All of them?"

"You were the only one we found alive."

"Then it was real." He clenched his eyes shut, opened them again. "I was sitting against a rock and everyone around me was dead."

"How much do you remember?"

"Most of it. Do you want me to tell you what I saw?"

"Please," said Stefan. "It's of the highest importance."

Jerre nodded, closed his eyes. "It was late afternoon. We were gathering meria seeds for the spring planting. I was under a tree, and someone near me looked up and said, "What in Earth's name is that?' I listened, and heard something very faint in the distance, a sound I can't describe. I stood there and listened, and the sound grew louder. After a few minutes it was deafening. All the people around me stopped what they were doing and looked north. I remember that some of the watchers took their guns and went toward the sound, and an old woman near me suddenly screamed and ran down the slope away from it."

He swallowed. "I don't remember the next few minutes very clearly. Gunshots, many of them, very fast. People screaming and dying all around me. A man I knew was shot a meter in front of me and stumbled into me, and I fell down. Then a machine came over the rise and down the slope." He stopped, made himself go on. "I think it was a battle-drone."

"Please describe it to me," said Stefan.

"Like nothing I've ever seen." Jerre opened his eyes. "All angles and bulges, painted blue and gray in uneven stripes, with guns in a turret in the nose. It floated about a meter above the ground."

Stefan reached into a pocket, frowned and turned to Amery. "Do you have your copy of the banned-tech manual with you?"

"Of course." She handed a pocket-sized book to Stefan, who opened it, turned several pages, passed it to Jerre. "Is this what you saw?"

Three drawings on the open pages showed top, side, and front views of a Type Ten drone, the most common model. Notes in fine print indicated gun turret, sensors, cooling units, lifters, vulnerable points. Jerre examined it and frowned. "Like that, but shorter and thicker, not so round here, and lower in front."

"Turn to the next page," Stefan told him.

The next page showed a different drone, the Type Eleven. Jerre shook his head, and at a gesture from Stefan turned the page again. There he stopped. "Yes. That's what it looked like."

Stefan took the book back, glanced at it. "That's most interesting."

"What was it?" Amery asked.

He returned the book to her without speaking, and she looked at it, at him. "The one I destroyed was also a Type Twelve."

Stefan faced Jerre again. "What happened then?"

"I'm not sure." The survivor closed his eyes again. "More gunfire, more screams. I remember lying still, hoping that the drone would think I was already dead. But someone—someone spoke." His face had gone white again. "Calling out four words I don't know." He forced them out. "*Shcha lyu ang chwem.*"

Stefan waited for a time, then asked, "And after that?"

"All I remember after that is sitting against the stone with the dead all around me in the night. I must have crawled away from where I'd fallen after the drone left. I don't know. After that, nothing at all."

In the silence that followed a flurry of rain splattered against the skylight. Finally Jerre spoke again. "Sen Halka, I don't think I ever knew much about battle-drones and I remember even less now. You'll probably think this is ludicrous. But whoever spoke those words—he was talking to the drone, sen Halka. I'm certain of it."

"I know," said Stefan.

Jerre stared at him. The older sen Halka said no more. Amery glanced at him, then turned to Jerre and said, "Sen Amadan, we learned about the four words within days of the killings. You repeated them when you were still in withdrawal. Since then the Halka have known the drones might have been under someone's control."

"Drones?" Jerre asked, the gray horror returning to his eyes. "More than one?"

"Six attacked the camp. One of those has been destroyed, and there's a Halka patrol hunting the others right now.

But we've had very little to go on, and for that reason you have my thanks for telling us what you remember."

"And I think we'll leave you with Tamar now," said Stefan, breaking his silence. He rose to his feet. "I need to contact the Halka circle at Talin, and let them know about this. Tamar will have more for you to do. But you have my thanks also." He faced Jerre for a moment, his expression veiled, and went to the door. Amery stood also, nodded politely to Tamar and Jerre, left also. The survivor's glance, troubled and touched with dread, went with them until the door slid shut.

Outside, the two sen Halka turned and walked up the corridor. When they had gone far enough not to be overheard, Amery sighed. "I wish I knew what to make of this."

Stefan glanced at her. "I know."

"The drone didn't just pass him by because he pretended to be dead. The sensors would have detected breathing and body movements in seconds. Yet he's not lying—I sensed no trace of deliberate dishonesty. Unless the controller of the drones just happened to call them off before they found and killed him ..." She left the sentence unfinished.

They turned the corner, went up three steps to another corridor leading in toward the Shelter core. Stefan frowned, mulling over the possibilities. "I thought of that," he said, "but I don't know what to make of it either."

Amery gave him a thoughtful look. "You noticed something I didn't."

"Maybe." He gestured uncertainty. "I'm wondering about those Type Twelve drones. I don't know much about them, and I have a feeling I need to know more."

"They were one of the final types, weren't they?"

"Yes. They went into production in the last year of the Insurgency."

The last year of the Insurgency: something coiled like smoke around that phrase, something that Stefan could not make out but that set the innermind in motion. Subtle awareness flared, and through it the core images of his vision—darkness, light, sound, shadow—rose up with shattering force.

Reflexes backed by an effort of will contained these last and forced his mind clear, but the effort raised cold sweat on his forehead. The effort, or the fact that it was necessary? He could not tell.

Abruptly he became aware that he'd stopped, and that Amery was watching him, puzzled and uneasy. He drew in a ragged breath and started walking again. "I'm sorry," he said. "More of this—" A curt outward gesture made the rest of the sentence unnecessary. "Would you mind greatly, seeing to the message for Talin? I need to find a history of the Insurgency, a good one. It may be of some importance."

"Not at all," said Amery. She was still watching him. "What are you looking for, or do you know?"

"I'm not sure." In the deep places of the innermind, shapes still moved. "Something that happened in the last year of the Insurgency. Beyond that, I'm not sure."

She nodded. Other questions moved behind her eyes, but—thankfully—she asked none of them. A few more paces brought them to one of the Shelter's main stairs, and he managed a farewell, turned aside toward the library.

CHAPTER 3

THE BOOK OF CIRCLES

1

"It took some work to get the protective ring clear of moss." Amery gestured toward the bare metal ahead of them. "But the rest was simple enough. Eighty per cent of the drone traps were in good working order, and it took only three weeks to get all the others repaired."

Carla Dubrenden, walking with her, nodded. "That's been our experience elsewhere."

"Beyond that, the Shelter council and I have worked out an emergency plan in case we're attacked, and the radio message center's set up and staffed. That's what we've done so far."

The moss around the two sen Halka sparkled with rain, though pools of standing water in hollows in the ground reflected only the sparsest of clouds and the concrete and glass of the Shelter behind them were already more than half dry. Another thunderstorm, the fourth in two weeks, had broken over Mirien in the night; the noise of it had roused Amery from an uneasy sleep. In the darkness the thunder echoed through the Shelter's ventilation system like a memory of Shalsha's fires.

"And the Shelter folk?" Carla asked. "Are they well enough armed to matter?"

"Better than I'd expected. The Shelter arsenal has eighty rifles in usable condition and just over nine thousand rounds in rifle caliber, all properly stored and tended. This area still had trouble with outrunners thirty years ago."

"The Council was supportive, then."

"They've given us everything we could have asked."

They splashed across an area of sodden ground and came to the inner edge of the protective ring. Before them a strip of dark rustproof metal ten meters across, like a river of iron between banks of pale blue meadowmoss, closed off the Shelter's periphery with a barrier no drone could cross. At intervals around the outer edge, only half visible even in the clear light of morning, seams in the metal traced out lifter field detectors and the innermost ring of drone traps.

Carla considered the ring for a moment and then turned to Amery. "Have you helped set up a Shelter defense before?"

"Before this one? No."

"You've done remarkably well, then."

Amery looked surprised. "I followed the standard procedure."

"True." She turned back to the protective ring. "Quickly, capably and without any lapses I've seen so far, which is another thing altogether. Mirien ought to be safe against anything short of a field army of drones." Her expression tensed. "I wish I could say the same of the rest of the north country."

Neither of them spoke for a time. "What do you think of Stefan's vision now?" Amery asked at length.

"Now? I'm even less certain than I was." They began crossing the protective ring, their boots striking dull resonances from hollow places under the metal. "I spent most of yesterday evening talking with him. We sat and drank tebbe and discussed, very calmly, the destruction of our world. It was unnerving." A jewelfly flitted past them, sparkling in the morning light. "He seemed entirely reasonable about it, and I didn't detect a trace of delusional thinking."

"Tamar thinks he's avoided visionary psychosis."

They stepped from metal onto moss. "So she told me," said Carla. "Yes, I spoke with her, and also with the survivor. I wanted another perspective on Stefan's claims before I discussed them with him." She shook her head. "Some of the people at Talin were against my coming here at all because of my friendship with Stefan. No one objected openly, of course, but the feeling was common enough that I have to be cautious."

"So they've set aside Stefan's vision?"

"For the most part." Water splashed under their boots, and a cloud of jewelflies danced around them and flew off. "Inevitable, I suppose. Talin Shelter has become a very busy place since you and Stefan left it. There are more than a hundred sen Halka there, and as many more in each of the three or four Shelters closest to it. The command circle meets daily; there are strategists, legalists, some of the most famous sen Halka on Eridan advising it now. They're all experienced, sober, sensible people, and of course Julian is woven of the same thread. They've considered Stefan's vision in great detail, and decided that he's simply another of the false visionaries our order produces so often. There's plenty of precedent for that, of course. Do you know anything about the last time the Orange Sky code was declared?"

"No. It was before I took baya, wasn't it?"

"Just less than fifteen years ago. The sen Halka who did it was shot by order of a judgment circle three weeks later. I don't know all the details, but he claimed he'd found the location of Bredin Shelter."

Amery looked puzzled. "I'm not familiar with that."

"No? It's a hill country legend, one of the stories they tell on winter nights to chill your bones to the marrow. There are a hundred different versions, but they all start with a traveler on his way through some distant area just before the beginning of winter. He comes to a Shelter and the Shelter folk welcome him, but warn him to stay in the common areas and especially to stay out of the workshops on the lowest level. Of course he becomes curious, finds an unguarded stair, and goes to look. He finds the people there building and repairing battle-drones, and when he listens to their talk he realizes that all the people in the Shelter are descended from survivors of Shalsha. They see him, he makes his escape, and runs through falling snow all the way to the next Shelter. When he leads a party of sen Halka back the next morning, the Shelter's deserted; there's no trace of the people—or the drones."

"The sen Halka thought the story was real?"

"Apparently. According to the legalist who told me about this, it's happened to others within living memory."

Amery shook her head, laughed uneasily. "In a way I understand that. Can you imagine anything that better captures the worst nightmare of the Halka?"

"No. You may want to consider, though, how close the idea at that story's heart is to the themes of Stefan's vision."

They walked on in silence to the edge of the forest, stopped beneath the first trees. "That's true," said Amery, "and worrisome. I wonder if Stefan knows the story."

"I don't intend to ask. You can be sure the command circle at Talin knows about it, and has discussed the parallels with Stefan's vision. I suspect that played a large role in convincing them to set his vision aside."

"What did they think of Jerre Amadan's memories, then?"

"That was another matter." Carla gestured ambivalence. "When you sent word to Talin about what he'd said, the circle seriously considered the possibility of war for the first time in weeks. Later, though, there were second thoughts. All we know for sure is that the one survivor of the killings heard someone say four unknown words. Everything else is speculation. So we're back where we started."

"Is that why the command circle sent you?"

Carla turned to face her. "The command circle wanted someone to come here and assess Jerre Amadan's story. I offered to go, and though some of the circle members were against it my offer was accepted. My reasons for volunteering, though, were my own and not those of the circle." She paused. "This is to go no further for the time being."

"Of course."

"Amery, I think they're making a hideous mistake. I grant that a war for the restoration of Shalsha is unlikely in the extreme—but it's possible. During the last few weeks I've found myself thinking again and again of plausible ways it could happen. There are at least three."

Amery motioned her to go on.

"First, a group of renegade technicians could have discovered a place where intact drones were abandoned, and deciphered their control systems. Second, someone—technician or otherwise—could have stumbled across a written key to control language, and taken command of drones at large in the far north. Third, one of the outrunner bands could have preserved scraps of lore from before the destruction of Shalsha and finally figured out how to put them to use. Motives and strategies would differ, but in each case they would need one thing to have any hope of victory—the failure of the Halka to take the threat seriously and prepare to face it."

"Which is what the command circle's doing."

"Essentially, yes."

Amery nodded slowly. "You've discussed this with them?"

"Several times. A few members of the circle are sympathetic but the rest want evidence."

"Do you expect to find that here?"

"No. I came to listen to Stefan and the survivor, and decide if there are grounds for a supplementary judgment in dissent. I know that's a drastic step, but I don't know of another way to force Talin to face the situation."

"They have the right to refuse."

"If they do, they'll have to deal with my judgment not as a supplementary but as a full formal alternative. I'll stand with it, if it comes to that."

Amery stared. "That would mean calling an alternate command circle."

"If eight other sen Halka declare support for it, yes." She stopped, looked embarrassed. "I'm sorry, Amery. I'm assuming your support without even asking for it."

"You have it," Amery told her. "Of course you have it."

The older sen Halka regarded her for a moment, then smiled. "Then we'll attempt it, if we can meet the requirements and they won't listen. The circle at Talin will have to deal with the circle at Mirien, like it or not." The smile thinned. "I don't think they'll like it much."

A jewelfly darted between them, hovered momentarily in a ray of sunlight. Behind, within the protective circle, Shelter folk were moving. "No," said Amery, "I imagine not."

2

Paper rustled in Tamar's hands. "And before that, nothing?"

"Nothing," Jerre acknowledged. "I wish there were more."

"I know." She set the papers aside, took a flat hand-sized box from a pocket. "We'll see if the Sequence deck has anything else to tell us."

As the sen Halvedna took the cards from their box, concentrated on them, and began to shuffle, Jerre let his eyes go shut. The effort needed to drag one memory after another out of the mist and darkness of his mind left bands of pain around his eyes and temples that he could set aside but never quite drive away. For the tenth time that afternoon, he slowed his breathing, slipped into the relaxation drill Tamar had taught him, willed rigid muscles to loosen one after the other. The pain faded, but not much.

"The first card," Tamar said, and set it down on the floor with an audible slap.

Jerre opened his eyes and looked at the card with as much concentration as he could manage. A circle trapped by three intersecting lines, the whole in a larger circle: like all the Sequence cards, white lines on a black background, with a number at the top. Restriction, he thought he remembered, and tried to push the recollection out of his mind. The image remained silent, lifeless. After a moment he shook his head.

"*Kel eshonat nen-na-tekke*," said Tamar, "nineteenth glyph of the Sequence, the image of Limitation." She glanced at Jerre, at the card. "The second card."

The image she placed next to the first showed three circles in a vertical line, two overlapping, the other a short distance away. Jerre looked at it briefly, shook his head again and looked at Tamar.

"*Kel eshonat ken-na-dedekke*, twenty-fifth glyph of the Sequence," she told him. "The image of Departure. Is there any response at all?"

"Only things I've remembered already."

"We could stop now if you wish."

"No." He motioned toward the deck in her hand. "Thank you, but no."

"The third card."

He stared at the glyph for a time, shook his head once more.

"*Kel eshonat an-na-fadekke*, forty-first glyph of the sequence, the image of Conflict. The fourth card."

The lines and circles, entangled, suggested nothing to him but his own weariness and confusion. He shook his head.

"*Kel eshonat tre-na-tredekke*, thirty-third glyph of the Sequence, the image of Frustration." Despite herself, she smiled. "Appropriate, I suppose. The fifth and last card."

One circle, lines radiating from it, pressed against the upper part of a surrounding circle as if trying to break free. Jerre glanced at it, began to shake his head, then stopped and stared at it again, eyes narrowing.

"What do you see?" Tamar asked him.

"A bowl." His gaze did not move from the card. "An upturned bowl. Something was tapping on it, tapping from beneath. I don't know what it was."

Tamar waited, watching him. After a time, his face bleak, he looked up at her. "That's all. A bowl and something tapping on it. I can't even remember what color the bowl was."

"*Kel eshonat sho*," Tamar said quietly, "eighth glyph of the Sequence, the image of Containment."

Jerre nodded and closed his eyes again, drawing inward against the pain in his head. The relaxation drill, when he tried it, seemed to play across the surface of tensions that drove into him like spikes. He heard the rustle of Tamar's robe, and a moment later the sound of a cabinet door opening, but the sounds remained distant, meaningless.

Again cloth rustled near him. "We shouldn't have gone on so long," Tamar said. "Drink this. It'll ease the pain."

He took the medicine cup she gave him, drank the contents, felt tingling spread over his tongue and the back of his throat. Presently the pain dimmed and was gone. He rubbed his eyes, opened them. "Thank you. What was that?"

"The drug? A short-term analgesic." Tamar stood again, took the medicine cup back to her cabinet. "Be careful standing up for the next fifteen minutes; your sense of balance won't be quite right until after then." She vanished into the next room, returned after a minute with two bowls of tebbe. "Here," she said, giving him one. "As Stefan likes to remind me, this is one of the minor medicines, and it blends well with the one you've just taken. It's good for relieving muscular tension. You'll have a great deal of that just now."

He sipped at the tebbe. "What causes that?"

"The tension? Pure effort. After chemical catamnesis, some memories come back easily, some can be brought back with intense concentration, and some are permanently lost. Bringing out the second kind always causes tension and pain."

"And I've come to the end of those now."

She glanced up from her tebbe. "That's my guess. I'm sorry, Jerre." After a pause to judge his mood, she went on. "I can tell you what you remembered with the last card, though."

That caught his interest. "How so?"

"The bowl and the tapping are more than enough." A smile creased her face. "It's a game children play with jewelflies—have probably played since humanity first came to Eridan. They take a bowl, hold it over a jewelfly at rest, and startle the fly with a shadow or a movement. The secret is that jewelflies always fly straight up when they're startled, and so long as the bowl stays above them they'll keep being startled and flying straight up into it. They can be held that way for hours. Do you remember it now?"

"Dimly." He struggled with the image. "I recall hoping that just once the jewelfly would realize what was happening and free itself. If it folded its wings and fell, it would be out of the trap. I remember how sad I felt when I learned about instincts and neural-release mechanisms, and understood that it's impossible."

Tamar nodded. "You learned more about them than most people do. In the Halvedna outer circle training we use that as a metaphor; it makes a good example of the dangers of rigid patterns of thinking."

"I suppose that's true." He drank tebbe and watched her. "It might not be easy, setting a jewelfly free once it was trapped like that, especially if you couldn't just turn the bowl over." He swallowed. "Perhaps you could give it something that would paralyze its wings for a while, make it fall, and hope that once the drug wore off it would get out from under the bowl and not fly right back up into it in panic."

The sen Halvedna said nothing at all.

"And perhaps the only thing you could give it was something you knew would damage it in some way, not enough to kill or cripple but enough to cause pain and fear. That might be more difficult still. The jewelfly might fly back up into the bowl because of the fear and the pain all by themselves, or because of that combined with everything else. Even if you succeeded, even if the jewelfly escaped the bowl, it might fly at you and try to bite you, knowing only that you'd hurt it, not realizing that you had no other way to get it out of the bowl. That might be the most difficult part of all."

"Not so difficult as all that," said Tamar.

Jerre went on as if he hadn't heard. "I said some bitter things last week, when you told me about the catamnetic. I'm sorry for that, Tamar. I was angry and frightened, and the thought of having most of my memories gone forever was still new enough to make me lose my balance whenever I thought of it. I ..."

"Jerre?"

He stopped short.

"Do you think you're the first patient who's spoken to me in those terms?"

He thought about that for a moment. "I suppose not," he said. "How many people have you taken through catamnesis?"

"Forty-two, counting yourself." She drank from her bowl, looked at him across the rim. "Every one of them responded with feelings of anger, hurt, and betrayal when they learned that their memory loss was a result of the treatment." Her tebbe finished, she put the bowl down. "All of it's quite justified. Chemical catamnesis is a brutal therapy, closer to the edge of the Affirmation than most sen Halvedna will go. It's surgery with a blunt instrument, and the only reason we use it at all is that we don't have anything better."

"You don't use it often, then."

"Only in the most drastic cases of withdrawal, regression, or psychosis, where nothing else will serve, and even then only when the patient's young enough to have a full life afterward, or when the problem's the result of some drastic shock to the mind."

Jerre managed a bleak smile. "I must have been the perfect patient."

"In a sense, yes." She folded her hands. "In your case, though, the Halka needed to know what you saw during the killings. Normally I would have used a different catamnetic, one that would have erased the entire experience, and let your other memories return at their own pace rather than breaking through the catamnesis as we did."

"Would that have been better?"

"It would have been easier for you. Beyond that, the results would have been the same, and we would have had this same conversation around the middle of autumn or a little later." She shifted, and picked up the manuscript next to her. "You might ask Amery Lundra about that, if you're curious. Her treatment went along the more usual path."

"The sen Halka? She was a patient of yours?"

"Four years ago. Stefan brought her to me, as he brought you." With a wry look: "He does that; it's his way of staying in contact." Then, serious again: "Like all the Halka, he goes where there's death and pain. Where you find those you find shattered minds as well."

"What happened to her?"

"You'll want to ask her about that."

After a moment, he nodded uncertainly. "I'll do that."

Tamar acknowledged that with a gesture, turned to the manuscript on her lap. She went through it page by page in silence, pondering what was on certain pages for a minute or more, merely glancing at others. Jerre watched her, and waited. Finally, when she'd finished with it, she handed the sheaf of paper to him and said, "You'll want to keep this, and read it through several times in the next few days. That will help fix your memories in place."

He looked at the topmost page. On it, words in his own handwriting described the few fragmentary memories he'd been able to salvage from his childhood. "With the time and pain this cost me to write, I don't think I'll ever forget anything in it. I'll read it through, though."

"Thank you. There's one other thing." She rose to her feet, motioned for him to stay when he moved to do the same.

"A gift of sorts. One moment." She went into the next room, returned a moment later with a slim book bound in plain black cloth.

"This is the Book of Circles," she said, handing it to him with a hint of formality. "I'm not sure if you remember much about it."

"Nothing at all." He opened it at random, found himself looking at one of the Sequence glyphs. Beneath it and on the facing page, a commentary that seemed to make less than no sense was itself commented on, in no less cryptic terms, and the whole summarized in a poem of four lines more baffling than either.

"The Book of Circles," said Tamar, "was written by a man named Loren Frederic during the first decades of the Directorate. Other than his name, we know almost nothing about him. We do know that the glyphs and the first commentaries came from Earth, and the rest was his own work. He passed it on to students, and one of them passed it to Judith Mariel when she was in hiding with the hermits at Andarre, after her break with the Directorate. According to our tradition, it was by studying the Book of Circles that she came to understand what had gone wrong with Shalsha, and thus the need for the Insurgency."

"I recall a story," Jerre said, "about Mariel and a mountain hermit who gave her a book."

"This was the book. Her copy is in a glass case at Zara along with the documents of the Convention, and you'll still find hermits at Andarre and the country around it, though of course they're sen Halvedna now. I spent three years there after the end of my training." She stopped, smiled ruefully. "But we were speaking of the Book of Circles. Only the Halvedna study it much these days, and that's always concerned me. When I first became a mindhealer I took up the habit of giving a copy to each of my patients when they finished their treatment."

Jerre turned one page, another. "I'm to study this?"

"If you like. I'd like to ask that you read through it once, and consider working with the cards—there's a deck of them inside the back cover in a pouch, with instructions for using them. Whether you go any further beyond that is up to you."

He nodded again, lapsed into silence. Tamar waited. Finally, with a shake of his head, he said, "And so it's finished. My treatment, I mean. Do you know, I hadn't even thought about what to do next."

She allowed a gentle laugh. "Once the jewelfly's out of the bowl, it has to decide for itself where it wants to fly."

"I suppose that's true." He got to his feet, pocketed the Book of Circles. "Whatever I said last week, Tamar—thank you. For all of this."

"You're of course welcome—and you're welcome to come talk to me any time."

He nodded, but his thoughts were elsewhere. "Thank you."

The door slid open, shut. Tamar sighed, shook her head.

I affirm the infinite potential of the human individual, community, society, and species for wisdom and creativity, joy and forbearance, compassion and grace. Words worn smooth as riverbank stones turned in her mind. *I affirm the value of conscious action in unfolding these potentials, and the responsibility upon those who follow this path to renounce coercion and violence of every kind.* She'd embraced those words and the path they offered with all her will. *I affirm my own lifelong commitment to this work.* Why did the words of the Affirmation seem so frail as she considered them now?

After a moment, she reached for the Sequence deck, lying half forgotten on the floor. The five cards she'd dealt out for Jerre slid smoothly in amid the others. A practiced shuffle, a gesture of awareness to attune her mind to the cards, and then she dealt out a single card face down. "What am I afraid of?" she asked it, then turned it over.

The image of Conflict gazed up at her. She nodded unwillingly. Stefan always brought a challenge on his visits to Mirien, if only some patient shattered by violence to remind her of a choice he'd made and she'd renounced. This time, though, his news and his own troubling vision honed that challenge to a fine point. If the war he foresaw came about, what of the Affirmation? What could renunciation of violence offer Eridan in the face of killing machines?

She slid the card back in among the others, got to her feet and went into the next room.

3

"I began with the Type Twelve drone," Stefan said. He leafed through the stack of papers at his side, extracted one sheet and handed it to Carla Dubrenden. "These are the specifications, and everything else I could find about the type."

"This is from the Shelter library?" Carla asked.

"Part of it. The rest came from a friend at the historical library at Embran."

She read through the notes and then handed them to Amery.

"Notice the dates," said Stefan. "The first Type Twelves were deployed in the last month of 82, and more than half came out in the year before Shalsha was destroyed." He searched for another sheet of paper, found it. "The last factory camps at Sharru and Keltessat were liberated in the spring of 81 and the last mining center in the hill country was blown up by saboteurs at the end of 80. After that the Directorate had no metalworking capacity except for two small mills in Shalsha itself, and no source of raw materials except stocks on hand and salvage."

"How did they make up the deficit?" Carla asked.

"Not very well." He examined his notes. "Outputs of most industrial products went down eighty to ninety per cent because materials were in such short supply. Most production went to the war, of course, but the shortfalls were still enormous, especially where the more exotic alloys had to be used."

More paper passed from Stefan to Carla and Amery, caught the light of the room's one hanging lamp.

"The question of alloys is important," he said then. "Drones need some unusual metals—indium, tantalum, thorium, half a dozen more—for the hull, the power core, and the electronics. Have either of you heard of the Type Fourteen drone?"

Fractional motions of his listener's heads told him they had not.

"Nearly a thousand of them were made in the eight months between the fall of Werelin and the destruction of Shalsha, as a desperation move. They had steel armor and anything for a power core the Directorate could salvage. They're not in the banned-tech manual, because any of them that survived Shalsha corroded away into streaks of rust more than a century ago."

"And the Type Twelves?"

"Varied. Early production runs in 82 and early 83 were as good as anything the Directorate ever built; by midway through 84 they weren't much better than Type Fourteens. The power cores were the great weakness, though." More paper rustled. "High-energy isotopes were in such short supply that almost eighty per cent of the Type Twelves had simple irradiated cores with a ten year lifespan. Only a few hundred of them would still be functional now even if every Type Twelve ever made had been hidden away in a cave somewhere."

"Which they weren't," Carla said. "After the floods four years ago any number of wrecked drones washed out of the river mud near Werelin, and I spent better than three months with the Halka teams that cleared them away. There were plenty of Type Twelves."

"Even so. Now consider this." He took a map out from under his notes, unfolded it, spread it on the floor. The ragged wedge of Eridan's northern continent sprawled before them, indigo and white against green oceans. "Before the first Type Twelves were deployed, the entire Annan valley was in insurgent hands. The mountain passes had been closed off by 75 or 76, the hill country was lost before then, and Werelin was as far north as Directorate forces dared go by 80. So I'm left wondering how the Type Twelve that attacked the foraging camp at Talin made its way from here—" He pointed to the area north of Shalsha. "—to here." He moved his finger to the wild country north of Talin Shelter, more than three hundred kilometers further north.

Carla studied the map for a long moment, her expression puzzled at first and then settling into a deeper disquiet. "And the last serious Directorate forays into the north country took place before Amris fell and the southern front opened up."

"In 79. Exactly." Stefan picked up his notes and began sorting through them. "So we have unlikelihood on top of unlikelihood, and both of them riding a single drone—if the one Jerre saw and the one Amery destroyed were one and the same. If they were two different drones, the problems double." He shook his head. "My vision tells me that all six of the drones at Talin were Type Twelves. Make of that what you will."

He set some of his papers aside. Carla picked them up, looked at them, and then gave him a questioning glance. "What are these?"

"I'm not sure," said Stefan. "When I was studying the map two weeks ago, the innermind kept overlaying it with curved lines. I tried to copy them, but the lines shifted constantly. These are approximations."

Carla studied each of the drawings in turn, then passed them to Amery.

"That's the whole of it," he said then. "What it means I still have no clear idea."

"What does your vision say?" Carla asked. Her tone was casual, but her expression could not hide the edged clarity of Halka judgement mode.

Stefan glanced up at her. "About all this? Almost nothing. It insists that something of terrible significance happened during the last year of the Insurgency, and it brings me images of Type Twelve drones and moving lines on a map. That's essentially all."

Carla nodded, accepting this, and Stefan began gathering his papers. As he reached for the map of the northern continent, Amery set the drawings of lines down on top of it. "There's one thing," she said tentatively. "The two of you probably saw this already."

Stefan motioned her to explain.

"All of these patterns have something in common." She spread the drawings across the top of the map. "Think of ripples in a pond. The stones that made them fell here, here, and here." Her fingers touched places where the lines tangled around one another. "The same three places on each drawing. Can you bring the lines back into awareness, Stefan?"

He looked at the map. "Readily."

"Where are the three points?"

After a moment, he pointed to three points near the middle of the continent.

"That's what I guessed." Amery leaned over the map, gestured at the points. "Do you see it now? One of the points is Talin or close to it. This one to the east is another Shelter in the far north, perhaps Arremal, and this last one to the west will be one of the new Shelters on the far bank of the Annan, close to the sea." Her finger traced a line west from the mountains to the coast. "All along the northern edge of settlement. If you were the controller of the drones and looked at those three places, what would you see?"

Carla considered the map. After a moment her eyes widened. "Invasion routes."

"That's what I saw," said Amery.

"There would be three columns, then." Carla picked up one of the drawings, another. "The two in the east are the main thrust—look how much further south the lines reach there. I'm not sure about the one in the west."

"A diversion to keep Halka forces pinned down in the hill country,"

"Possibly." Carla nodded. "Possibly. But the main force would drive south through the gap between the mountains and the hill country, and break out into the plains south of Werelin."

"Going right past us here at Mirien in the process," said Amery.

Carla glanced up from the map to Amery. "True."

Stefan's gaze had never left the map. "If these are drone movements," he said, "there's more to the plan than ordinary strategy, I think." He touched the map gingerly, as though a clumsy movement could scatter the lines of his vision. "There's an underlying pattern. I don't know what it is but it's there."

"That's part of your vision?" Carla asked.

"Some is vision, some interpretation." His finger traced a wandering line southwards from the north country, where it had first touched the map, to Shalsha. "The two interweave. I'm not certain I could untangle them if I tried."

"Of course." Carla fell silent for a time, her thoughts veiled. Then: "There's something you need to know, Stefan."

He looked up.

"I'm preparing a judgment on the events at Talin." Her tone was measured, quiet. "A supplementary judgment in dissent. For two months now I've listened to all the arguments for inaction and they don't convince me. I'm left feeling that the command circle at Talin has chosen a course that's both dangerous and irresponsible."

"Those are extreme words," said Stefan.

"This is potentially an extreme situation."

"Tell me this." His expression went flat, unreadable. "How likely do you think it is that my vision is accurate?"

"Extremely unlikely," Carla said at once. "Maybe one chance in ten thousand. The fact remains that it exists, and it's not being dealt with."

He turned to Amery. "And you?"

"I'd rate it higher by a factor of ten."

Carla leaned forward slightly. "How would you rate it, Stefan?"

For a long moment he did not answer. Finally he said, "I've tried not to think about that. The vision demands absolute acceptance, but I don't dare give it that. I've thought it best to avoid the entire issue."

"You have that freedom," Carla said. "The rest of Eridan doesn't."

"I know." He looked down at the map again, staring at the interplay of lines neither Carla nor Amery could see. "For whatever it's worth, I do think war is a possibility, and that Julian and the others are wrong to dismiss it out of hand."

"Then we're in agreement." Carla paused. "I'll need the loan of some of your papers, and the names of the sources you used. All this about the Type Twelve drones is new to me, and it deserves a place in my judgment."

Amery picked up the drawings of lines on the map. "Will you need these?"

"I shouldn't," said Carla.

She turned to Stefan. "I'd like to borrow these."

"Of course." He glanced at the drawings, at her. "Why?"

The lines twisted and curved like living things as Amery tilted the drawings, examining them again. "I'm not sure," she admitted. "There's a pattern underlying them, just as you said. I want to figure out what that is. It—" She stopped. "I don't know. It may be important."

For a moment, only the whisper of Shelter air vents broke the silence of the little room. Outside, darkness covered half a world. "Let me know what you find," said Stefan. "If my vision shows you anything else, I'll tell you at once."

4

Morning light danced across the glossy backs of the Sequence cards, flickered in pale reflection on the ceiling. "And again," Jerre said aloud.

He cut, shuffled, and then dealt out one card, face down. After a moment he turned it over: Transition. The abstract symbol represented, or so the Book of Circles claimed, one of the basic categories of human thought. According to the Book, study of the cards led to wisdom. He examined the glyph—a small circle passing through the upper edge of a larger circle—but found nothing but confusion. He picked up the card, returned it to the deck, shuffled again.

His hands remembered the motions almost at once when he'd placed the cards in them, though he could not recall handling cards before: another unexplained skill, like his talent for fixing broken machines. Wisdom, he thought, and shook his head. If there was wisdom to be had from the Sequence, it wasn't quick to show itself. Still, he kept shuffling, watched the glimmer of sunlight on the cards though it hurt his eyes. If there was wisdom to be had, he needed it desperately.

He finished, dealt a single card again, turned it over. The glyph of Transition faced him again, gnomic and uncommunicative. He began the inner search for patterns, trying to recall what he'd read of the Book of Circles, but his mind kept straying onto other paths. Memory brought him images of firelight and motion, the beat of clapping hands, the wailing of the kyrenna. After a time he sighed, and picked up the card.

Recollections of the night before remained with him as he began shuffling once again. It had been a good sama, as good as any of the few his splintered memories still recalled: more than four hundred people at its height and the last dancers not gone from the samahane until the night was more than half over. He'd been among those last, the lonely ones seeking solace, the troubled seeking absolution, the ecstatics with their bright dancing-robes and amulets of wood and crystal seeking union with the energies of the innermind. A young woman he knew slightly from Shelter work had approached him, then, and in the moment before she spoke he'd wondered which one she sought. It had been, he reflected later, something of all three.

But was that the answer to his questions? He thought not.

He cut the deck, shuffled, dealt a single card. Once again, Transition faced him.

He frowned, then reached for the shelf next to him. Tamar's gift lay there along with a dozen other books from the Shelter library. He opened it, glanced at the number on the top of the card. Transition was *kel eshonat sen-na-tekke*, seventeenth glyph of the Sequence. He found the right page and read:

17: the image of Transition
First Commentary

Next, Transition. The circle closes, the one path remaining leads beyond it. Do not cling to what is past. Do not try to ordain what is to come. The universe, in accordance with its own patterns, will provide for both of these. Especially, do not pretend to grace. No new thing was ever done, except awkwardly. It is like a person going down a long hallway with doors on either side, trying each one. If it is locked, abandon it. If it is not, attempt to open it. If it opens, pass through.

Second Commentary

After Fulfillment and the end of the first cycle comes Transition, the passage from one state to another. At the lowest and highest levels the continuity of the universe breaks down; an electron leaps from energy level to energy level with no intervening steps; the voyage of *Journey Star* from Earth to Eridan crossed light-years of empty space.

So, too, human affairs. The shift from one way of thinking, acting, relating is as often sudden as gradual. Too much continuity is a source of danger; one who tries to stand on both sides of a doorway at once will be hurt when the door is closed. In a time of Transition, accept change and the loss of the familiar, be aware of the demands of the situation, and do not insist on knowing the end of a road at its beginning.

Once a philosopher on the last day of his life asserted that the continuity of things is forever unbroken, that each state from first to last melded into the next without break or division. Having said this, he clutched his chest, fell down and died. His own heart had refuted him, thrusting him across a boundary that admitted of no intermediate states.

Summary

The circle has one break, the chain one weak link, the wall one open door.

That door links reality to reality, joining and separating two worlds.

One door opens among many that remain shut. It will open once only,

Briefly, and close. There is no time to seek explanations, only to enter.

Jerre read through all this twice, the first time puzzled, the second with growing dismay. Sudden change, the abandonment of the known? He'd had more than enough of that in the last few months, more than he wanted to see again in the rest of his life. He began reading the text again, hoping for some other way of understanding the card's message. Halfway through, finding none, he shut the book and looked at the cover with a look that changed slowly from dismay through deep uncertainty to anger.

Abruptly he hurled the Book of Circles across the room with all his strength. It struck the far wall, fell onto the rumpled bedding beneath. He stared at it for a time, then slumped and lowered his face into his hands.

5

The door to Mirien Shelter's radio room slid open with a whisper of wood on metal.

"... have already discussed this at some length." The voice, blurred by loudspeaker hiss, was Julian Mereval's. Two figures in Halka black stood by the message center, listening intently; on the far side of the room, the shift operator had turned in her chair and was watching in silent apprehension.

"That's true." Carla's voice. "The circle has chosen to set it aside each time."

"The circle has chosen to follow the evidence, rather than the visions and speculation you offer. You doubtless find that assessment harsh, but it's the considered judgment of the circle."

The door slid shut. Near it, shadows shifted, darkness against darkness.

"Do you share that view?" Carla asked.

"I do. It seems to me that neither you nor Stefan has offered anything more than that."

"Then I request a formal statement of your intentions toward my judgment."

The low rustle of static did nothing to fill the silence that followed, or hide the tension in the voice that broke it. "For myself and the circle, I acknowledge it but will disregard it. If you request, I will submit the matter to the individual members of the circle."

Amery took the microphone. "That won't be necessary, Julian. We question your choice of action, not your fairness."

"You plan on sending out your judgment as a formal alternative, then?"

"That's our intention." Carla's tone was unyielding. "If the circle at Talin won't deal with the possibility of war I have no choice but to call together a circle that will."

"Have you considered an arrangement for primacy, or will you contest that also?"

"Carla and I have discussed the issue," Amery replied. "Neither of us has any desire to see a divided command, now or in the future, or to go through with an adjudication of primacy if there's any other choice. We're willing to grant primacy to the circle at Talin, on the condition that you agree to release it to us if war begins, or there's proof that war is imminent."

Another silence, longer, passed. Static muttered. The two sen Halka, silent, watched the loudspeaker grille, Amery with a worried frown, Carla with the focused intensity of a sen Halka facing an armed opponent. Across the room, the shift operator looked on, visibly distressed; in the shadows by the door, a movement began and instantly checked itself.

"That will be acceptable," Julian said at last. "Have you drafted an agreement?"

"It leaves with tomorrow's mail," Amery replied, "along with the letter of formal dissent and the other documents. We've prepared other copies for Linda Meridun at Kerriol, and Zara."

"Even so." Another pause. "I'll review the agreement as soon as it arrives and present it to the circle. We should be prepared to respond formally in a week."

"Thank you," Amery said. "We'll await your response."

"Very well. *Halka na.*"

"*Halka na.*"

The link with Talin Shelter closed down in a burst of loudspeaker noise. Amery turned off the transmitter, looked to Carla. "So that's over," she said, "and you were right. I didn't think she would agree to the primacy arrangement."

From behind them both, Stefan's voice: "It's as well that she did."

They turned. He stood, arms folded, not far from the door. Eyes weary with the weight of futurity looked at them and through them. "I know I said I wouldn't be here. The situation's changed. I had to be certain an arrangement for primacy would be agreed on."

"What's happened?" Carla asked.

"I saw …" He stopped, his voice fading into the background noises, the hiss of ventilators and the mutter of distant signals over the main receiver across the room. More clearly: "An hour ago I was thinking about the supplementary judgment and Talin's response to it. My vision came then, and changed—blurred, split apart into two paths, with different beginnings and different endings. The point of division was here." Again his voice went low. "Now. The paths began with Julian's acceptance or rejection of an agreement for primacy. With her acceptance, my vision continues as I've seen it. With her rejection, the innermind tells me that everyone in the north country would have been dead within one year."

"Bright Earth," Amery murmured.

Stefan did not seem to hear. "Even so, I might not have acted on it, but—" He stopped, shook his head. "The vision aside, a contested primacy could be fatal if anything actually comes of all this. If she'd refused, I would have formally accused her of prejudice and forced an immediate adjudication."

"You would have been shot." This from Carla.

"Very probably." A faint smile. "It seemed worth the risk."

Carla gave him a long appraising look. "What interests me most about all this is that you saw two different futures. That's uncommon—in fact, I don't think I've ever heard of it before."

"Nor I," said Stefan. "But there it is."

They turned to leave. Amery stayed a moment longer, then shook her head and followed. As she came to the door, sensing someone's gaze on her, she glanced back. The shift operator was staring after them, horror in her eyes. Her gaze met Amery's briefly, then broke away.

6

Stefan turned the page, read:

> anticipated the insurgent thrust against Werelin, but could do little to forestall it. Efforts to find the forces Thomason knew must be gathering against him, ranging

from ground patrols to orbital reconnaissance from *Journey Star*, brought back nothing. At the same time, few of Thomason's superiors agreed with his assessment, and fewer still were willing to have forces drawn off from the southern front or the defense of Shalsha itself.

Thomason was on his own, then, although he failed to realize this. Documents captured at Werelin included copies of his letters to Planetary Director Emmer, pleading for reinforcements. The first of these are calm, reasoned, diffident. The last, a cry of desperation, was written within a week of the first assault. By that time no help could have reached him in time even if any had been sent. The fate of the city had already been

Someone knocked at the door.

Stefan glanced up from Kregeth's *History of the Insurgency*, surprised, and then set the book aside. He expected no visitors; Amery and Carla would still be with the Shelter Council, he was sure of it, and it had been weeks since he'd spoken to Tamar. Subtle awareness brought him only the fact of presence. "Please come in," he called.

The door slid open and Jerre Amadan stepped into the room. The troubled look on his face brought back memories of the emptiness of withdrawal. "Sen Jatanni? I'd like to speak with you, if you aren't too busy."

"Not at all." Stefan motioned him to a cushion. "Please."

Jerre closed the door behind him and sat. He did not speak at once, though his mouth opened twice and shut again. Finally: "Is it true that there's to be a war?"

Stefan regarded him carefully. "We don't know. Where did you hear this?"

"I've heard little else for the last two weeks."

"Rumors?"

"Dozens of them, sen Halka. Some people are saying that there might be hundreds of battle-drones hidden in the north.

Some say that someone's controlling them, like the one—" His voice faltered, recovered. "Like the one I saw. Many are saying that the whole north country may be attacked." Then, almost unwillingly: "And some claim the Halka are divided about all this."

"The last is true enough," Stefan said "As for the others, some of us think they may be possible. Others don't, thus the disagreement."

Jerre's eyes widened. "What will come of that?"

"The disagreement? We have procedures for dealing with such things, and we've already settled the question of command. The difference of opinion won't get in the way of fighting the drones if it comes to that."

"That's welcome news." The younger man paused, shifted. "Would it be proper to ask what's being done? Everyone's talking about battle-drones but no one says anything about how they're to be stopped."

"Of course you may ask. It's a Halka matter, but we have no secrets—and you more than anyone else deserve to know." He paused, searched for the right words. "Just after the attack on the camp I declared Orange Sky, one of the high emergency codes, and a judgment circle confirmed that a few days later. Do you remember anything about the Halka codes?"

"Not to speak of."

"They announce a potential or actual threat to the Six Laws. Orange Sky means potential danger on a regional level. The procedures have been worked out for more than a century. For Orange Sky we ask the local Shelters to ready their own defenses, we set up a message net, we bring sen Halka in from other regions and heavy weapons up from the arsenals in the south."

"And that's all been done?"

"We finished more than a month ago. I don't have exact figures but there are between six and eight thousand sen Halka in the north country now, and the last shipment of heavy weapons came past Mirien six weeks back."

"That's reassuring," said Jerre, and said nothing more for a time. Stefan watched him and wondered just what moved behind the survivor's eyes. Clearly he hadn't come just to ask about the status of the north country defenses, and despite his words, little reassurance showed in his posture and movements, the myriad little cues that subtle awareness caught and interpreted. Whatever was on his mind gave him little peace, had probably given him none for days. And its nature? Stefan could not tell. He folded his hands, waited.

"Sen Halka, I don't know." Jerre's face tensed into an approximation of a smile. "I hope I don't annoy you with questions. It's just …" The smile failed. "I can't stop thinking of the drones. Tamar said I should put what happened behind me, but it won't go away."

"I imagine not. Did she give you the Book of Circles?"

"Yes." After a moment: "How did you know?"

"That's the Halvedna way." He shook his head, his expression touched with familiarity and old distaste. "First comes the Book of Circles, then the Affirmation, and if those catch your interest there's more. There's always more." Stefan shrugged. "As I said, it's their way. They believe it's possible to shape human society toward perfection, if only enough people can be guided into the right ways of thinking and acting. Their healing work is part of that, and so is Tamar's advice."

"To put it behind me." Jerre looked up, hollow-eyed. "What would be the point? The battle-drones are still there. If I forget about them, that won't make them forget about us. It terrifies me, sen Jatanni."

"You fear for yourself?"

"I fear for Eridan." After a pause: "I think about what I saw, and then I think about what could happen if the rumors are right and there are hundreds of those things somewhere in the north. Fear for my own life is the least of it." He laughed, shakily. "I've had a dream, sen Halka, several times now, of battle-drones killing every last human being on Eridan except me. I begged them to shoot me and they wouldn't." He looked at Stefan for a moment, and then his gaze fell. "Sometimes I wonder if it might have been better if the drones hadn't missed me."

"In my judgment," Stefan told him, "that's not the case."

Jerre looked up.

"Your memories warned us that the drones might be under human control, and that alerted us to the possibility of war." Stefan allowed judgment mode to shade his voice. This one, he thought, this one will take consolation only from words that don't seem to console. This one has seen far too much evil to accept a good that looks too plausible. He smiled inwardly, and thought: we're alike in that, perhaps. "Without that we might have had no warning at all."

"I suppose that's true." Then: "If I'd been killed in the attack, would any preparations have been made?"

"Minimal ones," Stefan said. "A judgment circle would have been called and one of the minor emergency codes declared. A few hundred sen Halka would have come north, some patrols sent out, and a small cache of heavy weapons brought north to Talin. That's all." Which was not true, not quite; there would also have been a judgment circle a little later for a visionary whose obsessing images of war and disaster would have had nothing at all to give them the least scrap of credibility. Lacking the support of four remembered words, he would certainly have been judged deluded, and probably shot.

"Then maybe it was best," Jerre said. "I don't know, sen Jatanni. I just don't know."

Watching him, Stefan wondered again what haunted him. Then, abruptly, understanding came: a whisper from the inner-mind: *shaddat baya*. The sen Halka held his expression neutral only by an act of will. Possibly, he thought, possibly. Aloud: "I think there's a question you wish to ask."

Jerre, startled, said, "Yes. Yes, there is." He hesitated, then: "If you don't mind the question, sen Jatanni, why did you join the Halka order? What made you choose that?"

"Baya?" It was not the question Stefan expected, but it was close, close enough that he knew for certain the other would be asked before Jerre left the room. "That's what we call the first drinking of the dwimmerwine, the ceremony that binds a candidate to the Halka order: baya. You may want to remember that." Too obvious? It scarcely mattered now, he told himself, and went on. "I took baya a little more than thirty years ago, sen Amadan. As for why, I'll tell you the story of how it happened, if you like. That's as close to an explanation as I've ever been able to come."

"Please." Jerre shifted, listened.

"It was just over thirty years ago, as I said, that I took baya and entered the Halka order. Two years before that, I began study with a Halvedna master." He gestured, deprecating. "Yes, I was a sen Halvedna, or would have been. I spent those two years studying the outer circle of Halvedna lore, and it would have taken me four more to pass through all three circles and wear the many-colored robe, but that was my goal. I'd wanted that since I was a child. I wanted, in fact, to become a sen davannat. Do you remember much about them?"

"Nothing but the name."

"They seek to fuse their minds completely with the innermind. If you've been to the samahane since you recovered, you met ecstatics and spirit dancers." Jerre nodded, and Stefan went on. "Sama music uses atonal patterns to stimulate the nervous system. It's designed to imitate the effects of a very mild dose of dwimmerroot."

"I don't think I knew that," said Jerre.

"Most dancers don't, but that's why the Halvedna developed it."

"I'm sure I didn't know that," said Jerre. "Sama was a Halvedna creation?"

"One of many. They're always trying to shape the world closer to their ideal." Then: "The sen davannat are like ecstatics, but the dwimmerroot pushes them far beyond the places sama music can go. They live in two worlds at once, the world of ordinary consciousness and the innermind's world, and they know all the hidden pathways between the two. That's what I hoped for myself.

"At that time I'd nearly finished the outer circle training, and tasted the dwimmerrroot four times. The one thing I wanted in the world was to finish my training and go to Andarre, to the old hermitages in the mountains. Then I received a letter from an old friend who lived at Istal Shelter, where I was born and where most of my family lived.

"A few weeks earlier that spring the Morne flooded. The chapter house where I was in training stayed above water only because we filled sandbags day and night for most of a week. Old flood channels that fill up once in a hundred years were full to overflowing, and in one of these, twenty kilometers from Istal Shelter, the waters washed a battle-drone out of the mud."

"In the flood channel?" Jerre asked. "How did it get there?"

"Drones have their weaknesses," said Stefan. "One of the most important is that lifter fields won't bear weight over a conductive surface. Put a drone over a sheet of metal or water, and it falls. Probably the drone blundered over the flood channel during the Insurgency, when the Directorate stripped the hill country of trees and the erosion sent the Morne over its banks nearly every year. It might have been decoyed over water by insurgents; that's a strategy they used often. If that's what happened the insurgents probably thought the drone was gone forever.

"But battle-drones are remarkable machines. They have hermetically sealed hulls made of alloys nobody's been able to duplicate since, proof against every kind of corrosion. They carry huge stores of ammunition in sealed bins full of nonreactive gas. Their power cores use high-energy isotopes that stay functional in standby mode for centuries. They're self-repairing, internally guided, and very difficult to destroy.

There's not much to praise about the Directorate but I'll say this much: they knew how to plan for the long term.

"This particular drone was fully functional, and once the floodwaters left it behind and its sensors told it that it was free, it returned to whatever mission it was following when the waters swallowed it. That brought it westward to the main track south to the Gathering at Halleth. It met a group of travelers going toward the Gathering, killed them, and went south on the track to the next Shelter. The Shelter folk there hadn't yet finished clearing mud and sandbags from the protective ring, and so the drone got across and attacked, firing through windows and skylights, while the Shelter folk ran for the deep levels. The Halka were alerted at once, and a few hours later three sen Halka reached the Shelter and blew the drone into scrap metal.

"The whole affair cost ninety-one lives. It so happened, though, that the Shelter the drone attacked was Istal Shelter, and every last member of my family happened to be among the victims. That was what I read in the letter I got that spring. A week later I left the chapter house and the Halvedna order, and a month after that I went to a sen Halka I knew slightly and asked her to take me as a candidate for baya."

Jerre stirred. "I'm not sure I understand."

"It's simple enough. The Halvedna teach that it's possible to make human society perfect by following their Affirmation, which forswears all acts of violence. I believed in that wholly, but that was just because I'd never thought through the consequences. It's one thing to dream about a perfect society, but reality includes things like drones, outrunners—and Shalsha. The Halvedna way pays no attention to those. It leaves them to the Halka. I realized that the Affirmation was dishonest, that the Halvedna could give up violence and dream of a perfect society only because the Halka, using violence, put their own lives at risk to defend them."

He allowed a rueful smile. "It seems so easy to say now. At the time, that cost me days and nights of struggle. I don't imagine it's ever easy to realize that you've built your life on a lie." His shrug dismissed the smile and the memories it carried. "Beyond that, I couldn't go back to the life I'd been living. That the things had happened at all was monstrous. That it might happen again at any time was more monstrous still. I couldn't ignore that. I had to do something about it, and I realized eventually that meant taking baya."

Jerre was nodding slowly. "How many sen Halka come to the order that way?"

"From some personal experience with violence? More than half, I think."

"Did sen Lundra ..."

"Amery? Yes. She had a brother, a helicopter pilot, who made a forced landing in the mountains and was killed and eaten by outrunners."

"And sen Dubrenden?"

"Carla as well. In fact, she was wounded in the attack on Istal Shelter, and we took baya within days of each other." Again the rueful smile appeared. "Of course that's not the only option. I think Carla and I were the only two people affected by that affair who took baya. And there's another choice as well." The smile tautened. "Tamar's choice. We were close in those days, but she'd thought of entering the Halka order for nearly as long as I'd dreamed of becoming a sen Halvedna. She was there at Istal when the drone attacked. A month later, she went to the Halvedna chapter house I had left, and took the outer circle initiation. I don't pretend to understand her choice, but there it is."

"But baya is open to people in a case like that?"

Carefully now, Stefan thought. "It's open, yes."

"And if I wanted that, what would I need to do?"

"There's a traditional form for the *shaddat baya*. First, I'd ask certain questions."

Jerre swallowed visibly. "Ask them."

"How long have you considered this matter?"

"A week, maybe more." After a moment: "I first thought about it the day I learned that sen Lundra went through the same therapy I did, and after that chose to—to take baya." He stumbled over the phrase. "That was more than a month ago. For the most part, it's been this past week."

Stefan nodded once, went deeper into judgment mode. "In your estimate, what role do feelings of pride or guilt or self-interest play in your decision?"

"Pride, some role. Guilt—" A flicker of tension touched his expression. "Some role. Self-interest, no role that I'm aware of."

Stefan nodded again. "In your estimate, what role does the wish to die play in your decision?"

Jerre did not speak for a long moment. Finally, in a whisper: "I don't know."

The sen Halka nodded a third time. "Acceptable," he said. "Now attend. Once you speak the words that formally begin the process of seeking baya, you'll have set in motion an irreversible series of events. You may stop that series at any time before baya, but if you do that, baya will be closed to you and you'll be forbidden from seeking it again from any sen Halka under any circumstances whatsoever. Do you understand?"

"Yes."

"Then I give you the words of the formal request: *shaddat am baya*, I ask for baya. You may speak them now or at any later time. Think well before you speak them."

Jerre did so. After a silence minutes long, he drew in a breath and repeated the words.

"Even so." Distant now, wrapped in the absolute clarity of judgment that tradition demanded of him, Stefan went on. "Listen now with all your attention, and do not speak again until I request it. Until and unless you choose to leave the path that leads to baya, and you may do so at any time, you will be bound by the traditions and conventions of the Halka order, and you will be subject utterly to the instructions of your sponsor among the Halka. At this moment I am your sponsor, although you have the right to choose another at a certain point in the future if this is your wish. If you are instructed to do anything, and you fail to do that thing to the best of your ability, your training will end at once.

"Your training will last ninety days. At the end of that time, if you still wish it, you may take baya, testing your inmost self against the dwimmerwine. If you choose that and survive, you will be bound for the remainder of your life by the traditions and conventions of the Halka order, and subject to the penalties these provide." The austere perfection of the judgment mode slackened briefly. "Those penalties are generally death by gunshot. I might add that you have roughly one chance in three of dying during baya, thus never having the chance to be shot in the first place." Then, returning to full clarity: "During your training you will be expected to learn these traditions, conventions, and penalties, so that you have full awareness of the commitment you are making in advance of your final decision. Once again, you may end your training at any time, and your sponsor may also end your training for certain reasons which will be explained to you. If your training has been ended, and you feel this has been done unfairly or with insufficient reason, you may consult with any other sen Halka, and you may request any sen Halka to summon a judgment circle to consider your case. All this I am required by Halka law to tell you, and be sure that you understand fully. If you have questions, you may ask them now."

"I have none," said Jerre.

"And you're resolved to continue?"

"Yes."

With that the judgment mode faded, and a weary middle-aged man considered Jerre for a time and then nodded once more, curtly. "You must use the formal words again, then. Once you do that, you must go somewhere else at once.

Don't discuss your decision or any of our conversation with anyone else. If you're still resolved to pursue this seven days from now, come here again and make the same request to me once more, and we'll begin the next stage of the process. Do you understand?"

"I think so," said Jerre. A moment later: "Shaddat am baya."

CHAPTER 4

THE WAY OF THE GUN

1

Footsteps whispered down a dark corridor. The open door at its end drowned shadows in a flood of light.

Amery paused outside the doorway, then went in at a pace slow enough to keep from appearing hurried. The room beyond it, the common room of Mirien Shelter's Halka quarters, had been cleared of what little furniture it normally had, and a circle of cushions had been arranged around the center. There, caught up in silent contemplation, all but one of the members of the new command circle sat. None looked up as Amery came in, though subtle awareness told her that her presence had been noted and a place made for her in the circle groupmind.

She walked around the circle, found an unoccupied cushion, sat. Three deep breaths and a murmured phrase cleared her mind somewhat, and triggered the shallowest level of trance, just deep enough to allow her to enter into rapport with the other members of the circle. As channels opened up between mind and mind, flickers of greeting came to her from several directions at once. She responded, then withdrew to the outermost edge of the rapport. Carla, on the far side of the circle, caught her gaze, nodded fractionally. After a moment, Amery returned the nod.

Then nothing remained but the waiting.

Minutes later, footfalls echoed again through the open door. Amery resisted the urge to turn and look. The soft mutter of sound broke gradually into two distinct paces and stopped. A moment later the door slid shut.

"Sen Halka." The voice, Stefan's, seemed to come from far away. "Jerre Amadan asks your permission to speak with this circle."

To Amery's left, an old man wrapped in the black robes of a Halka legalist looked up. "Bring him forward, Stefan." After the low noises of movement rose and subsided: "You may speak with us. First, though, I must ask you to answer certain questions."

"Of course," Jerre said.

Now Amery did look at him. Pale but intent, he stood just beyond the circle of cushions, his plain gray robe fitting an old symbolism so perfectly she wondered for a moment if he could have chosen it deliberately. Behind him, Stefan waited, a watchful shadow.

"Have you requested baya three times from a member of our order?"

"Yes."

"Do you understand the implications of that request, as they were explained to you?"

"Yes."

"Having considered these things, do you still seek baya?"

"Yes."

The old man nodded, acknowledging. "Please be seated. My name is Benamin Haller, and I've been named Speaker for the command circle here at Mirien. Stefan asked me to witness the beginning of your training, and give you what advice I can. For my own part, since you're part of the matter this circle was called to consider, I call the whole of the circle as second witness. Is that acceptable to you?"

Jerre settled on a cushion. "Yes."

"Then we'll proceed." The Speaker turned to the young sen Halka next to him, and was given a locked cylinder of metal and black plastic. "This contains one standard dose of the dwimmerwine. I witnessed its preparation and can guarantee its potency and purity." He set the cylinder on the floor before Jerre. "You have the right to drink it now if you wish."

"Now?" Jerre gave the Speaker a startled look. "Sen Jatanni told me that ninety days of training came first."

"We offer the training, sen Amadan. By the Convention of Zara we're forbidden to compel you to take it. If you ask for baya now, at this moment, we have no choice but to give you the dwimmerwine."

Jerre thought about that for a moment. "Sen Jatanni told me," he said then, "that a third of those who take baya die of it. How many of those refused the training?"

"Those are counted separately," Benamin told him. "The figure Stefan gave you is the fatality rate for properly prepared and screened candidates. For those who take baya without preparation the rate is just over ninety-eight per cent."

"Oh." With half a smile: "I think, sen Speaker, that I'll take the training."

"Very well." Benamin handed the container of dwimmerwine back to its keeper. "The thought of dying in baya disturbs you, then."

"Somewhat."

"You may not know that there's an alternative to baya."

"What do you mean?"

"We offer our training to everyone who formally requests it, as you know. Nearly half those who go through it decide not to take baya afterwards. They learn the two great branches of Halka lore, the use of weapons and the study of law, but choose to use one or another outside the Halka order. They're highly valued for their abilities; you'll find many of them serving on Shelter councils or working as arbiters for Gatherings or trade networks. If that appeals to you, there's a course of training available to you that aims toward those ends rather than baya."

"If I choose that course of training," Jerre asked, "will that bar me from taking baya?"

"Yes."

"Thank you, then, but no. I'll take the ordinary training." Then: "Before you go on, sen Speaker, may I ask why you're trying to keep me out of the Halka order?"

A smile creased Benamin's face. "Good, sen Amadan. Very good." Serious again, he went on. "We've found it necessary to test all our candidates with every means at our disposal. Not everyone who seeks baya does it for a good reason. Some seek their own deaths; others seek prestige, power, respect. We give the first the dwimmerwine before they're prepared to take it, and they get what they want. We give the second a way to feed their vanity with less risk, and so they get what they want. We do that because it allows us to get what we want, which is an order made up of people who aren't driven by such motives."

"And you suspect that they drive me?"

"Not necessarily. As I've said, we've found it necessary to test all our candidates. We can't limit our testing to those who show some obvious distortions of purpose, just as we can't rely on a single test."

"Then I'll be tested again."

"And again, and again."

"I'll be careful."

"That would be wise." The Speaker nodded once, as though that settled something. "I think we may proceed to the last part of the ceremony. Has a book of laws been provided?"

On the far side of the circle, a young woman with burn scars disfiguring her face came up out of rapport, took a slim volume from a pocket inside her coat. On its cover, white on black, the triangle-in-circle emblem of the Halka blazed. "Yes."

"Has this copy some significance?"

"Yes. It belonged to my teacher, the legalist Maren Corey."

"Let it be given to Jerre Amadan. Has a gun been provided?"

Before anyone else could move, Amery reached inside her coat and brought out a plain Halka handgun. "Yes."

"Has this gun some significance?"

"Yes. It belonged to Toren Dall, who died fighting one of the drones who attacked Talin Shelter's foraging camp."

A moment's silence, then: "Let it be given to Jerre Amadan." Book and gun passed from hand to hand around the circle until they came to Jerre.

"These things mark your acceptance as a candidate for Halka training," Benamin told Jerre then. "Consider them carefully. Between them, they'll take up most of your waking hours between now and the day you take baya, and define most of your work if you survive baya and take your place among us.

"At present your sponsor of record is Stefan Jatanni. You may keep him as your sponsor for training, or you may choose any other sen Halka at least seven years past baya. Once you choose, your choice is irrevocable, so think carefully on this."

"I've already done so," Jerre replied. "I would prefer to have sen Jatanni as my sponsor."

The Speaker turned to Stefan. "Do you accept the task of training Jerre Amadan in the Halka path, so that he may take baya if he chooses with the best preparation you can give him?"

"Readily."

"Word will be sent to the archives at Zara." Turning back to Jerre: "Earlier I told you I would give you advice. Some of that I've done already, in one form or another. Here is one last piece. Look at the robe you're wearing."

Jerre glanced at it, at Benamin.

"You may not be aware of it, but gray garments have an ancient meaning to the Halka. During the Insurgency we needed clothing that blended in with forest and meadow, and so the first sen Halka wore gray, not black. Later, after the end of the Insurgency, after the schism between Halka and Halvedna and the Convention of Zara that settled it, our order changed its color from gray to black. When you leave this room and start your training, you'll be making a similar transition. You'll find it useful to compare the two, and think about the reasons that governed the first of them. That's all."

Stefan stood up then. A quick burst of innerspeech, partly screened from the rest of the circle, passed between him and the Speaker. As it finished, he turned to Jerre. "Then we'll begin. Come with me." Jerre got to his feet, and the two of them left the room.

When they were gone, Benamin glanced once around the circle, closed his eyes and entered rapport. The circle group-mind carried his thoughts to the others: *His testimony is the last thing we must assess. You've seen him. How would you evaluate him now?*

Amery paused, considering, then told the groupmind: *No response. I can't answer impartially.*

Acknowledged. The groupmind, she reminded herself, was simply a mental construct, a controlled collective hallucination put in place to help keep personalities from standing in the way of the business of judgment or command. Still, to Amery's mind each one she'd experienced had a personality of its own. This one, for instance: it spoke in brisk tones, precisely phrased, and its summaries rarely strayed into subtleties or contested details. Another might have asked her about the reasons for her response, or tried elicit an answer from her despite them. This one, fortunately, had other habits.

The circle is of more than one opinion, it said now, *but a consensus exists.*

Present it, Benamin instructed.

So, in the still center of awareness, the voice of the groupmind:

First: *Jerre Amadan appears honest and perceptive, and can be expected to tell the truth as he knows it. His testimony in most conditions is likely to be reliable.*

Then: *A number of factors have been proposed which might produce false testimony. All of them are possible, but no firm evidence supports any of them.*

Finally, consensus: *In the absence of other evidence the possibility that Jerre Amadan's testimony is valid cannot be eliminated.*

Fourteen sen Halka pondered this in silence. After several minutes, Benamin asked: *Is this the considered judgment of the circle?*

The response was swift and unanimous: *Yes.*

We have three tasks, then. We must try to determine just what we may be facing; we must develop a legal structure for Halka actions based on visionary evidence; we must plan and make ready for the possibility of war. Each of you should decide which of these interests you most, and begin work. We meet again at tenth hour tomorrow.

He broke rapport. Others followed. By the time Amery blinked and looked around, half the circle's members had already left, and she and Benamin were the only ones still seated.

"Amery," the Speaker said quietly.

She looked at him.

In the innerspeech: *Stay. We should talk.*

The others filed out the door. Carla, among the last to leave, gave Amery a questioning look but went out anyway. When the last sounds of movement had faded, Benamin turned to her and said, "I assume you know we'd already found him a gun."

"Yes."

"Perhaps you'll explain, then."

"Of course." She'd rehearsed the words, readying herself for this moment, but now that it had arrived they came only with an effort. "Jerre Amadan has been through chemical catamnesis. So have I. Thinking over my own experience, I realized the ordinary range of tests for false purpose might not be enough. Someone just finished with catamnetic therapy has another motive to seek baya: the desire for lost memories."

Benamin nodded. "I see. You'll have meant the gun to remind Jerre of what happened to its last owner, to balance his desire with a precisely placed fear."

"Essentially."

One eyebrow twisted upward. "Why didn't you propose it to the circle beforehand?"

"I'm far from sure the other members of the circle would understand."

"As it happens, Stefan and I discussed this matter of memories a week ago."

Startled, Amery managed a wan smile. "Then my plan was wasted effort."

"Not at all. You saw something that needed doing, and did it. That is the Halka path." He rose to his feet. "Your stratagem has much to recommend it: more subtle and more efficient than the one I had in mind. When I spoke to Stefan just now, I said as much. When it's time for you to train candidates of your own, Amery, you'll do well." He turned to go, then glanced back at her. "I know we stress again and again the need for consensus and cooperation among Halka, especially to the young. Those are—" He gestured. "Helps on the path. Personal action and personal responsibility *are* the path. You might wish to meditate on that."

"I'll do that," said Amery.

Benamin nodded once and left the room.

2

Later, looking back on the ninety days of his training, Jerre recalled the time before baya as a seamless blur of images and events, each one blurring at its edges into all those around it, with his acceptance by the circle at its beginning and baya at its end framing it. At the time, though, every fragment of Halka lore mastered and every test passed seemed to mark a boundary in his life as absolute as those the drones or the catamnetic had imposed. That was intentional, he realized, and the details of training had been carefully crafted to reinforce that feeling in ways he could sometimes perceive, but the awareness did not keep those from having their effect.

Thus on the first day of his training he was given black Halka garments, a holster for his gun, and a few austere items for his daily use. All his own possessions were locked away for safekeeping, to be returned only after his training was over. His room returned to the Shelter's open list, and he moved into a bare little cubicle in the Halka quarters only just large enough for the bedding they gave him to be unrolled.

Just outside, in the common room where the circle met, he had his first lesson. In silence, Stefan showed him how to take apart, clean, and reassemble the heavy Halka pistol, then had him do it over and over again until his fingers no longer stumbled over the curves of cold metal. Next Stefan taught him to load the ten-round magazine and empty it, and had him repeat that until Jerre lost count of the repetitions. Then, breaking silence, the sen Halka taught him how to clear a jammed round from the action, and had him repeat that, too, until he could do it without thinking. Finally, Stefan had him load the magazine again, this time with the light rounds the Halka used for target practice, and when he'd finished, motioned him to stand and led the way outside.

The day was clear and cool, late summer touched with the first breath of autumn. Trees within sight of the door had begun to bud with their winter leaves, pale against the deep indigo of the summer foliage. Shelter folk moved among the trees, inspecting the bark, and Jerre realized with a start that the meria harvest would be only a week or two away. A year ago, he recalled, he'd worked long days helping bring in the harvest at Talin. The memory seemed alien, as though it belonged to someone else. Another boundary, he thought, and hurried after Stefan.

They walked westward through the forest for most of a kilometer in silence, on level ground at first and then up the first low slope of the hill country. The slope crested and dropped away, and the trail turned south, joined another that came from further west, and curved down through tree-shadows to one side of a clearing.

"There," Stefan said, gesturing to the right. Maybe fifteen meters away, a massive wooden post pocked with bullet-marks rose up out of the meadowmoss. "That will be your target. Have you used a firearm before?"

"Not that I remember."

"Good. Those who learn to shoot in the ordinary way commonly spend weeks unlearning their old habits before they can begin learning the Halka way of the gun." He glanced at the younger man. "Pay close attention. Everything you'll learn in the next ninety days will come down to this one thing.

"Look at the target." When Jerre did so: "Your conscious mind and the innermind both see that target. The first of those is what you've probably always considered your inmost self. The second you've probably never experienced at all, and for now you'll have to take its existence on faith. But the first, as you look at the post, sees only the post. The second sees everything in front of you: the post, the fallen log beyond it, and the second target off to the left. Did you notice those latter two?"

"No," Jerre admitted.

"If either of them was a drone you'd be dead now. That's the risk of remaining in the outer awareness, as Shelter folk do when they use guns. The first Halka did the same before the dwimmerwine opened our eyes, but the innermind, not outer awareness, guides us now. The gun must be an extension of the arm, the arm an extension of the mind, the mind an extension of the innermind. Remember that."

Jerre nodded, uncertain.

"Now for the practice. Face the target, and stand this way."

Jerre copied the stance awkwardly. Stefan examined him. "That will do for now. Center your weight between your feet, and don't lock your knees. Good. Now, without looking down at it, reach for your gun and draw it slowly."

Sweat moistened Jerre's palm as he curled his hand around the pistol grip. The weapon slid out of its holster smoothly, almost without effort.

"When the muzzle clears the holster, swing it forward, and turn off the safety catch with your thumb. That way, yes. Now bring your hand up and forward, until your arm is straight. Don't tense it. Now hold."

He stepped forward, adjusted the angle of Jerre's shoulders, stepped back. "Look at the target, not at the gun. Don't try to aim. Just look at the target, let your outer awareness focus on the target, and pull back slowly on the trigger."

Jerre stared at the post for a long moment, and fired. Recoil jerked the gun up and back, jolting his arm and nearly tearing the pistol from his grasp. The post was untouched.

"Put on the safety catch," Stefan told him, "and put the gun back in the holster. Check your stance, draw, and fire again."

The younger man drew, paused, pulled the trigger. The pistol jumped again, less wildly.

"Again," Stefan said, as echoes from the shot came back to them.

After the fourth shot, Stefan stopped him. "You're beginning to aim. Look at the target, not at the gun. Let the innermind take over."

"How do I know when it's doing that?"

"You can't. You'll simply have to trust it. Draw again, and fire."

Six more shots sent echoes ringing through the quiet air. The next to last clipped one edge of the post; the others vanished without any trace Jerre could see, though Stefan seemed to be able to follow them. As he returned the gun to its place, Jerre shook his head. "I don't know, sen Jatanni. Do most beginners miss so often?"

Stefan glanced at him. "Does that matter?"

It wasn't the answer Jerre expected. "I don't know."

"Don't speak of it again." Without another word Stefan turned and left the clearing. Jerre looked after him, startled, and followed.

The rest of that day went into studying and memorizing passages from the book of laws, and repeating the drills for cleaning, loading and clearing the gun, one after another well into the night. After a few hours of sleep, Stefan woke him with a tap on his door, waited while he dressed and ate a cold breakfast, then had him load the pistol and six extra magazines with target rounds. By the time dawn broke, the two of them had returned to the clearing. Once again Jerre drew and fired over and over, corrected every few shots by some terse comment of Stefan's, and once again nearly every shot missed. Though he remembered the sen Halka's injunction and did not voice his feelings, frustration spoke in every line of his body as he inspected the post grimly, then followed Stefan back to the Shelter.

That afternoon, after wrestling with the text and commentaries on the First Law and learning what Stefan told him was the first in a series of concentration exercises, he and Stefan returned to the clearing. Stefan watched in silence as Jerre faced the post, took up the shooting stance, drew and fired. The shot missed, and Jerre looked at the target in dismay for a moment before slipping the gun back into the holster. He wanted to aim, to fire just one shot that would hit, but what would be the point? That would be just as much a failure as missing again. At length, for want of anything better, he drew again, thinking: and this one will miss, too, and the next, and the next. Then, as the muzzle cleared the holster and his thumb disengaged the safety catch, a second thought: and if that happens, what difference would it make?

He pulled the trigger, and splinters flew from the middle of the post.

Jerre stared, slid the gun back into its place, drew again. That shot missed, and the one after it, but by the third shot he'd found his way back to the small space of clarity where it didn't matter whether the bullet hit or missed. As he drew back the trigger he knew the shot would hit, and it did, square in the middle of the post two centimeters away from his first mark.

"Hold," said Stefan. A fractional smile slipped past the precise detachment his face usually wore during training sessions. "Can you repeat that?"

"I think so."

"Can you describe what you were doing wrong?"

Jerre paused, fumbled for words. "I was trying too hard, I think." Haltingly, he explained about the space of clarity and how he'd stumbled onto it.

"Good." The sen Halka nodded. "Now attend." He drew his own gun in a fluid blur of motion, pointed it at the post. "At the moment you fired, your arm tensed like this." His wrist canted minutely to the left. "As a result..." He pulled the trigger and missed. "Nearly all your bullets went four to ten centimeters to the left of the post. You'll find the holes in the moss if you look for them. How many rounds do you have left?"

The question was an awareness test, one Jerre had failed before. This time he was ready. "Fifty-five."

"That should be enough. Be aware of your wrist, and relax the muscles that aren't needed to aim or brace the gun. Now that you've learned from the mistake, there's no need to repeat it." He put his pistol away. "Begin."

Jerre drew and pointed the gun, caught the tensing of muscles before it could affect his aim, fired. Splinters of wood flew from the post. He let new habits return the weapon to its place, draw it again, fire. Within, the space of clarity remained, minute but bright, like a spark in slow tinder. At its heart the pressures of emotion and the demands of memory fell away for the first time since a dim image of light ended the whirling darkness of the catamnetic.

Another boundary, he thought. Another bullet struck the post.

3

Amery spread her map across the concrete, pushing Stefan's drawings away to either side. "This is my reconstruction," she said. "The red lines are drone movements. Each break is the end of twenty-four hour's travel at cruising speed."

The terrace around her basked in noon sunlight. Above, one of Mirien's wind turbines turned lazily in a breeze from the distant ocean. Two of the three sen Halka sitting with Amery moved closer, studied the map and the lines with more than ordinary interest.

Carla spoke first. "Has Stefan seen this?"

"Not yet. He's been busy with Jerre Amadan's training. I admit I haven't been anxious to disturb him."

"Understandable."

They turned back to the map. Another of the sen Halka, the young woman with the scarred face who had given Jerre the book of laws, traced one of the lines in the east with her finger. "This would be the main line of attack?"

"That's my thought."

"Given enough drones, they could be here within days."

"Exactly," said Amery. "That's the core of our problem."

"Perhaps." Carla was frowning. "There's another difficulty, though. Benamin's been in contact with Shelters across the north country, and he says maybe one in twenty is willing to make the sort of preparations we have in mind. Most of the Shelter councils trust Talin's assessment."

"I was expecting that," Amery told her. "It may not be as much of a problem as it looks. Notice the blue circles." She pointed them out, about two dozen of them scattered randomly over the north country. "Those are Shelters that have contacted us and offered their support. We've been discussing a defense in depth, which is sensible, but we've also been talking about strengthening every Shelter in the north country, which may not be. Our resources aren't unlimited, and for all we know we may face time limits as well. What if we accept the situation as it is and turn the Shelters that support us into strongpoints?"

The others pondered the map for a time. "That's reasonable," said Carla. "That's most reasonable. I would support it. Tena?"

The scarred sen Halka nodded. "Good. If the drones attack the strongpoints they risk heavy losses, and if they don't they'll have to deal with significant forces behind their lines."

"Exactly," Amery said. "They'll also have to be resupplied, and strongpoints behind their lines would put that at risk." At Tena's startled look: "Remember we're considering a war, not just wandering drones. Whoever our enemies are, they'll have to keep their drones from running out of ammunition."

"That's true," Tena said. She turned, then, and looked at the fourth member of the group. After a moment, Amery and Carla did the same.

Old eyes, heavy-lidded, glanced up from the map; a wizened face lined and wrinkled into a caricature of itself regarded them. Allan Berelat had been the master strategist of the fight against the outrunners of Wind Gap, a legendary figure among Halka, and his decision to join the Mirien command circle brought it a credibility nothing else could have done. So far, though, he'd held his silence except for a few words of agreement. At times, talking of strategies in his presence, Amery wondered if the mind that had defeated the largest concentration of outrunners in Eridan's history had been defeated in turn by age.

Now, though, the old man cleared his throat. "One question. How much reliance do you place on your map?"

"Some," Amery said carefully. "I may have misinterpreted Stefan's drawings, or the vision itself may be wrong. Still—" She met his gaze. "The shape of the land puts limits on what drones can do, and the best line of attack southwards is here."

She pointed to the main line of attack. "If I were our enemy's strategist, this is where I would attack."

"I see." His face remained almost expressionless. "I will support your plan." The pale eyes closed, and silence fell around him like a wall.

"Thank you," Amery said, and began gathering up her papers and maps. "We can present it to the command circle tomorrow, and see what the others have to say."

"Before then, we should talk to the sen Halka in some of the Shelters that support us." Carla got to her feet. "We'll need some sense of what they need. I can contact them by radio today if you like."

"I would be slow to do that," the old man said abruptly.

The others looked at him, startled. His eyes were wide open, and fixed on Amery. "You reminded us a moment ago that this is war, not simply raids by solitary drones. That has consequences you haven't discussed yet. One is that anyone who can command drones presumably can listen to our radio communications as well."

Amery blanched. "When did you think of that?"

"I was aware of the possibility before I joined this circle."

"And you said nothing?"

"So far the circle has simply followed standard procedures. The enemy doubtless knows those, and radio silence would only make them suspicious. It's the variations from standard procedure that have to be concealed."

"The strongpoints," said Carla.

Allan glanced at her. "Those above all."

"Yes," said Amery. "You're right, of course. In fact, I can think of a way to use the radio net itself for that."

"Can you?" For the first time, a flicker of interest showed in the old man's eyes. "Good. Work it out in detail and we'll discuss it tomorrow." He blinked, then, and all at once the barriers returned. The others watched him as he rose to his feet with a visible effort, turned, walked away.

"The message network?" Tena suggested when he was gone. "That ought to be secure."

"True," said Carla, "though I don't relish all that writing. Didn't they have copy-making machines on Earth? I'd welcome one just now."

Tena laughed. "It's a long walk there. I'll help with the writing, if you like." Turning to Amery: "So you think we can trick the enemy with the radio net? I'd like to hear more."

Amery was still looking the way Allan Berelat had gone. "He's amazing," she said after a moment. "Did you notice? He's planning strategies around our reactions and the enemy's alike. I thought he was senile and all along he was twenty kilometers ahead of me." Then, to Tena: "I have the seed of an idea, nothing more than that. I'm still not sure what to do with it." She gathered up the last of the papers, stood up. "Give me a little while to work on it."

4

"Below us," Stefan said. "What's unusual about it?"

They stood at the top of a gentle slope. To the right, dark hills cloaked in mist rose up into the morning; to the left, the sun had just cleared the mountains. Below lay a valley full of soaring purple trees Jerre didn't recognize; in the middle distance the trees gave way to blue meadowmoss reaching southward to the edge of sight. Jerre struggled to clear his awareness of thoughts so that patterns could surface from the innermind.

The two of them had left Mirien two days before through the pale mists of an autumn morning. Stefan said nothing about their destination, and Jerre knew better than to ask. The sen Halka set him awareness exercises as they walked but otherwise said little. They spent the night at a Shelter whose name Jerre could never remember afterwards, and started south again at dawn.

Now Jerre blinked back the morning sun, tried to use the lessons he'd been studying for most of two months.

"There's something odd about the trees," he said after a time. "They're—they're too regular. That's it. They're arranged in lines."

"Good." Stefan started down the slope. Jerre caught the first signs of motion and went with him: another awareness exercise. "We're approaching Werelin," the sen Halka told him.

"The Gathering?"

"Yes. Do you recall anything about the battle here?"

"No." Cautiously: "During the Insurgency?"

"Not long before it ended. Werelin was a city and a huge military base in those days. The Directorate commander here was Marc Thomason, probably the best tactician they had. He warned his superiors that the Halka meant to attack. They didn't believe him. That cost them the base, the city, and eventually the war."

Trees clothed the slopes around them, and only jewel-flies moved in the drowsy air. War could not have seemed further away.

"Look with a warrior's eye," said Stefan. "Werelin's in the middle of the valley, where the tall trees are. Can it be defended?"

Jerre considered that as they descended. Slopes surrounded the valley on three sides, and on two of them heights further back made the slopes impossible to defend. "Only against an attack from the south. If the attackers win the high ground, no."

"Good. If someone told you to hold it anyway, what would you expect?"

After a silence: "I wouldn't expect to survive."

"Thomason didn't," said Stefan.

They reached the bottom of the slope finally, followed the track onto the floor of the valley. The purple trees Jerre didn't recognize soared a hundred fifty meters above them, twice the height of a tall thilda. Fog still shrouded the valley bottom, turning the trees around them into ghosts and the heights to either side into dark presences more sensed than seen. After a short distance the ground beneath them changed. Jerre glanced down and found himself walking on weathered concrete.

"The streets of Old Werelin," Stefan told him. "Look at the way the trees follow them." A gesture pointed out long rows of trunks fading out into the fog.

"Did somebody plant them?"

"Good. Yes. After the Insurgency, when they stripped the city of building material for the first Shelters in this area, they brought daula saplings from the south and planted them here. The daula forests suffered hideously during the fighting; the Directorate used defoliants and fire to hunt for insurgent bases. This is north of daula country but as you see, the saplings thrived."

Gray spires topped with a purple canopy, the daula trees loomed overhead, catching most of the sunlight; what passed through them slanted down through the fog in bright shafts. Stefan and Jerre walked on. "Is this where the Gathering's held?" Jerre asked.

"A month ago you'd have found tents, trade goods, and people covering every square meter," Stefan told him. "But they're careful about the Second Law. There's been trouble at Amris and Halleth now and then, but never here."

He fell silent again. Jerre glanced around as they walked. City, battle and Gathering alike seemed insubstantial as phantoms in the mist. He tried to imagine the people who lived there in the city's crowded streets, those who fought and died there during the Insurgency, those who traded there in the long years of peace afterward, and ended up feeling as though he and Stefan were the only living people in a world of ghosts.

Two traders heading north, hauling a trail cart heaped with gaudily wrapped trade goods, offered welcome evidence to the contrary. They greeted Stefan by name with broad smiles, and stopped by the trailside long enough to exchange pleasantries and ask about conditions further on. When the traders started on their way again and the creak and rattle of the cart was muffled by the fog, Jerre asked, "You know them?"

"Yes," said Stefan. "We've traveled the same road more than once." They walked on in silence for a time. "Most sen Halka who know their work talk with traders as often as they can. Traveling folk get news sooner than anyone else, and they know it's our doing that they can travel safely. When Shelter folk violate the Six Laws we usually hear of it from a trader first."

"Does that happen often?" Jerre asked, startled.

"I've investigated only two cases of that kind in thirty years." Stefan glanced at him. "One dispute between Shelters that turned briefly violent, one technician who salvaged banned machinery. Six people had to be shot. Two of them were younger than you are."

Jerre gave him an appalled look, but Stefan walked on in silence.

Not much before noon, when the last wisps of fog had burnt off, they left the main track and headed off through the trees. An indistinct murmur turned into the sound of water splashing over rocks. A little later, they came to a stream, crossed it on a wooden bridge, rounded a cluster of meria trees, and stood facing a building of gray concrete. Narrow windows looked down on them from above, and a heavy ironbound door in front of them stood just slightly open.

"A technician?" Jerre asked, surprised.

"No ordinary technician." Stefan stepped up to the door, raised a fist to knock on it.

"Come in," boomed a deep voice from within.

Stefan pulled the door open, and he and Jerre entered. Dimness inside after the bright morning left Jerre unable to see anything at first but looming shadows. One of the shadows spoke in the same deep voice: "Stefan. Well. It's been a while."

"Four years now."

"With a candidate, I would guess."

"Yes. This is Jerre Amadan. You'll know his gun, Tom."

"I know it already." To Jerre: "Show me."

The shadow shifted, came forward. As his eyes adjusted to the dim light, Jerre made out workbenches and hanging tools around him, and a great barrel-shaped figure of a man approaching. Long unkempt hair and beard, black going to gray, spilled over heavy barkcloth garments; small black eyes that glittered like stones regarded him. The man reached out a hand twice the size of Jerre's. Jerre drew his gun and handed it to him grip first.

"Well." A low meditative rumble shook the room, perhaps laughter, perhaps not. "An early piece of mine, winter of '52, made for Marc Toben—you recall him? Shot by a judgment circle in '69. Rebuilt it in '70 for Anna Merreth, and fixed mistakes I didn't know enough to avoid in '52. Balanced it in '79 for Toren Dall after Anna died up in the mountains. What happened to Toren? Blood's touched this steel, and not Anna's only."

"He was killed by a drone, north of settled country this spring."

The big man nodded slowly. "Sooner than I hoped, but not sooner than I feared. He had too much anger in him to last long."

Jerre took in all this in silence. Stefan turned to him while the other examined the gun minutely. "Tomas Mord is the best master gunsmith on Eridan today," the sen Halka said.

"Only by default," Tomas rumbled. He handed Jerre's gun back, faced him squarely. "You're wondering what business you have with a gunsmith, eh? You have your gun, you pull the trigger and it fires, you need nothing else from me. If you live through baya you'll think otherwise. Give me your gun hand."

Jerre did so, and the gunsmith took the arm in his own hands, probed it as though exploring an unfamiliar machine. "Feel the tensions here, and here." He found tight muscles and pressed massive fingertips into them, sending spikes of pain up Jerre's nerves. "You have grief in your muscles, grief and guilt. Feel how this muscle wants to strike out, this one wants to pull back. Toren, now, his body had rage and fear in it, and these muscles here—" Another jab. "—these were loose, not tight as yours are. Your wrist pulled to the left early on, I think."

Jerre nodded, and the gunsmith made another rumbling noise in his throat. "The gun's balanced for a shorter arm, a smaller hand, a different mind. That can be fixed." He handed Jerre something that looked like a stick. "Grip this as you would a gun, but harder."

Jerre took it, clenched it in his fist and felt it shift beneath the pressure as Tomas' huge hands moved back and forth on his arm, probing tensions and angles. "There," said the gunsmith after a time, and took the stick back, marked by Jerre's fingers. "Now draw, slowly." Jerre did so. "Return, and draw as though your life depended on it." Blur of speed, the gun leapt out of its holster with an ease Jerre had struggled for nearly two months to achieve. "Good," said Tomas. He turned and shouted: "Cara!"

A moment later a young woman in baggy clothing looked out from a door on the other side of the room. "These two need food and I need them out of here," the gunsmith told her. "Take them somewhere."

She motioned for them to follow, and a few moments later they climbed a stair out of the dark workroom. "You won't take offense, I trust," she said as they reached the top and sunlight poured down from skylights in the slanted ceiling above. "He's like that."

Stefan allowed a laugh. "Indeed he is. I've had my guns worked and balanced here for twenty years. You're his new apprentice?"

"That I am." She motioned them to a massive wooden table, began setting out dishes. "Do you know Jo Tannath, lives west of Annan-mouth?"

"I used one of her long rifles against outrunners in the forests past Wind Gap," Stefan said. "A good sturdy weapon; it saved my life more than once."

The apprentice grinned. "Jo's my mother. I'll tell her that when next I'm home." Thick slices of fresh green bread with yeast paste, bowls of stew, and herb beer made up the meal. All through it Stefan asked questions about the summer's Gathering and the doings of technicians he knew, and Cara answered artlessly enough. Jerre ate, listened, and said very little.

Not long after he finished, Tomas' booming voice sounded up the stair, though Jerre couldn't make out the words. He and Stefan went back down to find the big man polishing the pistol's wooden grip with a rag that had seen many better days. "Here," the gunsmith said, handing the gun back to Jerre. It seemed subtly different, and the grip was new. He turned to Stefan then. "You've trained him on real rounds?"

"He's used them."

A rumble of disapproval set tools vibrating on the walls. "Target rounds. The Halka of our grandparents' time would have laughed at them. Well." To Jerre: "We'll see how much you've learned. Come."

They went out into the bright afternoon and circled around the house. Behind it, open ground reached past a wooden target post twenty meters away to steep overgrown slopes behind. "Try it now," Tomas said.

Jerre took up shooting stance, checked the magazine. Ten long rounds gleamed in the sunlight, tipped with jacketed bullets that could pierce a drone's armor or pass through a tree to kill someone hiding behind it. He closed the magazine, returned the gun to its place, drew and fired. The gun came out of the holster and rose up in an elegant curve that startled him by its effortlessness, but the shock of the recoil nearly pulled the grip from his hand. Wood chips exploded from the target post as the report echoed back, and an instant later a low *thump* told of bullet meeting clay on the slopes behind.

He returned the gun to its place, drew and shot again, repeated the drill until he'd emptied the magazine. The gun seemed to move by itself through each movement, as though responding to his thoughts.

"The gun's an extension of the hand," said Tomas then, "the hand of the mind, the mind of the innermind. Yes? But all depends on having a gun that can do its part."

"Equally," Stefan replied, "on a hand and a mind that can do theirs."

Laughter rumbled like summer thunder. "That's your task to worry over, sen Halka. Mine's merely to see to the gun." Then: "You'll stay the night?"

"Unfortunately not. We have a long walk still before us." A shrug. "Next spring, maybe. You know the way of it, Tom."

"Too well." A slow nod, the black eyes glinting. "I'll get the papers, then."

Stefan signed for the trade credit, and he and Jerre said their farewells and started back through the daula grove toward the main southward track. When they'd gone far enough not to be overheard, Stefan glanced at the younger man. "Good. You have a gun that suits your hand, and I don't have to worry that an old friend might be shot for breaking the Fifth Law. Tom's come close to that more than once, and I was glad to hear that he's become more careful."

It took Jerre a moment to make sense of that. "When you talked with Cara—"

"I asked about things that would make her think of banned technologies if she knew anyone was working with them, and I listened to her voice, not her words. If she'd had anything to hide I'd have known it at once."

Jerre nodded but said nothing in response. Stefan glanced at him again and then stopped and turned to face him. "Ah. I thought we'd reach this moment soon. You asked for baya with the thought of fighting drones, but you've seen another side of our work, and it troubles you. Am I right?" Jerre managed another nod, and Stefan went on. "And it should trouble you. If it didn't, I'd dismiss you from training for that alone."

The sen Halka turned half away, looked off into the forest. "Shelter folk think fighting drones and outrunners are the heart of our work. They're mistaken. When the last drones have been blown apart and the last outrunner band has been hunted down, the Halka will still have more than enough to do, because drones and outrunners aren't the greatest threat to our world."

"You're saying that Shelter folk and technicians are?"

"All of us are." Quietly, then: "Shelter folk, technicians, traders, sen Halvedna, sen Halka, anyone who might let the concerns of the present blind them to the hard lessons of the past. For two hundred years now, people on Eridan have had peace and freedom, more of both than their ancestors ever had on Earth. Yet in every single one of those two hundred years, at least one person's tried to get past the barriers that make that possible." He faced Jerre again. Though his voice stayed quiet, his gaze focused on the younger man with a terrible intensity. "Most of them have good reasons. That's the bitter thing. They never think they're starting down the road to Shalsha. They simply want to solve a problem, or redress a grievance, or give people a choice they wouldn't have otherwise. They're always sure the situation justifies setting aside the Laws, just this once. They never understand that to us, the reasons can never matter."

Meeting the sen Halka's eyes, Jerre wondered if that was the way Stefan looked at the people he was about to shoot. One certainty came through the confusion of his thoughts. "You want me to ask you why."

"Good. You're starting to learn." Then: "But there's only one place on Eridan where I can answer that question, and it's the place we're going next."

"Where is that?"

Stefan allowed a fractional smile. "Come and see."

5

"Here," Stefan said. "You may remember this."

He and Jerre stopped at the trail's edge, looked west across the plain. Before them broken concrete pavement, half buried in meadowmoss, marked the course of an ancient road.

"Dimly." Jerre stared at the cracked surface, struggled with his memory. "It's from Shalsha's time, isn't it?"

"Yes. All the old roads were built by the Directorate."

"Where does it go?"

The sen Halka glanced at him, then stepped onto the old road. "Our destination."

All around them moss plains stretched away into distance, violet-gray edged with blue. Five more days of walking south from Werelin had brought them well into the lowlands, so that the forests that swathed the north country made only an indigo haze on the hills ahead of them and a band of the same color at the feet of the mountains behind. Here, in the settled heartland of Eridan, Shelters stood as close together as the Second Law allowed; to the east, the wind turbines of eight communities rose above the moss. To the west, though, nothing broke the plain from the trail to the edge of the hill country tens of kilometers away. Jerre noticed this, puzzled over it briefly. A pale fragment of remembrance flitted past him; had he been here before, or walked a nearby trail? He could not tell. An eyeblink later the memory vanished.

"As we walk," Stefan said, breaking the silence, "watch for windflowers of that type." He pointed to the side of the road, where a slim feathery flower rose out of the moss, white against violet, a springtime shape starkly out of place amid the autumn hues of the plain. "Note where they grow, and in what numbers. Don't speak again until I request it."

An awareness exercise, Jerre thought, and made the minute gesture of assent he'd been taught. The special quality of attention those demanded came to his mind with practiced ease.

On the way south from Werelin, Stefan had set him one awareness exercise after another, forcing him to push his mind
beyond its ordinary limits, and in the process making conversation all but impossible: just as well, Jerre thought, since the
questions he most wanted to ask were the ones he knew Stefan
would refuse to answer.

Moss rustled beneath their boots as they walked. The road
ran on, compass-straight, level despite the gentle curves of the
plain. The pale windflowers appeared here and there at first,
half-concealed in hollows in the ground. As Stefan and Jerre
walked on and the sun crept westwards with them, the distance between one flower and the next became shorter and
small clusters of white showed here and there among the moss.
The hills at sky's edge came no closer. Against them, though,
tiny irregularities now stood, too widespread to be a Shelter's
wind turbines, too ordered to be the work of nature.

Afternoon deepened and the shapes grew closer. The flowers became a white carpet across uneven ground. The sound
of moving waters came from somewhere ahead, faintly at first
and then with growing strength until it drowned out every
other sound.

Then the plain broke away into riverbank, and the road ran
straight across on a massive bridge of concrete and corroded
metal. Ten meters below, a great river flowed southwards,
curling and splashing against the pilings. Beyond the bridge
low mounds of moss-covered rubble and weathered masses of
concrete lined the sides of the road, and reached away into distance in three directions.

"Do you know where we are?" Stefan asked.

Jerre turned to him, wide-eyed. "This is Shalsha."

"Eastbridge, on the edge of the city." The sen Halka gestured ahead, into the heart of the ruins. "The buildings on the
other side were the Eastbridge fortifications and the headquar-
ters of the Fourth Field Army." Indicating the road behind:
"This was Highway 9, which ran eighteen kilometers east to

the factory camp at Tol Edri. Candidates for baya went there before Shalsha was safe to enter, but that was long ago. There's nothing left there now except the monument to the dead." He motioned to Jerre to follow him, and started across the bridge.

Jerre caught up with him a moment later. "But—what about the radiation?"

"It reached background levels on the surface over a century ago. So long as we don't disturb the soil there's no danger."

They picked their way across the bridge, staying clear of the places where the decking had begun to give way. Below, the river rushed past. "Halka teams survey the ruins with radiation counters every three years," Stefan went on. "It's a formality, really, but it comforts the local Shelter folk. Of course there's reason for caution. There can be no digging here, no planting or harvesting for human use. There are dangerous isotopes and chemical wastes underground, and the groundwater's still very toxic."

They stepped back onto solid ground on the far side of the bridge. Stefan knelt and plucked one of the white flowers, gave it to Jerre. "Look at it," he said. "Study it, contemplate it, burn its image into your memory. Do you know its name?"

"I did once." Jerre stared at the flower in his hand, sensing again the stirring of a memory that refused to surface. "But I don't—"

"Fireflower."

Jerre's lips formed a silent "oh."

"A curious plant of more than scientific interest." They began walking again, deeper into the ruins, past the crumbling remains of massive sloped walls. Everywhere an ankle-deep layer of white windflowers blanketed the rubble, wrapped the feet of Shalsha's failed defenses. "You know about the plants prospectors use, the ones that cluster where there's some mineral beneath the soil? Fireflower is much the same. Normally it's rare to find two in a square kilometer, but some fluke of biochemistry makes it flourish in soil tainted by atomic fallout."

The sen Halka gestured outward. "Elsewhere it flowers for a week, maybe two. Here, it flowers seven months out of the year. A mutation, perhaps."

The crumbling walls gave way to low mounds, the remains of lighter structures. "Many years ago," Stefan went on, "the Halka considered taking the fireflower as its symbol in place of the circle and triangle. Philosophical thinking prevailed, but the principle's still good." A low mound of moss and corroded metal that might once have been a vehicle blocked half the road. They went around it, kept going. "For most of Eridan's people, this is a place of fear and death."

"But not for the Halka?"

"No." Wind rippled across a sea of fireflowers. "For the Halka, it's a place of memory."

To either side of the street, aluminum poles broken off at knee level and warped by great heat rose out of whiteness like rotting teeth in a skull. Stefan pointed them out. "Two centuries ago those were thirty meters tall, taller than the buildings, and each one carried the green banner of the Directorate. This was the main avenue of Shalsha. Armies marched along it, parades, formal processions, from Eastbridge through the city center to the main government buildings in the west. By all accounts it was a grand sight: the bright face the Directorate showed the world. The dark face was elsewhere." A gesture outwards. "Tol Edri, Sharru, Keltessat, Annum Tal. The factory camps where four and a half million people died." He stopped, turned to face Jerre. "Imagine it as it was, if you can. Imagine it, and remember that this is the thing the Halka came into being to destroy."

They started walking again. "That was Judith Mariel's true gift to us," Stefan went on. "The conception of the Halka as a wholly negative force. Does that phrase surprise you? The point is that we don't have a political program of our own. We stand against certain things, and that's all. What other people stand for is their concern. What they do is our concern only if they violate the Six Laws, and even then, their motives and purposes mean nothing to us.

"There's a story about that, sen Amadan. You'll hear it, as every candidate for baya hears it, here in the ruins of Shalsha." He fell silent for a time, then said, "There's more to it than that. Ultimately, whether you'll survive baya or not depends on what happens here." He glanced at Jerre. "Now."

Jerre gave him a startled look but said nothing.

"The story begins far from here, in the southern mountains where the Insurgency started, and it begins in the last year of the Insurgency." That last phrase sent echoes moving through the innermind again, echoes Stefan tried to ignore. "Werelin had already fallen and closed the gap between the hill country and the mountains. The last of the factory camps had been freed months earlier, and the plains south of Halleth were in insurgent hands. The Directorate had controlled every square centimeter of the planet twenty years earlier; but when this story begins all they still held was Shalsha itself and the plains around it."

The road stretched on. This far in, only uneven ground beneath the fireflowers showed where buildings had been. The flagpoles dwindled to blackened stumps visible only when the wind disturbed the flowers around them.

"The Directorate was fighting for survival, and losing. The historians say that Carl Emmer, the last Planetary Director, expected the final assault on Shalsha itself within months. Security Command still had troops, aircraft, drones, but not enough of them. The insurgents outnumbered them many times over, and they'd learned how to counter Directorate technology well enough by then that Security forces didn't dare risk open battle.

"So Emmer ordered raids on suspected insurgent bases, to retake the initiative and draw forces away from the assault on Shalsha. Soldiers and drones went by air to points deep in insurgent territory, did what damage they could, and left.

It was a desperation move, and it wouldn't have had any effect on the war except for an accident."

Ahead, just visible in the distance, a wall of rubble several meters high rose up from the plain, curving away on either side into the shadows at the feet of distant hills. Fireflowers blanketed it like snow.

"One of these raids happened to find a minor insurgent base in the southern mountains—a base like dozens of others, except just then Judith Mariel was using it as her head-quarters. She was wounded in the attack, and someone in the Directorate force recognized her and got her onto one of the aircraft. In the confusion none of the insurgents realized she'd been captured until the raiders left and she couldn't be found.

"Her loss was a disaster. She'd been the heart of the Insurgency for twenty years, its chief strategist, the diplomat who held its different factions together. Worse, she alone knew all the details of the planned assault on Shalsha. Whether she could keep those secure in the face of Directorate drugs and torture was a question nobody wanted to answer."

Jerre stumbled on uneven ground, caught himself, pushed the fireflowers aside with one foot. Beneath, rubble lay over the road. He glanced at Stefan, began walking once again.

"You'll understand, then, how desperate the situation was. The Insurgency had been on the brink of victory and suddenly had to face the possibility of defeat. Arguments over the chain of command began as soon as the news got out. The other commanders knew that something had to be done at once, but they weren't able to agree on a common plan.

"At that point, a handful of the younger commanders decided on a plan of their own."

Debris grew thick beneath their feet, covering the road completely. At closer range, the wall of rubble proved to be a slope four or five meters high, blotting out the hills, casting a long shadow toward Stefan and Jerre.

"Before Werelin fell," the sen Halka went on, "the Director-ate had nearly a third of its aircraft there, and several atomic weapons with them. One of the latter fell into insurgent hands intact. It was hidden away, and very few people knew about it. Mariel wasn't among them; she stood firm against weapons of mass destruction, and while she still led, those who had the device didn't dare use it. Her capture removed that obstacle."

They reached the foot of the slope and clambered up it. Around them, the remains of Shalsha spread outward, redden-ing in the light of the setting sun.

"The Insurgency had agents in Shalsha, some of them high up in the Directorate. They smuggled the atomic weapon into the city and hid it inside the core complex of government build-ings. As soon as the agents had time to escape, the weapon went off. The result ..."

They clambered up the last steep part of the rise, stood on the crest.

"... was this."

Before them the ground fell away. A crater more than a kilometer across had been blasted out of the plain, its harsher edges rounded by fireflowers, its depths hidden beneath the dark waters of a lake. Where sunlight touched the water at the lake's eastern edge, swirls of orange and gray scum showed on the surface.

"This is as far as we go," said Stefan, and sat down on the edge of the crater. "The water down there's very toxic, and the air's not much better."

After a moment, Jerre sat down next to him.

"The explosion killed nearly a quarter of a million people," Stefan went on, continuing his story. "A third of them within seconds, the rest over the next two weeks from burns, injuries, radiation. I don't know if anyone has ever calculated the num-ber of wounded, but it was many times larger. Emmer himself and most of the Directorate hierarchy died instantly. There were so few unhurt that the city couldn't have been defended even if the defenses hadn't been wrecked. The surviving officials tried to organize relief, but they had so little food and medicine that when insurgents came to Eastbridge and offered those in exchange for surrender, what was left of the Directorate accepted. Before anyone quite realized it, the Insurgency was over.

"Just over a year later, after the Provisional Council had dissolved and the meetings that drafted the Convention were under way, a Halka tribunal met at Zara to judge the commanders who used the atomic weapon. The members of the tribunal considered all the circumstances—the desperate situation, the risk of defeat, the hundreds of thousands of insurgent lives that had been saved, the total victory that had been won—and after long debate, decided that none of those things mattered. Ultimately, they ruled, the only issue was that the people under judgment had used an atomic weapon against human targets. For that act, the tribunal ordered them to be shot." Stefan turned to face his student. "Do you understand why?"

Jerre, troubled, shook his head. "Not at all."

"The commanders who ordered Shalsha's destruction let belief in their cause override everything else, and committed a monstrous evil. That they did it for the best reasons doesn't make it a fraction of a millimeter less monstrous." The sen Halka looked back into the crater, where the last edge of sunlight had begun to creep up from the waters of the lake. He went on in a more reflective tone. "On Earth, I've read, there was a legend about a place called Hell, a factory camp for the ghosts of people who committed wicked acts. The saying was that the road leading there was surfaced with good intentions." Facing Jerre again: "To condone the destruction of Shalsha would have condoned any excess, any abuse, in a supposedly good cause. That way, the tribunal realized, lay a tyranny equal to Shalsha's. So they ordered the execution of the people who defeated Shalsha, and affirmed Mariel's vision of the Halka in a way no future legalist could ever disregard.

That decision more than anything else kept the Halka from becoming a new Directorate."

"I thought," said Jerre cautiously, "the dwimmerwine did that."

"The dwimmerwine keeps out the unfit," Stefan replied. "Those who come seeking ego satisfaction of one sort or another. Those aren't the only ones who turn to oppression. Idealists are as dangerous as egotists, or more so. Thus the precedent, and later decisions following it."

"Later decisions?"

"There have been quite a few."

"And sen Halka have been shot?"

"Of course. You know we apply our laws to ourselves first of all."

Jerre looked away. Below, the shadow of the far rim climbed the wall of the crater. The sun burnt crimson over the silhouettes of rugged hills, kindled a scattering of low clouds to incandescence. Stefan waited with a hunter's patience.

"What happened to Mariel?" Jerre asked finally.

"No one knows. The Directorate announced her capture, and a week or so afterward Carl Emmer issued a proclamation that she'd been convicted of crimes against the state and sent to Sohallen Prison. That's the last record of her anyone has ever found. It's possible she might have lived until Shalsha's destruction, but few people believe that now. Most people who were sent to Sohallen died within days."

"After the explosion, did they find ..."

"Do you see the masses of concrete along the crater rim, there?" The sen Halka pointed.

Jerre looked, nodded.

"That's what's left of Sohallen Prison. There wasn't much more two hundred years ago."

The younger man stared at the rough shapes of concrete amid rubble stained by the evening light. Muscles tightened at the corners of his mouth. Stefan watched him; after a time, the sen Halka stood up, but motioned to Jerre to remain seated.

"Stay," he said. "You'll remain here in contemplation through the night, until I return at dawn. Draw your gun." When Jerre had done so: "Set it in your lap. Consider it, and consider the fact that if you take baya and survive, you'll use that gun to kill people who violate the Six Laws. Many of them will believe that what they've done is justified, and you'll have to kill them anyway. Think about that."

Before Jerre could respond, Stefan turned and started back down the slope behind him. The sound of his boots on rubble continued for a while, and then faded. Jerre looked at his gun, then at the broken remnants of Sohallen Prison, subject of whispered stories even his shattered memories recalled. Finally, muttering the triggering phrase he'd been taught, he entered the first level of trance and focused on Stefan's words.

6

My friend,

I hope you'll forgive the brevity of this letter and the unconventional manner by which I've sent it. I hope, also, that you won't find my intrusion into this matter out of place. Our Affirmation doesn't often justify involvement in such things, but this case is out of the ordinary.

Jori recently came back from a year's retreat with the hermits near Andarre. When we talked last week, she told me of a troubling movement among the sen davannat there, and that brought to mind your letter of several months ago. A large number of our visionary brothers and sisters have begun to report the same visions of war and disaster your letter mentioned, and some of them have left the hermitages in the last few months and are traveling north. Jori hasn't been able to learn their intentions. Other sen davannat have begun preaching to the Shelter folk nearby, speaking of the coming of war. So far none of them seems to have left the Andarre area, but rumors are flying here at Setneva and elsewhere.

I've been contacting friends all through this past week, and almost everyone who has contact with sen davannat has similar stories. Several of us have formed a network to collect accounts of these visions and keep watch on the movement. There's real potential for trouble here, Tamar. Jori gave me a summary of what she heard from one of the preachers, and it sounds as though two centuries and the Affirmation itself have dissolved like mist. The imagery is all of fire and struggle, and it's not meant as metaphor.

So there it is. I wanted you to know about this, partly because you're already involved in it to some extent and partly because you live on the edge of the north country. Beyond that, I'm told that Mirien has become a base for the Halka response, and I would like you to bring what's happening to the attention of the sen Halka there. I know this is most irregular. I feel sure you'll understand my reasons, though.

Please contact me as soon as you can and let me know what you think of all this. Any responses or questions the sen Halka might have would be more than welcome.

I remain, as always,

Your brother in Halvedna,

Barra Johanan

Amery looked up from the letter. "Bright Earth. How long ago did you get this?"

"Just this morning." Tamar, kneeling at the kitchen unit on the far side of the room, looked up. "Barra sent it with a sen Halka who stopped at Setneva on her way to the north country. That was the odd manner of sending he mentioned."

"With a sen Halka?" The younger woman went over the letter once again, shook her head. "That's something more than odd, I think."

Hot water hissed, and the scent of tebbe blended with that of Tamar's favorite incense. "It's unprecedented," the sen

Halvedna said. "Like the letter itself. I wish I could think that Barra was simply overreacting, but he's one of the most sensible and perceptive people I know."

"Is this sort of thing common among sen davannat?"

"Prophetic movements, yes. Nothing on this scale or with this content."

"I'm reminded of the sen davannat who helped with Jerre's examination."

"Daval." Tamar looked up again. "I was thinking of that myself."

The sen Halvedna stood, then, and brought two bowls of tebbe across the room. Amery accepted one gratefully and sipped at it. "Thank you, Tamar. After the last week I need this."

Tamra set her own bowl on one end of a cluttered table, found a cushion, settled onto it. "The command circle?"

Amery drank more tebbe. "We had to reach consensus on strategy. Everyone had some issue or condition or argument that had to be dealt with, and no one wanted to spend anything like the credit necessary. There were harsh words. A few people insisted that we should postpone deciding on a strategy until we find evidence we're not just chasing phantoms."

"That seems risky to me."

"To me also, but I understand their thinking. Eight months ago the drones attacked Talin's foraging camp. Since then, what has happened? Nothing. What have our patrols found? Nothing. Where have the drones gone? We have no idea. Do they exist at all? We have to assume so, but what evidence is there? Again, nothing."

"Except visions."

"Except visions." Amery sighed, folded up the letter. "I'll bring this to the command circle, tell them what you've told me. Maybe we can get information from Andarre."

Tamra waited, sipped from her bowl, then asked, "Has Stefan seen anything more of his vision, do you know?"

"I've seen him maybe four times in the last two months, and then only briefly. As for the vision, I don't know. He's told me nothing new."

"He's withdrawn into himself again?"

"That, and into Jerre's training."

"How do you feel about that?"

Amery didn't answer at once. "I'm not sure," she said finally. "I've done a great deal of thinking about him, about myself, about some of the things you said when we talked about him. I still care for him deeply, but it's not the same. It's like ..." She fumbled for words, fell silent.

"A gap?" Tamar suggested.

"Not at all. As—as if a gap has been filled." She finished her tebbe. "Part of it was just the bond between student and teacher, misunderstood. I realized that only when I found another teacher—Allan Berelat, the strategist. Maybe you've heard of him ..."

"Allan Berelat?" The sen Halvedna looked wistful. "Yes. Oh, yes." With a soft laugh: "When I was a girl, during the last years of the fighting at Wind Gap, I used to go to the radio room in Istal Shelter and sit there for hours, daydreaming, listening for messages from the command circle at Abbesan. I still remember his voice." She laughed again, shook her head. "And now you're studying with him—strategy, I imagine. There was a time when I wanted that for myself, you know."

"I know," Amery said. "But it's a matter of blunt necessity, Tamar. Allan's very old and his health isn't good at all. If he dies before this is over there needs to be someone to take his place. He seems to think I can do that. I have serious doubts, but ..." She shrugged. "He makes his own choices."

Tamar said nothing, and her expression tautened. After a moment Amery gave her a worried glance. "What is it?"

"Nothing relevant," the sen Halvedna said. After a moment: "Thinking about Stefan, and the choices we both made. So much bitterness came from it, and yet there's no other choice I could have made, then or later."

"He said the same thing to me once," Amery said.

"Did he?" A wan smile touched her face. "He hasn't mentioned the subject to me in thirty years. He comes to stay here at Mirien every few years, we talk about anything but that, and he goes his way. I know his feelings haven't changed, and neither have mine, but there's the thing we don't discuss, and it's always between us."

Amery paused, asked carefully, "Have you ever tried bringing it up?"

"No." A moment passed. "I've never found the courage." Tamar sipped at her tebbe.

The sen Halka picked up her bowl, finished the tebbe, set it down. A moment later her expression changed. "I'm forgetful," she said then. "Stefan did have something new appear to him, the night we settled primacy with Julian Mereval. He said he saw two futures at once."

The sen Halvedna choked on her tebbe. "*Two* futures?" she forced out, still coughing. Then, her throat clear: "Tell me all of it. Please."

Amery, startled, recounted what had happened in the radio room. As she described Stefan's words, Tamar's eyes went round.

"I need to speak to him," Tamar said when Amery was done. "Now, if that's possible."

Amery spread her hands. "I wish it was. Jerre will be taking baya three days from now and he and Stefan are both in seclusion."

Tamar gave her a dismayed look, then nodded. "Three days, then. That should give me time to contact Barra and the wardens at Andarre, and read the literature."

"Perhaps," Amery ventured, "you could tell me what that means?"

"Of course. I'm sorry, Amery." She paused, found words. "There's a theory, an old one, about visionary states that show more than one future at the same time—the technical term is 'polyphase vision'. It's extremely rare, and that's limited our chances to study it and find out ways to foster it. The theory is that it might be possible for visionaries to measure choices against their visions on a moment-by-moment basis, to move the future toward a desired state. If Stefan's become a polyphase visionary, even briefly, it might be very important."

Amery nodded. "If you find out anything the command circle needs to know, you'll pass it on to me?"

The question hung momentarily in the air between them, tracing out the lines of a barrier: the wall the Convention of Zara had raised between Halka and Halvedna, painful but necessary, a balancing of opposed forces set in place by people who had seen the results of unchecked power. Old prerogatives and constitutional struggles stirred in the still air of the room, and for a flicker of time Tamar and Amery faced each other not as friends but as sen Halvedna, sen Halka, the powers of Eridan.

"Of course," Tamar said, and the moment passed. "Let me write to Barra and see what the literature has to say. I should be able to tell you something within a week or so."

7

Jerre blinked and opened his eyes.

Autumn light fell through the hallow room's one window, gleamed dully on the metal traceries of the floor. Silence lay heavy as stone. The ancient symbols of the Sequence curved around the place where he sat, half legible in the dim light. Nothing except the light had changed since the beginning of his vigil nearly twenty-four hours before. Yet certainly something had roused him from trance. He wondered about that, and remembered: the sign.

We'll send you a sign, they told him just before leaving him here. *When the time comes, you'll know.* He had puzzled over that, using questions he could not answer to hold his attention and drive away the need for sleep until the questions became meaningless and the clamor of body and mind alike fell silent. The space of clarity he'd first found at shooting practice opened wider and wider still, until even the thought of what lay ahead no longer touched him.

He unfolded his legs from *ten sedayat*, the posture of contemplation, and stretched slowly, mindful of the aches twenty-four hours of perfect stillness had left in his muscles. Joints cracked, the sound startling in the hallow room's quiet. After the pain faded he drew his feet under him and stood.

As he did so, the door behind him slid open.

Light from the corridor beyond turned the window before him into an imperfect mirror, silhouetted three figures in Halka black as they filed into the room. Although Jerre could not see their faces he recognized them at once: Carla Dubrenden, Stefan Jatanni, Benamin Haller: the three sen Halka who had tested his competence in the teachings of the Halka order and now would witness his final test by the dwimmerwine.

He turned, faced his judges. Impassive, they observed him, as they did through six unbroken days of examination: questions on law and legal procedure, the full day he'd spent on the practice range, the tests of awareness and concentration, wilderness skills, Halka traditions and lore, armed and unarmed combat. They had spoken only to tell him what he had to do, and only when they brought him to the hallow room to begin his vigil had he known for certain that he'd passed. He glanced at each face in turn, said nothing.

"Your vigil is complete." Stefan spoke. "Nothing remains but baya. Are you still resolved to seek it?"

"Yes."

"Then repeat the formal request."

"*Shaddat am baya.*"

"Witnessed," said Carla, and Benamin: "Witnessed. Come with us, please."

They turned and left the room. Jerre followed, closing the door of the hallow room behind him. The corridor beyond ran past several doors before it reached one of the main stairs, and there the sen Halka turned left, downwards, leading him past one landing after another into the deep levels of the Shelter. Bare electric lamps lit the way at intervals, and sounds of water and steam in pipes drowned every whisper of their footfalls.

They stopped only when the stair bottomed out ten flights down at the Shelter's deepest level, the emergency refuge level. Blast doors held open by magnetic locks guarded the passage in from the stair's foot. Past them, a short hallway led into a room the size of a helicopter hangar, empty except for a cushion at its precise center.

The crossed the floor to the cushion. "Once you take this seat," Stefan said then, "you may not rise from it again until you've taken baya. Once you take this seat, you'll have entered the Halka order, and for the rest of your life you'll be bound by its traditions and laws. If you're going to turn back, you must do it now. Do you understand?"

"Yes."

"Do you still wish to go on?"

"Yes."

"Then remove all your clothes and be seated."

Jerre slipped out of his clothing, gave the garments to Stefan, sat. Air moved around him in sluggish eddies, chilled his bare skin. Dust stirred from the floor as he settled his legs.

Benamin took the clothing from Stefan, slipped it into a black bag, turned and left the room. Carla unslung a cylinder of dwimmerwine from her shoulder, set it on the floor in front of Jerre, and left also. Stefan watched them go, then sat down on the floor just beyond the cylinder and said, "You're now permitted to ask me any questions you wish—anything at all."

Jerre glanced at him, then at himself. "One thing. Why did you have me undress? Is it symbolic?"

A wry smile broke through Stefan's reserve. "Purely practical. During baya you're likely to vomit or foul yourself. Clothes make it harder to clean you afterwards."

"Oh." After a moment: "Is there anything you can tell me that might help?"

Now it was Stefan's turn to be silent for a time. "I'm not sure. You have an advantage in baya, just as Amery did. It may be easier for you to face some of what you'll have to face. That's not a guarantee of safety; one student of mine with that same advantage died during baya. Still, it may help." He paused, looked pensive. "You'll want to resist the urge to follow your first instincts. That's all."

Jerre nodded slowly. "I don't have any other questions, except..." He reached for the cylinder of dwimmerwine, examined it. "How do I open this?"

"The combination is three, one, eight, six. Set the wheels, then pull up on the cover and turn it to the left."

"Three, one, eight, six," Jerre repeated.

"Yes." Stefan got to his feet, brushed dust from his clothing. "When you come out of dwimmertrance, come to the foot of the stair. We'll be waiting there." He regarded Jerre for a moment, then turned and walked away.

When he was gone Jerre drew a deep breath, began turning the wheels of the lock. The cover, when he pulled it up, rose with a click that echoed and reechoed in the emptiness around him. He took the cover off, sniffed. The dwimmerwine had a faint earthy odor. Before his fears could begin to urge second thoughts, he lifted the cylinder and drank. The cold fluid splashed down his throat, brought a dull ache to his stomach that reminded him how long it had been since he'd had food or drink. He cleared the thought from his mind, set the cylinder down, waited.

The ache in his stomach faded. Around him the world dissolved into darkness.

8

Within darkness, darkness...

A first level: emptiness. No flicker of light stirred the night upon the great deep. Memory, thought, self had vanished utterly. Somewhere in an abyss without limit, a mote of awareness that might once have been Jerre Amadan turned, rose, fell.

... within darkness, darkness ...

A second level: stirrings. Wind blew across unlit waters, the ripples that it raised the first dim murmurings of mind. Fragments of memory, glimpses without name or context rose and faded. Their passing sent tremors through the deep, called up others, disturbed a peace still not wholly broken. The image of a white windflower, the feel of hair between stroking fingers, the crack of gunfire, the impact of hard stone against booted feet, the taste of fear, the warmth of sunlight; colors, scents, moods, textures, words; all these touched the mote of awareness, filled it, and vanished, leaving behind some faint shadow of itself, something from which the consciousness that might have been Jerre's could begin to rebuild itself a world.

... within darkness, darkness ...

A third level: remembrance. Memories of events stirred the dark waters, passed through the mote of awareness on the way from silence to silence. A young woman turned, smiled, asked one question while her eyes answered another; her voice faded into wind-whisperings, and these swelled into the howl of a winter storm and the rattle of hail on windows. Hot tebbe scalded a throat the mote could almost recognize as its own, and then wide eyes stared upwards into a starlit sky, tracking a bright point of light across the southern constellations. Fire crackled as a kyrenna struck up a familiar-unfamiliar rhythm, catching a heart and feet that had never before danced to it. Sunlight streamed through broken clouds as a jewelfly darted past, impossibly brilliant. Pen moved over paper in practiced curves, tracing out the lines of a landscape on the edge of vast barren plains, catching the mood of a blue windswept land. Voices discussed some detail of the next day's work over the remnants of a meal. Other voices, softer, talked of promises and things of little meaning while hands fumbled with the ties of summer robes and shyly touched unfamiliar flesh, limbs tangled in darkness, warmth met warmth with coruscating joy. Rain fell on concrete terraces as a lone figure hurried toward a nearby door. Tears soaked a wadded blanket, arms clutched it tight against convulsive sobs. An old woman with bleak unforgiving eyes looked up from an outspread map marked with lines. Voices shouted, and a high grating whine rang out through forest, and the sun went down into a crimson ruin of clouds.

...within darkness, darkness...

A fourth level: pressure. The gyre of memories whirled faster, closer, flooding the mote of awareness with sensation to the very edge of bursting. Memory linked with memory, so that one sunset became all others, its colors brought to mind every thing red, orange, gold, black the eyes that had perhaps been Jerre's had ever seen, its circumstances called up every scene of quiet loneliness, every time of solitude recollection could find. More often, too, the memories touched centers of pain and anger and shame, stirred up others like them, flooded the deep with searing emotion. Bewildered and overwhelmed, the awareness struggled and turned and finally fought to close itself off from the flood of images.

With that, the swirling memories broke apart into shapes of raw energy and turned against the mote of awareness with shattering force.

...within darkness, darkness...

A fifth level: fear. Unreasoning and total, it drove the mote of consciousness to flight, upward, outward, away. Blurred streaks of force shot after it, multiplying, filling the infinite space of the abyss. Faces no longer human screamed wordlessly from the darkness. Images born of the innermind's deepest places shook themselves free of the night and sprang in pursuit. Yet the effort to draw inward brought a sense of identity back to the mote of awareness, a line between self and nonself, and with the little strength it could spare from its upward flight it began to search through the traces of memory, hunting for understanding as well as escape.

It hurtled on. Above, the limit of its speed began to take on a ghostly solidity, forming a barrier the mote could batter against but never penetrate. Below, the energies of denied memory surged upward, raging, chaotic. Groping in dimness, the awareness that could almost remember itself as Jerre sought for an image it sensed it had to recall: a limitation above, a fluttering against it, a way to freedom that could not be found along obvious paths. Words lost in the confusion pointed toward it. What had they been?

The mote remembered. It folded its wings and fell.

... within darkness, darkness ...

A sixth level: transition. The choice once made, momentum took over, sent the mote plunging into the heart of chaos. Sensations splintered beneath the pressure and fused into new forms. Energies flared as each memory and need and perception that had ever been repressed burst into consciousness and burnt itself out. The unleashed forces drove the awareness that now knew itself as Jerre onward into the hidden places of a mind laid bare. There, once again, images from memory caught at the inner eye, forced their way through barriers meant to hold them forever, and with them came a sudden knowledge, immense and terrifying. The mote clutched at that, held it to itself for a shaken instant of time, and lost it; found it again, and then lost it irrevocably as energies beyond all control hurled the awareness down into the heart of itself.

There forces fell away, images ceased, descent slowed and stopped. All sound faded into stillness. All thought dissolved in clarity.

... within darkness, darkness ...

A seventh level: ascent. Black waters parted around the consciousness that was Jerre as it rose, not by any strength or desire of its own but by the will of the abyss itself. Unfamiliar sensations stirred in the mote and around it. Above, dimly, something that was not darkness came filtering down through the waters, growing in strength as the mote approached it. A tunnel of darkness, the abyss rushed past, fell away finally into incandescence.

… within darkness, light.

Jerre raised his head. An empty room met his gaze in silence. The cylinder of dwimmerwine lay on the floor near him. He stared at it for a time he could not reckon, let the solid reality of it draw him back into the present moment. Then, shifting slowly, he drew his legs up under him, rose unsteadily to his feet.

Around him, the world exploded into meaning.

There, for instance: scuffings in the dust, dim marks of movement. Months ago they had been footprints, left by two people who brought some heavy object with them. One of them limped slightly, and halfway across the room—*there*, where the marks changed subtly—shifted the burden from one hand to the other. All this Jerre knew instantly as soon as the marks caught his eye. An instant later the knowledge vanished, overwhelmed by another perception, a subtle taste in the air that spoke of little-used machineries in a room nearby, and then another, and another. Somewhere in the confusion memory stirred: words of instruction, a place he needed to go. Footprints only a few hours old helped him remember, and he followed the tracks across the room toward an open doorway.

A dozen times in as many steps, he forgot his purpose in a flood of new perceptions, found his way back to it only after long moments of searching. Only the sparseness of sensory cues in the room and the corridor beyond gave him any hope of keeping his bearings, and when he reached the end of the corridor and figures in black rose up to greet him the rush of impressions overwhelmed him utterly.

The ones who waited seemed to expect no more. They guided him up the stair and down another corridor to a room of tile and bright metal, steadied him while warm water splashed over him, dried him. In another room across the hallway, deft hands helped into clean garments of tough black cloth and fastened a heavy weapon belt around his waist. One of those who helped him, a familiar face and voice, handed him a shape of metal and wood that blazed in his inner eye with significances he could only begin to name. Once this rested in its place at his hip, they led him out of that room and into another.

More of the ones in black waited there now, perhaps fifty of them, but their presence did not throw his mind into chaos as the first ones had. Already he had begun to sort out the confusion of new awareness and regain some measure of control over his mind. They gathered around him, and through the swirling chaos of impressions came an instruction, wordless but clear: *place your right hand out before you, palm down.*

He did so. The one who gave him the gun—Stefan, he thought he remembered, Stefan Jatanni—copied the gesture, putting his own hand atop Jerre's. Others, as many as could press in around him, did the same. One of them, he never recalled who, said two words aloud then, and the rest repeated them, while another message coming through the ebbing chaos of his mind let him know he should do the same.

"*Halka na,*" he said aloud. "*Halka na.*"

9

Turning, Amery pulled the door shut. Around her, evening on the terrace pulsed with kyrenna music, the beat of clapping hands. Somewhere nearby, what the weather-watchers said would be the year's last sama was beginning. The music touched feelings not yet extinguished; she paused by the door, looked toward the sounds, saw that she was not alone.

On the edge of the terrace, his feet dangling in air and a notebook and pen in his hands, Jerre sat watching the dancers below. Amery looked toward him for a moment, then went over and stood near him. He did not seem to notice. His pen scratched across paper, sketching the form of a whirling ecstatic on the samahane. About him, subtle awareness caught flurries of emotion and thought, marks of a mind not yet fully recovered from the shock of baya.

When the drawing was finished, she asked, "*Shona*?" The word meant *alone*, but also *alone by intention* and *busy, occupied*.

He glanced back over his shoulder, saw her, smiled. "No, not at all."

Amery sat next to him on the terrace's edge. "When I saw you here," she said, "I thought of the first time I heard sama music after I took baya—when I realized that it couldn't touch me again as it had. It wasn't easy. I don't imagine it ever is."

"No." Emotions swirled around him with the music: loss, sorrow, unwilling acceptance. "Did you dance often?"

"Every sama. Can you imagine me as an ecstatic, like the one you drew? I was one, for a while."

He looked at her, surprised, and then suddenly grinned and began drawing. Halfway through, he stopped, asked, "What did you wear?"

"A robe open to the waist," said Amery. "Four long strings of beads, and amulets on both wrists and my forehead."

He finished the drawing, passed her the notebook. "Like this?"

"Very like." On the paper a younger Amery whirled, arms outstretched, the hem of her dancing robe an arc of movement. The bead-strings around her neck stood out straight with the force of her turning, and the amulets swayed; her eyes were closed, all senses turned inward. "Very like indeed. How did you know I wore my hair long before I took baya?"

"I guessed. Most ecstatics do."

"I suppose that's true." She studied the drawing for some time. "Jerre, this is lovely."

"My thanks," he said, but seemed uncomfortable with the praise. Silent, he watched the figures turning on the samahane below, then said: "When I first heard the music this evening, and it was—music, nothing more—I was terrified that I wouldn't be able to draw again, either. I was wrong, fortunately. I've been drawing things since I was a child. It would have been hard to see that gone as well."

The sama music pulsed through the twilight around them, an overwhelming force to the dancers below, powerless to touch the awakened innermind. "Now that it's done," Amery asked, "was it the right choice, seeking baya?"

"I think so." With a quiet little laugh: "Of course I have every reason to think so. It's done, as you said, and there's no going back." He glanced at her, and in a quieter voice went on. "But I do think it was the right choice. I couldn't just go back to the life I'd been living, drifting from Shelter to Shelter and letting each day turn out as it did. After what happened, after the battle-drones, that's unbearable. Beyond that—" More quietly still: "—there are the rumors of war. If there's any chance those might come true, I know where I have to be."

She nodded. "And the chance is there."

"I know. I was up in the radio room yesterday, reading the message log for the last year." He looked away. "Stefan said I should give myself a chance to recover from baya before getting involved in the command circle's work, but I had to know what was happening. Three months was a long time to wait."

"I remember," said Amery.

"I imagine you do." Again the quiet laugh. "It's reassuring to know that someone else has been through all of this before me: the catamnetic, training, baya, all of it. Disturbing in a way, too; I'm used to solitudes."

"And yet you danced sama."

"Well, yes."

Now it was Amery's turn to laugh. "But you're right, of course. It's reassuring."

"Not disturbing?" He gave her an odd look.

"No, not really. Being alone isn't something I enjoy."

The last of the daylight guttered in the hills behind them. To the north, deep clouds blotted out the stars, moved southwards on the shoulders of a wind grown suddenly cold. Amery stirred. "This afternoon snow was falling in the north," she said. "That was the word from the radio room. I hope it holds off here a few more days."

"You dislike snow?"

"Cold. I'm not made for winters."

"No." Jerre shifted, regarded her for a time. "No. You'd be happiest in spring, I think." Once again emotions burst out from him into subtle awareness, but this time something else moved through them, a reaching outward that touched her in deep places.

Amery's eyes widened. Jerre caught this, looked away to cover his embarrassment. "Am I leaking emotions?"

"Yes." Quietly: "Perhaps I should leak you some of mine." And she did: his own feelings, or close to them, deepened through months of silent waiting. In the innerspeech, she said, *I've been drawn to you since I watched you wake from the catamnetic. There was a bond ... maybe the shared experience. I don't know.* Confusion, a tangle of emotions. *I want you.*

Then we share something else, he replied, shaken. *But you know that already.*

For a long moment neither of them dared to speak. Below, the sama whirled in a blur of colors. The kyrenna player let loose a run of high notes that cut the air like a weapon. Above, clouds grew heavier. *When you came here,* Jerre asked, *were you looking for me?*

I was on my way to the Shelter library, on an errand of next to no importance, and I came here mostly by accident. A smile flickered around the corners of her mouth. *But I was looking for you, yes.*

I thought so.

Had you been looking for me?

More emotions, conflicting, stirred the air around him. *I wish I could say yes. I wanted to go to you, speak with you, but ...* After a pause. *Pride, maybe. I've always hated looking foolish, and I really had no idea what to say.* He looked at her, went on in a whisper of innerspeech: *And I knew that if I opened myself to you there would be no way back, ever.*

Do you still feel that?

Yes. A long silence, then: *Yes.*

Then, said Amery, *we share something else.*

With that, the last of the barriers fell away.

Maybe an hour later, when a second kyrenna player had taken over from the first and a song nearly as old as humanity on Eridan took shape under the pounding of clapping hands, the two of them still sat on the balcony above. Neither spoke, or had spoken in most of that time. There are places beyond words, even when the words pass from mind to mind through subtle awareness. Only the innermind, joining each to the other, spoke, moved, saw.

A tiny fleck of white danced toward them on the wind and came to rest on the back of Amery's left hand. Cold at first, it turned damp against her skin. Amery blinked, looked at it as two more settled onto the balcony nearby. Below, luminous in the firelight and the glare of electric lamps on the samahane, more drifted past.

Look! said Jerre. *You won't have your wish, I think.*

I already have it, she replied. *But the poor dancers! They waited a day too long.*

Didn't you ever dance through the first snowfall?

Once. Memories tinged the edges of her innerspeech. *Once, much further south, and not in the teeth of a storm like this one. Taste the wind!*

A first flurry of larger flaked came whirling down onto the balcony. Jerre moved, faced the wind for a time and turned back to her. *You're right. The clouds are full of snow. And there's something else.*

What is it?

I don't know. A memory, perhaps. It's gone now: something about snow and the beginning of winter. He paused, searched. *It's gone.*

It will come back later.

I hope so. Another flurry began, harder. Wind muffled the kyrenna music. *We should go in. You feel cold.*

Freezing. She laughed. *I don't care. But you're right, of course.* She got to her feet, offered her hand as he started to do the same. He looked up at it, at her, in that moment all vulnerability, and took it.

CHAPTER 5

THE WINTER OF THE SPEARS

1

Stefan looked up from his book and glanced out the window. Light from inside made the glass a mirror against the darkness, but where his shadow fell on the pane he could see moving flecks of white drifting past. For six hours now, the snow had been coming down; the side of Mirien Shelter he could see from the window was half buried in drifts, the lights of rooms five meters away invisible if they still shone.

In all probability they did not, he told himself. Who else would be awake at such an hour? The question mocked at him. He pushed it aside, returned to the book:

> war of maneuver in the south had no one beginning. The insurgent forces under Daniel's command did not suddenly decide to face drones in open battle. Rather, insurgent units grew larger and better armed as Security Command adopted tactics that put more of its forces at risk. Sooner or later a collision had to occur. When it did, at Chandor Hal in the fourth month of 76, the crushing defeat suffered by the Third Field Army forced the entire Directorate to face a situation that had been building for years.

165

Details, details: the next nine pages had nothing to offer but the course of the fighting at Chandor Hal, the campaign that followed it, the insurgent response. He'd returned to Kregeth's *History of the Insurgency* partly to occupy his mind, partly to gain if he could some sense of how the Directorate had reasoned, and thus how its successors might reason if they existed. So far—and that was nearly two thirds of the book—he had failed at both. Again and again, his gaze wandered to the snow outside.

He paged past a map of the southern foothills around Chandor Hal and orders of battle for both sides, looking for the next reference to Directorate actions. All of his mind that could slip away from the task of scanning pages did so, toward what he was not sure; a watchfulness he could not explain had troubled the edges of his awareness since snow began to fall, making sleep and real study alike impossible. Earlier he'd chased after it into the depths of the innermind, tempted it with fragments of his vision, tried every means he knew to bring it into consciousness, all to no avail.

Here, he thought, and forced his attention back to the book in his lap:

> surprising that the Directorate had not anticipated anything like Chandor Hal. When the news arrived, nevertheless, it came as a devastating blow. Assistant Planetary Director Emmer reached Amris two days later to investigate the situation and repair the damage to Security Command. The worst damage, though, was beyond his control. For the first time, a Security field army of battle-drones had been met in open combat, and had been

It is beginning. A whisper from the innermind, unexplained. Stefan straightened, the book forgotten. What was this?

Now. A tension he hadn't felt before surged through the innermind. He turned his awareness on it, forcing himself to open to it and wait.

Then, agonized: *NOW!*

An instant later the images burst through, overwhelming, a whirl of fire and night, snow, battle-drones, gunfire, shouting, images of war. Through them pulsed a terrible immediacy.

And an instant after that, the knowledge he'd awaited for most of a year.

He was moving before the pulse of subtle awareness had passed, pushing the book aside, lunging across the room for his weapon belt and his jacket. He stopped for a heartbeat's time, then, realizing he had no idea what to do; the innermind pressed him in all directions and none; he forced his mind clear of vision, weighed the options. Only one made sense now, in the middle of the night, with no proof but his own awareness. He pulled the door open and set out at just less than a run for the radio room.

The corridors and stairs of the shelter were empty as old ruins. No one crossed Stefan's path, and even the machinery noises seemed muted, as though by time. Only his footfalls and the hiss of his breath, laboring as he clattered up stairs, sounded real to his ears in the night's stillness. The images of his vision had vanished as soon as he pulled the door to his room shut behind him. All that remained was watchfulness raised to an almost unbearable pitch.

At the door to the radio room he steadied himself, and entered. The room was nearly as quiet as the rest of the Shelter; he'd expected many things—confusion, voices over many channels or one, Halka codes from Yellow Sky on up—but not stillness, static muttering quietly to itself, an old woman in the shift operator's chair who looked up with sleepy eyes.

"Sen Halka?" She turned in her chair. "Is there something you need?"

"I'm not sure," he admitted. "Have you had messages—anything out of the ordinary?"

"Nothing so far tonight."

Nothing? Subtle awareness denied it, but the low hiss of empty channels and the blank face of the shift operator said otherwise. He nodded to cover his confusion, took a step toward the message center across the room.

Before he could take a second step, the loudspeaker of the main receiver spat static and let through a shouting voice. "Immediacy coding!"

Stefan spun to face the machine, battle clarity on him in an instant.

"This is Talin Shelter. We are being attacked by battle-drones. Immediacy coding for all Shelters. This is Talin Shelter, and we are under attack. Oh, bright Earth …"

Another voice cut in, calmer and measured: Halka by its overtones. "All Shelters copy and relay. This is an emergency message under highest Halka priority. Talin Shelter is being attacked by at least twenty battle-drones. Other Shelters in the north country and elsewhere may be in danger." A pause. "I am declaring Red Sky. My name is Kender Ban sen Halka. All Shelters copy and relay."

The voice vanished into a whisper of dead air. "The Shelter alarm—" Stefan began to say, but the shift operator was already reaching for the ring of keys on the wall beside her. One of them unlocked a nearby console, revealed a button marked with warning symbols. She pressed it, and somewhere nearby a siren began to howl.

That sound, familiar to Stefan from childhood, finally brought home the reality of it. For eight months he'd wrestled with the possibility of war, faced it day and night, watched the grim imagery of his vision unfold from the innermind, and yet none of that seemed to help him at all as he stared up at the loudspeaker, waiting for the next message. Emotions warred in him, and his eyes blurred. Part of it, he knew, was the realization that his vision had been proved true beyond all question, part of it memories of a letter he'd read on a spring day many years before. More than these, though, was the simple fact of the attack. Twenty battle-drones working in unison … He shuddered, and wondered what news the next message would bring.

The door slid open then, letting in a burst of silent noise and the first of the Shelter folk. Stefan noticed their arrival, but only briefly. His attention stayed elsewhere, far away. He heard the anguished voice of the shift operator, the horrified questions, the sounds of movement and some of the newcomers left and others moved toward little-used equipment, but these meant little. What mattered was the fighting some two hundred kilometers north. His inner senses strained toward that, and when they found nothing strained harder.

The door opened again, and subtle awareness caught a familiar presence: Carla Dubrenden, combat mode around her like a shadow of steel. He made himself turn away from the loudspeaker and face her, but could not speak. Her gaze, startled, assessed him and then tensed and turned away. A moment later she stood at the shift operator's console, talking with the Shelter folk, twice glancing back toward him, but words and motion meant nothing. All his perceptions drew together, focused on the loudspeaker, the static, the voice that would come—

Now.

"Immediacy coding," the loudspeaker spat.

Carla stopped in the middle of a word, looked up. Others moved, stared.

"All Shelters copy and relay." It was the second voice, still calm despite inner strains Stefan heard at once. "This is an emergency message under highest Halka priority. The attack on Talin Shelter is continuing. We estimate thirty-five drones are involved. We've suffered substantial losses. The command circle at Talin confirms Red Sky: all Shelters within one hundred kilometers of the northern edge of settlement are to prepare for defense at once. All Shelters copy and relay."

Silence for a moment, and then a familiar voice came over. "Mirien Shelter, please respond. Mirien Shelter. This is Talin Shelter command circle. Please respond."

Carla took the microphone. "Julian? This is Carla Dubrenden."

"Carla." Julian Mereval's voice tautened. "I'm ceding primacy to your command circle at Mirien. Talin won't be able to function as a command circle for much longer." Heavier, then: "You were correct, I think, and I was wrong. I hope I haven't cost us too dearly." Her voice nearly broke. Then, with rigid control: "Please acknowledge and relay."

"Acknowledged," said Carla. "We'll relay at once. Julian—"

Static hissed again over the loudspeaker. With that, suddenly, Stefan was released. As Carla cursed and turned away from the shift operator's console, he shook himself out of the visionary state and faced her.

Her look was halfway between shock and accusation. "You foresaw it."

"Just before it happened." Memories of the vision faded as he grasped for them, but one fact stayed with him. "Carla, Talin's not the only target. Other Shelters will be attacked before dawn. I don't know which ones."

She nodded once, accepting. "We'll declare Red Sun as soon as enough of the circle is here. You'll stay? Anything you see might help us."

"Of course." Subtle awareness picked out odd undercurrents in Carla's voice: a new level of respect, and something else, something like fear. Before he had time to wonder about that, though, something else came crashing through the innermind, overwhelming thought. "Now, or soon," he forced out. "Another—"

"Immediacy coding!" the loudspeaker blared. "This is Dolen Shelter. All Shelters copy and relay. We've been attacked by battle-drones, at least twelve of them ..."

Stefan turned away sharply, went across the room to an empty console. Carla looked from him to the loudspeaker, eyes wide, and then went back to the shift operator's station and the tense cluster of Shelter folk there.

"... over a hundred dead, and our wind turbines disabled. We're retreating to the refuge levels. We'll try to maintain radio contact for as long as we can ..."

"Curse this thing," Stefan whispered, looking down at blank metal and scraps of paper. "Curse it to Earth's fires." The vision: the attack: he could not at that moment have said which.

The door opened once again, and more people came in, sen Halka and members of the Shelter council. Carla's voice rose above the babble of sounds, briefing the newcomers. From their responses, Stefan gathered that Mirien's defenses were being readied, and that at least offered some scrap of hope.

"... of our supplies, but the rest are being taken down to the refuge levels. We should be safe for the time being. If any sen Halka ..."

Static snarled over the loudspeaker, sank to background levels. No more words came from Dolen Shelter. Stefan's hands drew up into fists at his sides; slowly, he forced them to relax, imposed the calm he'd need. Behind him, the inner senses told him, some of those who'd just arrived looked toward him, waiting for him. He turned and started back across the room.

2

The rest of that morning was the stuff of nightmares.

By dawn, when Mirien Shelter's defenses were ready, twenty Shelters on the northern edge of settlement had been attacked. Nine of them, Talin among them, were still fighting, but elsewhere the Shelter folk had been forced to barricade themselves in the deep levels and wait for help. Surprise and a heavy snowfall had left most Shelter defenses useless. So far, according to radio messages, the attack had cost at least four-teen hundred lives.

The command circle, or most of it, came into the radio room some fifteen minutes after the first alarm. It had formed first in the Halka quarters in the first few centers after the siren began to howl, sent two members to find out what was happening. Carla had been one of those. She'd returned to the circle moments after the message from Dolen Shelter had been cut off, came with the rest minutes later. Still others, sent to help arm the Shelter folk and direct an immediate defense if one was needed, returned over the next quarter hour. As the last of these came back, Amery arrived. The circle widened to admit her and no questions were asked. Carla, who was speaking, gave her and the other newcomers a quick glance and went on.

The problem is the snow. Review our strategy. From the groupmind, a flurry of concepts and images displayed itself and vanished. *The weather's cut into our mobility and rendered more than half our strongpoints' defenses useless. Our plan is badly weakened.*

Did no one consider the possibility of a winter war? someone asked.

Review our discussions. Again the groupmind responded with patterns of thought, a full record of the circle's debates in the flicker of an eye. *Apparently no one thought of it. You were there, Marc. Did you foresee this?*

Of course not. A pause, a crackle of frustration. *What are we to do about it?*

I wish I could answer that.

Benamin's careful innervoice cut in. *Are you saying that we have no functioning strategy at this point?*

That would be my view, Carla said. *Does anyone disagree?*

No one did. *The Red Sun code,* Benamin said, *includes a basic strategy to govern Halka actions until another plan replaces it. Is it our consensus that we should allow that to govern us for the moment?*

The groupmind paused, summarized the responses: *For the time being, yes.*

So be it. We have plenty to do. Unless something happens in the meantime, the circle meets again at noon. He broke rapport. The others followed, one by one.

Amery was among the last to shake herself out of trance and stand up. As she rose, Carla crossed the circle to her, asked in a low voice, "What happened?"

"I was on fifth level," she said. "The siren can't be heard from there, and so I didn't find out until the Shelter folk were alerted."

"Fifth level? But—"

A flicker of embarrassment showed. "With Jerre."

Carla, startled, paused for a moment before going on. "You'll want a summary?"

"Please."

Innermind touched innermind, and ten minutes' worth of description leapt across in an instant. When it was finished, Amery looked grim. "We're in trouble."

"I know. Tena and I have been trying to come up with a response since this thing began, with no results."

"Did Allan ..."

"Not a word." Disgust showed in Carla's tone. "Not a single word. He might as well have been asleep."

Amery shrugged. "We'll see. Do you know where Stefan is? I want to know if he's seen anything new."

"Over there." Carla motioned. "But you may have to wait."

Over next to an empty console, Stefan sat deep in conversation with Tamar. She had an armload of books and Halvedna journals with her, and several of those lay open on the console next to them. Their voices, low, vanished in the crackle of static and the murmur of Halka and Shelter folk discussion.

"I wonder," Carla went on. "You mentioned she'd been startled by what Stefan saw."

"She'd planned on talking to him about it a few days ago. I meant to ask her, but—" Her voice fell away. Then: "I have questions for both of them."

Carla gave her a thoughtful glance. More showed through Amery's voice and manner than Halka mental screens usually let out. Considering, Carla paused, then asked, "Where is Jerre now?"

An instant of unscreened emotion showed her the shot had struck home. "Periphery guard with the other juniors," Amery said. "He hasn't been given an emergency station yet."

Carla nodded, gave her a wordless touch of reassurance through the innerspeech. Amery responded with a troubled smile. At the far end of the room, Tamar's talk with Stefan seemed to be reaching its end. The two sen Halka went to join them.

Tamar turned as they came close. "Amery, you may kick me if you like," she said at once. "I decided to wait until I'd heard from Barra Johanan before talking to Stefan. I hope I haven't cost us too much. I came at once as soon as I heard, of course."

"A few days aren't likely to make much difference," said Amery.

"Maybe not, but a great deal could have been done." She shook her head. "How can I say this? Stefan is very probably on the edge of true polyphase vision. All the signs are there. If the theory is correct, and of course it's been tested indirectly, we might be able to open up the full polyphase talent, with proper development. But now—"

"What Tamar's trying to say," Stefan broke in, "is that she thinks she knows a way I could bring my vision wholly under control." He seemed remarkably calm now, almost detached. "To use them to test courses of action by their consequences."

"Useful," said Carla.

"An understatement. But the only people trained in the theory are sen Halvedna in the far south. In ordinary times it might take weeks to bring one here. Also, there are legal issues with anything that crosses the barrier between the orders."

Carla nodded. "True, though they're not insoluble. Benamin would be able to help."

"I mean to talk with him as soon as things are settled enough."

"There's another thing," said Tamar. The sen Halvedna looked as harried as Stefan was calm; what serenity she had left seemed clutched around her like a threadbare robe. "I haven't heard from Barra about Stefan's visions, but I had a letter from him in yesterday's mail, dated two weeks ago. It's about the sen davannat."

Amery nodded.

"They're in motion. Hundreds of them have left the hermitages, maybe more, and more were following."

"Where?"

"He wasn't able to find out. No one knows." She drew in a breath, steadied herself by a visible act of will. "You'll tell the command circle?"

"Of course." Another puzzle, she thought, and forced it away into her memory. To Stefan, she said, "If you see anything else I need to know about it."

"There hasn't been anything since the attack on Dolen," he said. "But if something else comes I'll inform you, of course."

"My thanks." She nodded to him, Carla, Tamar, then turned and hurried across the room.

Voices swirled around her as she moved past busy knots of sen Halka and Shelter folk, looking for a face she only half expected to find. Terse words and a muffled curse near the receiver told her that another Shelter had come under attack. She paused long enough to search the map by the message station and find the latest target, then went on.

She was nearly across the room before a cluster of sen Halka broke up in front of her and gave her a glimpse of the one she sought. A moment later, after dodging a running messenger and pushing her way through a group of staring Shelter folk, she came to the wall where he stood, watching. "Allan."

The pale eyes turned to her, but the old sen Halka said nothing.

Then Benamin was hurrying over toward them. "Amery," he called. "May I interrupt?" When she managed a nod: "You've had a summary, I trust."

"From Carla."

"You know how desperate our situation is, then." His voice lowered. "I'd hoped to speak to you before the circle met, and hear your proposals if you have any—and if there's anything beyond the Red Sun strategy we can do at this point."

Proposals? Amery stared at him blankly for a moment. "I don't know," she forced out finally. "I really don't know. It's possible that Red Sun is the best we can manage given what we have and what we're facing."

The Speaker waited for a moment, than nodded heavily. "Perhaps you're right. I—"

"Red Sun," Allan said then, in the quietest of voices.

Benamin stopped speaking at once.

"The Red Sun strategy will be known to our enemy." The old man's eyes fixed on Amery. "At this point, it is not strategy but the surrender of strategy. If that is the best we can do then in all probability we will lose this war."

Her gaze snapped up to meet his; anger, despair, a dozen other emotions pushed at the tatters of her shielding. Benamin looked on uneasily. Sen Halka nearby glanced up, gave the three of them startled looks.

A minute passed, and then Amery's eyes widened slowly. No trace of innerspeech came to the Speaker's subtle awareness, but abruptly Amery turned to him. "The drones out there," she said. "What type are they?"

Benamin looked puzzled, but said, "I'll find out." He stepped past another messenger, vanished into the crowd. Amery stood motionless, looking after him, her mind a torrent of thoughts and conflicting feelings.

"Very good," Allan murmured behind her. "I failed to think of that test."

She did not turn. "If I'm right ..."

"We will see shortly," he reminded.

A moment afterward Benamin returned, his puzzled expression tinged with a deeper disquiet. "Maybe you have some explanation for this, Amery," he said. "I have none. Every drone identified so far has been a Type Twelve."

Amery nodded. "How many?"

"Between two and three hundred by the latest count." More puzzled still: "You don't seem surprised."

"No. Our enemy knows how to manufacture drones, of course. I should have guessed that months ago." The one missing fact: given that, the rest came together at once, and the world shifted around her. "The makers had to go north into the empty lands. Where else could they have hidden what they were doing? And Red Sun depends on attrition, and that's useless if our enemies can make up for their losses."

The legalist spoke only after a moment. Habitual disciplines screened off much of what he felt, but not all. "That's true. Do you have another suggestion?"

She glanced at Allan, but the old man's gaze met hers flatly. There would be no help there. "Maybe," she replied. "I'll need a few minutes."

Nearby, the radio blared to life, reporting an attack on yet another Shelter. More messengers hurried toward the door. Here and there eyes turned to Amery, subtle awareness brushed her. The young sen Halka noticed none of this. She forced outside chaos and inside chaos alike to the edges of her awareness, cleared as much of her mind as she could. Presently, not without effort, a new pattern took shape.

"Yes," she said at last. "Yes, I think I do."

3

The messages went out, by runner through falling snow to the nearby Shelters, by helicopter in the brief daylight hours to further ones. Not one word concerning them passed over the radio net, and as they spread from Shelter to Shelter radio traffic fell away to minimal levels and the net came unwoven.

They had years to plan every detail of this war, Amery said to a silent command circle. *Years to learn all our usual strategies and craft ways to defeat them. So long as we keep following those strategies we play into their hands. Only if we turn to the unexpected do we have a chance to seize the initiative, to shatter their plans.* She reached for a map. *To win.*

In Shelters up and down Eridan's inhabited continent, Shelter councils met within hours of the time the messages arrived. Low voices, raised voices, angry voices, frightened voices debated nearly every word from Mirien, but in the end little choice remained. Votes were called, hands raised, Shelter after Shelter sent back the terse message: *we will comply.*

The structure of the Halka command circle itself is one of the weaknesses they counted on from the beginning. Yes, it's a weakness, though in other ways it's long been one of our main strengths. Most times, a command circle will follow precedent, tradition, past experience. Even now I can only hope that enough of you will understand what's happening, and agree with my analysis, to let this circle leave precedent behind and meet this thing as it has to be met.

Shovels cleared snow from prepared defenses, piled and packed it into bulwarks behind which people with guns could crouch and move. Further out, bonfires burned on metal scraped clear, and the heat spreading to either side sent steam billowing and rivulets of dark water streaming outwards from protective rings.

This is going to be difficult for everyone, Halka and Shelter folk alike. We are going to have to set aside many of our prerogatives and our familiar roles. For the first time in two hundred years the Halka order is going to have to admit that it can't maintain peace on Eridan alone. For the first time in two hundred years the ordinary people of Eridan are going to have to take an active role in their own protection.

Lights burned for the first time in decades in deep storerooms as hands pulled at the ties of long cloth-wrapped bundles, drew out weapons kept safe against highest need. Half of these, and half the ammunition from locked metal cases in nearby rooms, went to guardrooms and the hands of sentries in the prepared defenses. The rest went elsewhere.

Nor can we take back the initiative by some minor shift in strategy. Once our enemies realize what we're doing, they'll do their best to change their approach to match ours. Either we change our way of fighting so completely that they won't be able to respond, or change it so swiftly and decisively that they won't have time to respond. Amery looked from face to face around the circle. *I propose that we do both.*

In common rooms and Shelter council chambers, small groups of men and women talked quietly of guns, grenades, and battle-drones, and wrestled with a decision none of them imagined having to make just one day before. Sen Halka on their way north offered what information they could, and faced questions they and the questioners alike knew had no answers.

It has to be done quickly, and it has to be done in perfect secrecy. We can't expect to have a second chance. I wish I could say this is certain to work. All I'm sure of is that it will give us a chance of victory.

Through the hours of daylight, everywhere south of the war zone, helicopters rose out of landing bays and flew northward with weapons and ammunition, food and supplies, sen Halka from every Shelter on Eridan, and thousands upon thousands of plain Shelter folk in their warmest winter gear, with old rifles and grenade launchers in their hands. Other helicopters, empty, flew south to be filled again.

I've prepared a message to be sent out. She handed it across the circle to Benamin.

"Shall I read it to the circle?" the Speaker asked aloud.

"Please."

He nodded once, began. "Highest urgency coding. All Shelters copy and relay. Do not send or discuss by radio.

"By now news of the attacks on north country Shelters will have reached you. This marks the beginning of the first war on Eridan since Shalsha's fall. A group of people have preserved or rediscovered some of the banned technologies and are using them in an attempt to restore the Directorate's tyranny over our world. We cannot yet measure their full strength, but we know it is great enough that the people of Eridan must unite to overthrow it.

"We ask that all Shelters take the following actions:

"One. No mention of this message, its contents, or any preparations made in response to it, is to be made over radio. Where possible radio communication is to be limited to minimal levels, so that our enemies will be left ignorant of our plans and actions.

"Two. All Shelters without exception are urged to prepare for defense. Shelter councils should be aware that the Halka order will be wholly committed to the main front of the war and will not be able to offer help to Shelters elsewhere.

"Three. All those willing to take part in the defense of Eridan and the Convention against this threat are urged to arm themselves and gather at the assembly point named at the end of this message. Shelter councils are urged in the strongest terms to put half the arms and ammunition they have available at the disposal of those who choose to come to our aid. We know that this is a drastic step, but the situation is equally drastic.

"Four. Shelters are asked to assist the movement of sen Halka, their equipment, and all who join with us in this war to the assembly point with helicopters and other means available.

"With this aid we are confident that we can overcome our enemies and restore peace to Eridan. For the command circle at Mirien." The Speaker looked up at Amery. *You would have my signature there.*

If the circle approves, yes.

Then let the groupmind be established.

Amery entered rapport hesitantly, linking her awareness as little as possible with the others in the circle. The brisk competence of the groupmind's manner reassured her somewhat, encouraged her to hope that the harsh facts of the situation would override other concerns, force the circle and the rest of Eridan to drink the bitter medicine she offered. *No response*, she told the groupmind. *I cannot respond impartially.*

Acknowledged, it replied, and after that said nothing for a long time. Amery stared at nothing, waited. Around her innerspeech whispered and finally stilled.

The circle is of more than one opinion, the groupmind said at last, *but a consensus exists.*

Present it, said the Speaker.

The groupmind paused, then went on in its precise innervoice:

The proposal before the circle, if accepted, would mark the most radical change in relations between the Halka order and the rest of Eridan's people since the signing of the Convention of Zara. The future effects would be immense, and cannot be predicted in advance. Legal issues are of such complexity that none of the legalists present are willing to offer a definite opinion on the basis of past cases.

Amery nodded, mostly to herself. Though she'd had only the general legal training any sen Halka received, she had foreseen some of the difficulties, tried to find ways to work around the worst of them.

Several circle members hold that the proposal may violate the terms of the Convention itself. The balance of opinion of the circle opposes this claim, however, and a review of the Convention itself and related legal decisions does not support it. Other members of the circle believe that the proposal would prove wholly unacceptable to the majority of Shelter councils, but here as well the balance of opinion is against them.

Amery nodded again. Those two questions headed the list of her concerns during the few hours she'd spent wrestling with the details of her plan, after she'd torn herself away from the radio room and the widening disaster in the north. Those barriers passed, only one other remained—but that might well prove fatal to the plan, and quite possibly to its originator as well. She glanced around the circle, wondered if the blow would fall.

An objection more generally accepted is that the proposal violates several central points of Halka tradition, as an attempt to expand Halka prerogatives beyond the limits accepted at the time of the Convention. Review of the body of tradition and case law supports this claim, and historically serious violations of these traditions have been held punishable by death.

Amery tensed, then made herself still. She would not, she knew, have to wait long.

But the groupmind had not finished. *In the unanimous opinion of the circle, however, such a decision would be a serious error. Halka tradition exists to support and defend the Convention, and the present situation demands some redefinition of Halka prerogatives if the Convention itself is to be preserved. So long as the proposal does not itself violate the terms of the Convention, it should be carried out, and the matter submitted to formal judgment after the war is over.*

Benamin's innervoice cut through an almost tangible silence. *Is this the considered judgment of the circle?*

After a moment of meditation: *It is.*

The Speaker nodded, and handed the announcement to Amery. "Then this should be sent out at once."

Amery glanced at it, at him. After a moment, she collected enough of herself to say, "It needs your signature first."

"Perhaps not." He folded his hands together, considered her. "I'm a legalist, Amery, and for the last several hours I've been thinking that this matter has passed beyond me. With the circle's approval, I would like to relinquish the Speaker's place in your favor."

"No," she said at once. "Benamin—" Through her surprise, she struggled for words. "You've had decades of experience leading circles. I have none. More than that, we need a name on our decisions that sen Halka and Shelter folk both will recognize and respect."

Benamin nodded, after a moment. "I suppose that's true. If the circle agrees ..."

The response was swift and definite: *Yes.*

"Then I'll continue." He accepted the message from Amery, took a pen from inside his robe and scrawled his signature across the bottom. "This can go out at once," he said then, handing it back to Amery. "Do you plan on using the ordinary message network?"

"Partly. I also thought we could send messengers out to the assembly points to get this in motion as fast as possible."

"See to it." To the circle: *Unless there's something else, we meet again tomorrow at dawn. I'll be with the Shelter council for the next hour and in the radio room after that. Contact me at once if anything unexpected happens.*

He broke rapport, got to his feet. Amery did the same, and along with her the others. For a few moments the common room filled with motion as the members of the command circle went to their tasks, and footsteps and low voices echoed against concrete, but then silence returned, doors closed in the distance, and Amery found herself facing Benamin across an empty circle of cushions.

"You're aware," said the Speaker after a moment, "that we may all be shot."

Amery nodded. "Of course."

He bowed his head. "If you and the circle had accepted my resignation, I would have arranged to undergo trial by the dwimmerwine within a week or two. I can think of no other way to resolve this."

The young sen Halka said nothing.

"Paradox, Amery." He gestured, palms outward. "If we do what has to be done to preserve our traditions and our path, we destroy them. If we refrain, we'll see them destroyed. You're our strategist; how do you respond to that?"

"I do what I have to," she said simply.

"I know." Abruptly he sighed, crossed the room toward her and the corridor entrance. "That's the way Shalsha became what it was. I think about that sometimes late at night." Reaching the door: "Come. We both have too much to do."

4

Dim directionless light, pale as clouds or half-remembered dreams, set snow gleaming against dark trees: morning over Mirien Shelter. Watching it, Stefan Jatanni brushed snowflakes back from his thinning hair and faced the white blankness of the northern sky. One hundred fifty kilometers away, he knew, gunfire and death marked the furthest limit of the drones' advance, but the silent drifting of snow denied it, muffled reverberations that his inner senses should have caught even at that range.

Two sen Halka from the command circle had briefed him on the situation just after dawn. Nearly one hundred Shelters had been overrun in the first twenty-four hours of the war, most of them in the eastern part of the north country due north of Mirien. Talin had been silenced twelve hours earlier, the last radio link broken in a chaos of static and gunfire, Julian Mereval named among the dead two hours before. There as elsewhere, the survivors had to barricade themselves in the deep levels with any supplies they could gather and wait for help. The sen Halka had told him as well about Amery's plan and the first encouraging response from nearby Shelters, and they asked him—tentatively, and with the most careful of words—if his vision showed him anything that might bear on her strategy.

He turned their questions aside with the vaguest of answers. What could he have said?

In the still center of his mind, the place where visions are born, the same four images repeated themselves endlessly: darkness, light, sound, shadow: the stark symbolism of an event he could name but not yet place. Snow drifting past him settled on the edge of the balcony and his hands. He stared northwards, visionwards, into featureless white.

Amery's plan, he thought, and the plan of the nameless, faceless controllers of the drones. Ironic, that such abstractions should work themselves out in blood and fire across the

breadth of a continent. Ironic, too, that they should determine
the destiny of millions of people. He shook his head, thinking:
and behind them, more abstractions: the Convention of Zara
and its laws, the unknown hopes or dreams or desires motivat-
ing the drones' masters. And behind those?

Movement off to the left caught his attention, and he turned,
clearing his mind with a gesture of will. Out past the periphery
of the Shelter defenses, figures moved through the snow. Fifty
of them, more? Distance and drifting snowflakes left Stefan
uncertain of that and, at first, of their identity as well. Whoever
they were, they seemed to be heading north in a ragged line,
carrying poles or staves over their shoulders.

It was those latter, ultimately, that answered a question he
had not yet asked, and even so minutes passed before perception found memory and told him what he was seeing. When it
did, his hands tautened on the edge of the balcony; he stood
very still, then let out a long slow breath.

He turned abruptly, went to the door. Inside the air was
warmer, but something of the same winter silence remained in
the Shelter corridors as he made his way inward. Everyone in
Mirien not actively involved in the defense had been moved to
levels well below ground the day before, partly for their own
safety, partly to make room for some fraction of the thousands
of sen Halka and armed Shelter folk on their way north. Within
a day at most the first of those would reach Mirien, but for the
moment the upper levels were hushed, abnormally so, with
only the low murmur of machineries as background. The stillness reminded him of the night before the first attack, enough
to make him turn his attention inward, searching the innermind for patterns. Nothing rose to his awareness but the same
four images, endlessly repeating. He walked on.

Toward the Shelter core, movement and low voices gave
some semblance of life to the spaces around him. A group of
six sen Halka he didn't know came out of one of the main stair-
ways, greeted him with a flicker of innerspeech, went past.

Then, from the doors of the radio room, voices: familiar ones, pointing him to his goal.

He stepped into the room, crossed to the little knot of Halka over by one corner. Amery, Carla, Benamin, and two other members of the command circle stood there, listening to a young sen Halka who had melting snow on her hair and jacket. Nearby, shift operators sat at consoles, and a pair of technicians worked on some device Stefan didn't recognize.

Subtle awareness registered his presence as he approached. *A message from the periphery guard,* Carla told him in the inner-speech. *No immediate danger, but I haven't heard anything quite so horrifying in years.*

Stefan considered that and frowned. *I may have brought the same message.*

"… fifty-four of them," the messenger was saying. "They said others were following." In a tone that suggested she agreed with Carla: "Do we have better weapons to spare?"

Amery glanced at Tena, who gave a fractional shake of her head. "Everything we have is committed twice over already. And we have no right to reassign Shelter weapons."

The messenger nodded. "I'll inform the guard. Should anything else be done?"

"Let us know when more arrive," said Amery. "Beyond that, nothing."

The messenger nodded again, turned, left the room. When the door slid shut behind her, Stefan glanced at Amery, the others. "Drone spears," he said, dismay not quite shielded from his voice. "Whose thought was that?"

"We don't know." Amery's slight shrug spoke to Halka eyes of failed inquiries already made. "The sen davannat are arm-ing themselves with them. The band you saw was the first con-tingent of two or three thousand."

"The sen davannat?" He gave her a blank look, then recalled words Tamar had spoken, still half buried in the chaotic memories of the war's beginning. "That is …" He stopped, at a loss for words. "Unprecedented."

"Not quite," Benamin said. "Though the closest precedents date from the Insurgency."

"The hermits? I suppose that's true."

Puzzlement showed in some of the faces there. Benamin noted it, went on. "I spared twenty minutes after our last meeting to read what the Shelter library has on the sen davannat. The hermits at Andarre were the heart of the first risings against the Directorate and the seed from which the Halka grew, and the drone spear was always their weapon."

"A weapon of desperation," said Carla. "We're not that desperate yet."

"It's also one of the most effective weapons against drones," Amery replied. "The winter's taken away many of our defenses but it's given one thing back: people with drone spears can hide in the snow, where the drones can't detect them. And we *are* that desperate, Carla. We can't afford to turn away anyone's help."

Carla faced her, aghast. "You'll allow them into the war zone?"

It was Benamin, though, who answered. "We have neither the right nor the authority to turn them away." Gesturing: "They aren't bound by our traditions, Carla, and the Convention forbids us from interfering in Halvedna activities. As long as they don't violate the Six Laws we can't stop them."

She stared at him for a moment, then turned sharply away, crossed to the other side of the room. Silence followed, filled only with loudspeaker hiss. One of the technicians broke it at last, turning from the machine on the table to Amery. "Sen Halka? The receiver's ready."

"My thanks." She took a folded piece of paper from her pocket, opened it, handed it to him. "These are the frequencies we need watched. They haven't had normal traffic on them in two hundred years. If anything comes in, record it and send for me no matter what time it is."

"I'll do that." Paper crackled as he glanced at the numbers, turned back to the receiver.

Stefan had watched the whole exchange. *Should I ask about that?*

Of course. A flicker of surprise, almost dismay, came through subtle awareness. *The longwave receiver? An experiment of mine.*

He looked at the receiver again, tried to recall what little he knew of longwave radio: fragments, and the most recent of them decades old. The device itself looked as though it had spent years gathering dust. *Where did you find it? And why?*

They keep a few working examples at Zara; I had this one brought up by helicopter along with the latest shipment of weapons. As for why ... I've been wondering how the drones are being controlled. They may be following onboard programming, or guided by someone with them.

Like the one that missed Jerre.

Yes. Amery gestured her uncertainty. *But in Shalsha's time they were usually controlled by command language over longwave radio. If that's in use now, a receiver tuned to the old command frequencies might catch it.*

Good. Stefan nodded slowly. *Very good.*

Carla had rejoined the group; noticing, Amery and Stefan turned back to the others. "I apologize," she was saying. "But ..." A wordless motion of the innerspeech communicated her feelings with painful clarity. "I can't think of a more horrible way to die."

"Agreed," Amery replied in a quiet voice. "If it came to that, would you use one?"

The question startled her. "Of course."

"So would I." More quietly still: "The sen davannat have traditions older than ours, and this is one of them. Yes, it horrifies me too—but the drone spear is their weapon and I can't deny them the right and the chance to use it."

To that, Carla and the others had nothing at all to say.

5

Footsteps rang down the stair, hurrying. At the door to the Halka quarters, Amery paused to listen. Exhaustion or something not far from it blunted her perceptions, but she could sense alarm in the faint irregularities of the pace, a sense of threat not imminent but closer than she liked. As the footsteps came close, she tensed, half turned back toward the radio room.

No one appeared at the doorway of the stair, though. The footsteps continued, still hurrying, into the deeper levels of the Shelter. A message for the Shelter council? Amery did not take the time to guess. She pushed open the door, went down the corridor beyond.

The room at its end was silent. She hadn't expected that—the first group of reinforcements from the south, five hundred sen Halka and nearly three thousand armed Shelter folk, had arrived earlier that day and flooded the Shelter's upper levels with noise and bustle—but she welcomed it, as she welcomed the dim light after hours of sun's glare on snow. A handful of sen Halka, curled up beneath blankets or jackets, slept away the interval between duty shifts; closed doors around the common room, and a murmur of muted thoughts the innermind could detect, spoke of other sleepers nearby; a kitchen unit set into the floor in one corner kept tebbe and stew warm. That last reminded her how long it had been since she'd eaten, and she crossed the room, knelt, filled a bowl.

You may want to do without the tebbe, a familiar innervoice said. *Keren left it to steep for most of an hour.*

Startled and delighted, she turned. *Jerre.* With a sudden grin: *I can probably get some from Tamar. Did I wake you?*

Not really. He sat up slowly, pushing aside the jacket that had been serving him as a blanket. *Besides*—a little smile showed—*I'd rather be awake.* Had the dim light concealed him, or her weariness? She did not know, did not particularly care. *Are you free for long?* he asked.

An hour, maybe. She pushed a cushion next to him with one foot, sat. *And you?*

Three hours or so. Innermind touched innermind, gentler than any physical touch could be. They sat together in silence for a time, and then Jerre said, *I think your stew is getting cold.*

That earned him another smile. *Probably.* She disengaged enough of herself from rapport to start eating. *How is it on periphery guard?*

Cold. An image unfolded in her mind: trenches in the snow, dark figures with rifles huddled here and there, white drifts reaching away to the forest's edge. *Tiring. My mind is still only half settled from baya, and subtle awareness kept jumping at falling snowflakes. The others found that at least as tiring as I did.*

Amery nodded. *Under any other circumstances you wouldn't be allowed in a combat area until you were a month past baya.*

So Keren told me. He gestured. *When the second force arrives from the south I'll be put on messenger duty instead.*

Keren's idea?

And mine. Emotions still not perfectly shielded leaked into subtle awareness: embarrassment, mostly, for a mind not yet disciplined to combat mode. *My clumsiness could cost lives when the fighting starts.*

She nodded again, knowing there was no other consolation she could offer. Something else moved in his thoughts, though, or behind them. After a moment another image took shape in her mind, blurred by confusion and distress: a long line of robed figures moving through the snow, staves or poles in their hands. *You saw them?* she asked.

Something like two hundred of them, he replied, then fell silent. Finally: *Amery, I have no idea who or what they are, or what they're carrying. I wanted to ask, but—*He allowed a shrug. *Everyone stared at them as though they were walking ghosts, and I have no idea why.*

Recalling her own troubles with memory after catamnesis, Amery sent reassurance his way. *They are walking ghosts, or close. Those were sen davannat, hermits from Andarre, and the things they're carrying are drone spears.*

He repeated the phrase, baffled. *A weapon?*

The first weapon of the Insurgency, and barring only the last, the most terrible. Do you remember how drone traps work?

That called up a smile. *I helped repair dozens of them when the defenses here were being set up.* Again, imagery: a lifter field detector, an iron spike, a powerful spring. *Drive something conductive up into the lattices of a lifter element, the lattices fuse, and the insides of the drone turn into radioactive slag at about three thousand degrees.*

Now imagine that done with a spike on the end of a wooden pole.

He imagined it, and the blood went out of his face. *But the person who did that would have to be directly underneath the drone.*

Yes.

*And the drone would fall—*He fell silent for a time, even to subtle awareness. Amery waited. Finally, in a whisper of innerspeech: *What a horrible way to die.*

In the first decade of the Insurgency, Amery said, not without gentleness, *thousands of people chose that. For many of them, it was that or the factory camps.*

He nodded after a moment. *And the sen davannat think things are that desperate again?*

I wish I knew. They follow their visions. What those show I have no idea.

Another silence came and went. Amery finished her stew. At length, Jerre shook his head, looked at her. *I'd rather not find out,* he said. *And I know I'd prefer to spend time with you thinking about something else.*

So would I. She half-turned, managed a smile. *Since it's anyone's guess when we'll both be free again at the same time.*

At least one other possibility waited in the future, she knew, and sensed that Jerre knew it as well. Still, at the moment death could not have felt further away. She settled back against the wall, allowed tensions and worries to fall away for the moment.

Jerre smiled, then, and shook his head again. *We have terrible timing.*

She glanced at him. *What do you mean?*

You. Me. A quick movement of the innermind, untranslatable in words, for the bright nameless thing that joined them; then another, broader, reaching out to include the Shelter, the drones, the war.

Amery laughed, quietly, so as not to disturb the sleepers. *True*, she said, turning to him. *Very true.*

6

"Halvedna writings," Stefan said. "Everything Tamar was able to find on visionary states. She brought them over this morning."

Carla nodded, and Amery; the others did not respond. "Anything useful?" Carla asked.

Stefan glanced at the stack of books and articles, at her. "I wish I knew."

With five people inside it and the one window sealed against bullets with a steel shutter and sandbags, the little room felt cramped to the point of discomfort. Still, the others had not asked him to come elsewhere, and Stefan had not suggested it. When the knock had sounded at his door a few minutes earlier, ordinary reasoning no less that subtle awareness warned him that something of the highest importance might be involved. Now, as he considered the four sen Halka facing him—Amery, Carla, Tena, Allan Berelat, the strategists of the Mirien command circle and, effectively, the commanders of the defense against the drones—he was certain of it.

"So far," he said then, "everything I've read has either been theoretical, or a description of Halvedna visionary states. I may be missing something important, but—" A shrug.

Another nod from Carla. "Of course."

For a moment no one spoke. "Stefan," Amery said at last, "we need to ask about the details of your vision."

That, at least, he'd expected. "Certainly."

"What are you seeing now? Has anything changed since the beginning of the war?"

Stefan paused, stared past them at nothing anyone else could see: darkness, light, sound shadow. The words he sought came only with difficulty. "Since about twenty minutes after the original attack, all the secondary images have been gone. All the imagery of war—" His gesture cut the air. "Only the original image remains."

"The fire that destroyed Shalsha?"

"Yes." Darkness, light, sound, shadow: it hovered before his eyes, tangible as the wood and concrete of the Shelter around him.

Carla and Tena glanced at Amery. It was Allan, though, who cleared his throat and spoke. "The explosion. Is it the same one each time?"

Stefan looked at him, startled. The old man watched him from beneath half-closed eyelids, and the folds and creases of his face showed no hint of expression, but something moved within. "To the best of my recollection," replied Stefan, "the image is always the same, yes."

Allan nodded once, curtly. Stefan faced him a moment longer, and then allowed the beginnings of a smile. "So you thought of that," he said. "Good. I'd wondered."

"I?" The old man met his gaze. "No. That was Lundra's idea."

Amery looked as much embarrassed as anything else. "It was an obvious conclusion, once we realized our enemies could make drones. It takes an atomic reactor to make even the simplest sort of power cores. Atomic weapons are the next logical step."

"There is also," Allan added abruptly, "the nature and psychology of our opponent to consider. Shalsha's fate cannot have been forgotten, and revenge is a likely motive for this war."

Stefan considered each of them. "I'd thought of that. But if we face atomic weapons …" He stopped, left the rest of the question unasked.

"What do we intend to do about it?" This from Carla. "Stefan, you're forgetting your history. The Insurgency had strategies of dispersal and sheltering that made Shalsha's own atomics next to useless. We've already worked those into our current plans."

Darkness, light, sound, shadow: something rippled outward through the fabric of the vision. Stefan managed a nod.

"And there's another thing." Amery pulled a sheet of paper from an inside pocket. She unfolded it and set it on the floor before Stefan, who recognized it after a moment: the drawing he'd made months before, of lines moving south across the continent. "These were accurate for the first six hours of the war. After that …" She set another sheet beside the first, showing each Shelter that had been attacked, with the time of first assault noted, and red lines curving from Shelter to Shelter to show the drones' advance at hourly intervals. "The thrust in the west was abandoned, and the eastern thrusts were narrower and deeper than your vision predicted."

Stefan forced his mind clear, examined the papers. "So I see." Looking up: "What do you make of the change?"

"I think," Amery said, "they responded to the one significant change we made—the transfer of primacy from Talin to Mirien. Their original plan seems to have aimed at destroying the Halka here—" Her finger tapped Talin's position on the second drawing. "—and the dozen or so Shelters nearby where Halka strength was concentrated. The new plan, if I understand it, follows the same strategy."

"So the main force of drones is coming here?" Stefan asked.

"I think so, yes."

Darkness, light, sound, shadow: something in his vision blurred and changed, though he could not name the change, not yet. He considered her, the map. "And their primary goal is the destruction of the Halka."

Amery nodded. "We're the major obstacle to the creation of a new Directorate."

For a time Stefan studied the drawings. "If you're right and they have atomic weapons, Mirien is the most likely target."

"I know," said Amery. "We've asked all noncombatants here to leave for Shelters further south, and we've arranged a transfer of primacy to Kellath Shelter if Mirien is destroyed. Beyond that, the plans we've set in motion will continue whether we survive or not." She drew in a breath. "Once it's clear that our circle no longer exists, I've asked Linda Meridun to go to Zara and proclaim a new Insurgency."

Stefan stared at her. Darkness, light, sound, shadow: the images flickered through her words. "That is ..." He stopped, finding no words for it.

"Nearly all the sen Halka on Eridan who weren't in the north country at the beginning of the war are here," Amery told him. "If we fall, the Halka order falls with us, and the defense of the Convention shifts to the Shelter folk—the ordinary people of Eridan—and the old tactics and strategies that defeated Shalsha once before. If we can break this first assault, our enemies have lost the advantage of surprise, and lacking that they'll lose the war eventually. The Shelter folk can build their defenses, establish safe zones, trap and destroy future invasions, and eventually close on the controllers of the drones and crush them."

Stefan nodded again. Darkness, light, sound, shadow: the maps on the floor before him, vision and reality, might have been ghosts or dreams. Once again he fought his way back to clarity. "You're assuming our radio communications have been monitored."

"It seems likely." Amery frowned. "I wish I'd thought of the longwave receiver earlier, though. We might have heard ..."

She fell silent abruptly. Stefan gave her a questioning look. She responded with a quick movement of innerspeech, apologetic, and withdrew behind a mental screen. Even through the half-blinding presence of his vision, Stefan sensed thoughts moving behind her eyes at a furious pace, patterns created, discarded, transformed; sensed also Carla's surprise, Tena's concern, and—unexpectedly—a flicker of reaction from Allan. Stefan looked up at him, saw what might have been the faintest shadow of a smile at the corners of the old man's mouth.

A moment passed. Carla glanced at Amery, turned to Stefan. *If she's correct, we may hear command language on the old frequencies. Do you think Jerre Amadan would cope well with hearing that? It would be worth knowing if he recognizes the voice.*

Stefan nodded. *I cannot speak for him, but I think so.*

I'll ask him—Carla began.

"I'm sorry," Amery said aloud. Carla stopped in midspeech, and all the others except Allan turned to look at her. "I didn't mean to bring everything to a halt."

"I gather you thought of something," said Carla, with a smile.

Amery made as though to speak, then stopped, allowed a smile of her own. "Yes. The last piece of the puzzle. I'll need to talk to the legalists before acting on it."

Stefan barely heard her. Whisper in the innermind, something brushed his awareness, sweeping inwards from the edge of perception. Darkness, light, sound, shadow: the images of his vision had begun to take on a new dimension, one he recognized only after a moment.

Movement.

No longer abstract, the shape at the heart of his vision moved in space and time, plunged toward its fulfillment. He could sense it rushing through the night, swift angular shapes surrounding it, snow a blur beneath it, grating whine of lifter fields filling the darkness through which it passed. Around the images, his vision shattered into a blur of possibilities moving toward a single end: darkness, light, sound, shadow.

The others in the room watched him, and wondered. "The atomic weapon," he said finally. "I've seen it." He gestured northwards. "It's already on its way."

7

Footfalls, hundreds of them, sounded on the stairs and upper levels of Mirien Shelter, moving upward and out. Even through the closed doors and murmuring static of the radio room, Amery could hear them. The sound reminded her of summer thunder. Appropriate, she thought. If her plan succeeded, a storm to rival any of Eridan's weather was about to break.

If. She set the word in the forefront of her mind, a warning against overconfidence. Soon enough she would know for certain.

The radio room's door slid open, letting through a rush of sound, and closed. Amery turned to find Tena crossing the room toward her. "Weather?"

Tena's quick nod and the smile that twisted her scarred face gave as much answer as she needed. "The watchers say no more snow for at least forty-eight hours."

Other sen Halka in the room turned: members of the command circle and a few others, Stefan among them. "Good," Carla said. "And the forces at the other Shelters?"

"Ready," Tena said at once. "They've been sending messengers all evening."

Benamin, who was standing next to Amery, nodded. "Then we'll proceed. Unless there are objections, I'm declaring combat discipline, effective immediately. Amery, you're combat commander until and unless the circle relieves you."

She had argued against that, and been overruled by the circle. "I accept," she said, knowing she could do nothing else. Benamin extended his hand formally; she drew her gun and gave it to him. Halka tradition mandated that if she violated the rules governing combat command, she would be shot at once with her own gun. As the senior legalist present, Benamin had that duty, and he would stay at her side until he or the command circle ended combat discipline or relieved her of command.

"I'll inform the others," said Tena, and left the room.

When the door slid shut again and the noise of the deployment had faded to background, Amery went to the main receiver, stood behind the shift operator. Little more than static came over the loudspeakers: murmurings of routine traffic from the south, barely audible at this range, and a solitary voice from a second receiver nearby giving a terse situation report from a Shelter that had just been attacked. On the wall above, a large map of Eridan's northern continent and an old but functional clock defined the resources of space and time at her disposal. She gazed up at these for a few moments, then turned.

"There'll be a message for us shortly," she announced. "From Linda Meridun at Kerriol. You'll want to listen to it carefully."

Sen Halka around the room gave her surprised looks. Before any questions could be asked, though, static flared and spat behind her: timed to the second, as she'd hoped.

"Immediacy coding." It was Linda Meridun's voice; Amery, still facing away from the receiver, could see the flicker of recognition move from face to face around the room. "This is an emergency message under highest Halka priority. All Shelters copy and relay. A Halka adjudication circle meeting at Kerriol Shelter has formally relieved the command circle at Mirien under the terms of volume twelve, part twenty-eight of the General Code of Halka regulations. Primacy is transferred to the circle at Kerriol, also under volume twelve, part twenty-eight. All Shelters and sen Halka are to continue defense under the standard Red Sun strategy until new instructions arrive. That is all. All Shelters copy and relay."

Static punctuated the message, and for a time static was the only sound amid the stunned silence of the radio room. Finally another sound joined it: Benamin's quiet laughter. "Good. Very good, Amery. That was why you needed the legal reference."

"Exactly," she said with the beginnings of an answering smile. She pulled a sheet of paper out of an inside pocket, handed it to Carla, who was closest. "Here. This ought to make things a little clearer."

Carla, without a word, took the paper and unfolded it. Amery watched her eyes scan back and forth, then stop, widen, move on more slowly, as the expression framing them changed three times in as many seconds. "I have to agree with Benamin," she said finally, passing the letter to Tena. "Very good indeed." To the Speaker: "What's the reference?"

"The regulations on intentional dishonesty," Benamin said at once. "Specifically, the three situations in which a sen Halka may lie deliberately without penalty. The first of those is to mislead an opponent in a combat situation, of course."

Carla was nodding. "But why the General Code instead of the current Summary? No one but a legalist—" She stopped.

"Would have a copy of the Code available," Amery finished for her. "Quite a few people know their way around the Summary, and our enemies might be among them. Only legalists bother with twenty-two volumes of case law."

"Has this gone to the other Shelters?" Stefan asked, motioning with the letter.

"Every Shelter under combat command had it by this afternoon, and so did the assembly points and the secondary command circles. By now it should be most of the way across Eridan." She turned and crossed to the old device at the far end of the room. "I sent it by helicopter to be sure. No one who needs to know will be misled."

"And the commanders of the drones?" Carla asked then.

"We'll find that out shortly." Amery reached the longwave receiver, faced it. A technician sat before it, watching a long row of dials hooked up to the receiver by a tangle of make-shift wiring. Headphones brought her whatever came over the long-disused frequencies: not much, to judge from her face and the slight random movements of the needles on the dials. Behind the technician, considering the dials through half-open eyes, Allan Berelat waited.

He glanced up at Amery as she turned to the receiver. "The response will not be long delayed. Send for Jerre Amadan."

Amery gave him a startled look, then turned to Carla. Innerspeech moved in a quick dance between them; the older woman nodded and left the room. Once again the sounds of deployment surged into the space, drowned out the static, faded in turn as the door slid shut.

Amery turned back to the receiver, gave Allan a brief glance. The old man had retreated into silence, though, and whatever thoughts moved behind his face were his alone. Behind her, other members of the command circle gathered around the longwave receiver. One of them gave her a brief sheet of paper, and she gave it a puzzled glance before recognition came: Linda Meridun's letter, of course, a few quick lines giving the date and time of the radio message and instructing sen Halka and Shelter folk alike to disregard it. She folded the paper and pocketed it.

The dials in front of the longwave receiver remained next to motionless. Good reasons argued that they might stay that way. If the drones' masters simply hadn't been listening when the message from Kerriol went out; if they had never been listening to Halka radio traffic at all, and the change in their strategy had some other cause; if she had misunderstood their strategy, or worse, if they had anticipated hers: possibilities turned in her mind, scattered only when she cleared her awareness with an act of will.

Across the room, the door slid open, admitting another rush of noise. Subtle awareness announced Tena's return. Something had happened, Amery sensed that at once. Before she could turn, though, the technician at the longwave receiver sat up sharply and reached for the tuning knob. "Sen Halka, some—"

Whatever it was, it stopped her in the middle of the word. She turned a switch, and static exploded from a loudspeaker nearby. Through it, a voice:

"Jen thra num byen, ang dal. Kae brin am fyal, ang dal. Tyu lim fang shrey, ang dal. Tol, byel, aesh. Mrem fang do thra."

Amery, eyes wide, stared at the loudspeaker. Halka training set part of her mind to work analyzing the voice, assessing the unseen person behind it—old, female, precise, unforgiving—but a greater part responded, first with shock, then with something else. For months now the drones, their masters, the conflict of strategies and the looming war had been abstractions, to be shaped and mastered like the logic puzzles Tamar had given her four years back. The voice from the loudspeaker—*this* voice, *this* woman—was no abstraction, though. The response that came surging up through her as she faced it was no abstraction either: pure cold anger, intense enough to leave her shaken to a depth the voice itself did not.

"Shol chae num thwar, sye dal. Thun lyu aen fa, sye dal. Bren shcha ban threy, sye dal. Tol, byel, shra. Mrem fang am fal."

Static surged and fell. The syllables of command language continued through it. Amery, facing the loudspeaker as she might face an armed enemy, drew in a breath, forced her mind back to clarity: *tessat-ni-Halka shol ielindat.* Around her the others in the radio room—members of the command circle, other sen Halka, shift operators, messengers and members of the Shelter council—met the reality of their enemy in their own ways. Only Allan Berelat, his eyes barely open, showed no reaction.

"Tau fang rin shchae, mri dal. Zar mem sho thra, mri dal. Aeth fal chwem brin, mri dal. Tol, byel, shon. Mrem fang bae lun."

Abruptly a new emotional tone moved in the room: shock, pure and total. Amery detached enough of herself from the voice of the drones' controller to catch the movements of subtle awareness, sensed a familiar presence. She turned. Jerre stood in the doorway, Carla a silhouette behind him. The expression on his face was one she recognized instantly.

"Jerre." Benamin's voice carried over the command language and the static. "Do you recognize the voice?"

Jerre's expression—mind straining at the remnants of erased memory—deepened. "Yes," he said after a moment. "I've heard her voice before. I don't remember where or when. It's—" His gesture traced the limits of recollection. "Nearly lost. But I know the voice."

Benamin nodded. "My thanks." A quick flurry of inner-speech passed between them, an apology and a partial briefing. Jerre nodded, then, and went back out of the radio room. Carla came in a moment later, and pulled the door shut behind her. Only then did Amery notice the silence beyond it. The deployment was complete.

The old woman's voice, its edges blurred by another surge of static, still spoke the harsh monotonous words of command language. Amery gave a small fraction of her awareness to that, and the murmurs of innerspeech around her. The rest leaped forward along the track of the plan she'd designed. Her bait had been taken, that much seemed certain. Until she could measure the drones' response, though, the heart of her strategy remained a leap into mist and shadow.

"*Tso ban shreng mai, dal kra, mun ang. Zal, shol, chwem.*" A pause. "*Dau mrem bom thrai.*" Another. "*Chon.*" Then, silence, broken only by the hiss of the loudspeaker. Dials returned to brief fitful movements, and the technician leaned forward, twisted the tuning knob one way, the other. "I think that ends it, sen Halka," she said to Amery over her shoulder. "If anything further comes in I'll let you know at once."

Amery thanked her, glanced up again at map and clock.

"Well," said Allan Berelat. The word had the finality of a judgment. "I will be in my room if I am needed." He turned toward the door. Then, almost as an afterthought: "You have won. Now we see if any of us survive the victory."

When he had gone, the others turned to Amery. No one said anything. She moved to the main receiver, wondered how long it would take.

She had barely finished the movement when a loudspeaker crackled to life. "Urgency coding, all Shelters copy and relay. This is Ammath Shelter." Amery's gaze darted to the map, found Ammath: a hundred kilometers or so north of Mirien, on the western edge of the war zone, far enough north to know nothing of the request for radio silence. "We're no longer under attack. The drones appeared to go south and east. If any Shelter can spare medical supplies or a portable generator, we need them. We have over five hundred wounded and no power but core batteries. This is Ammath Shelter. All Shelters copy and relay."

Another message started as the first one ended. Amery listened just long enough to hear the source. She knew to the marrow of her bones what it would say, which direction the drones would be moving. The bait had indeed been taken, and taken as she'd hoped. The drones had done what she required of them, and they would shortly enter the jaws of her trap.

She turned, faced the others. Behind her, another Shelter reported drones withdrawing south. "We have maybe six hours before the drones reach us," she said. "A little longer, if they take the time to concentrate before they strike south."

Carla nodded. "You expect them to move against Kerriol."

That called up a smile. "I've done everything I can think of to lure them into moving against Kerriol—and the way to Kerriol leads straight past us. My guess is that every drone in the north country will be howling down our throats in six hours."

"If that's the case," Benamin warned, "we may not be able to stand against it."

"I know." Dance of patterns in her mind, the strategy included both those possibilities, flowed past them. "But Kerriol's far to the south, and if they mean to strike at it quickly, they can't afford caution. My hope is that they'll have no warning of our attack at all. If that happens, even if they win through, they'll lose most of their force doing it. Massed drones without infantry or aircraft—" Her gesture sent them into confusion. "Like Chandor Hal."

"And if they get through?" Tena asked. "What about Kerriol?"

Amery drew in a breath. "It's being evacuated. A few sen Halka will stay there and keep up the illusion that a command circle's present. Our enemies will vaporize an empty Shelter. We may have to do the same thing over and over again, as Mariel did."

For a moment static and the voice of another Shelter in the war zone reporting drone movements were the only answer she received. "A hard road to walk," Benamin said then. "In the meantime, we have a battle to fight."

"True enough," said Amery. "Carla, will you handle duty assignments? Tena—" She stopped, remembering. "You had news for us."

"Not formally." The scars on Tena's face could not hide her grim expression. "But yes, I did. Have any of you been out to watch the deployment?" Negatives in the innerspeech answered her. "The sen davannat aren't the only ones with drone spears. I saw close to a thousand Shelter folk carrying them."

"Instead of guns?" Benamin asked.

Tena shook her head once. "As well as guns." Then, with a slight shrug: "It's their right to choose, and I can't fault them for it. Still ..." She fell silent.

Next to her, another Shelter in the far north broke in to announce that the drones attacking it had gone south. Amery nodded. "Well." Then: "Tena, I'd meant to ask you to set up the innerspeech net."

"Of course. I can have it in place in three hours."

"The drones will be here in six." Amery turned. "Marc, Kel, I'd like you to handle logistics until the combat command is in place. Let me know what our immediate needs are."

"Besides time?" Marc asked.

Even with the tension there in the radio room, that summoned a laugh. "Besides time," said Amery. "We ought to have just enough of that."

8

Shcha lyu ang chwem: the words turned in darkness. Had he spoken them aloud, just then, or merely in his awareness? Jerre could not tell, and the turmoil in his mind and memory made the simple act of willed recall an effort beyond reach.

Around him, the silent workbenches of the helicopter repair shop rose up, dim shapes barely visible in the faint light from the door. With his own room housing newcomers and the crowded Halka quarters his sleeping place, the shop had been the one private silent space in Mirien Shelter Jerre had been able to think of, and he needed privacy and silence desperately. Once his duty shift as a messenger was over, he'd come there, sat on the bare concrete floor, allowed his mind to touch an awareness he'd held at bay since the door to the radio room slid open before him an hour before.

Shcha lyu ang chwem: whatever the words were, whatever they meant, they set off resonances he could no longer trace to the memories he knew. Alongside them, the words and the voice he'd heard in the radio room sent echoes down into the empty places of his mind.

He lowered his face into his hands, fought for clarity. The effort of recall sent spikes of pain stabbing through his eyes. A whispered triggering phrase numbed that, as it might numb a wound taken in combat.

Shcha lyu ang chwem: the words had meaning for him, and not just the meaning the memory of the foraging camp gave them. That was the heart of it, and the horror.

Clarity, he told himself, clarity. *Tessat-ni-Halka shol ielindat*: the first lesson of his training, the place of clear awareness in the Halka path. Given that, the resonances in his mind could be grasped, gathered, traced back to their source. Given that, he could face whatever the source might be. So he told himself, though the words rang hollow in his mind.

There in the almost-darkness, he turned back to the most basic of Halka disciplines, ran through the first of the awareness drills he'd been taught, the second, the third. Familiar now to his mind as his pistol's grip to his hand, they brought a first movement toward stillness to the chaos inside him. From that, the rest unfolded; skills forged in him by the order's training and strengthened a hundredfold by baya took over. The resonances fell silent, waiting, ready to be summoned back by a movement of will. He drew in a slow breath, began.

Shcha lyu ang chwem: the four words echoed again in his awareness. He let the echoes spread, merge, return. As they met again in the place of stillness at the center of his mind, images took shape, one after another.

First: the doorway to Mirien's radio room, and through it a dozen sen Halka gathered around a longwave receiver, listening to a message something in him struggled not to hear.

Next: Tamar's room up in the Shelter's upper levels, open and sunlit. He sat there, Tamar, Amery, and Stefan watching, as he handled the remnants of his own past.

Next: blood, a stark red blur on meadowmoss and cloth. Something hard pressed up against his back, and the fading light of evening turned even blood to darkness around him.

Next: screams, gunfire, the strident whine of lifter fields, the four words shouted by a voice shrill with fear.

Last: fleeting and dreamlike, the dim memory of a face.

Jerre paused, held that last image in awareness. No trace of name or place came with it, but that was common enough in his fragmented memories. Around it, though, was something that looked like a void but was not, something his probing awareness could neither penetrate nor define. Jerre frowned, probed again, drew back baffled.

The image of the face surfaced again, mirrored in the not-void as in water. The face, at least, he could comprehend. He focused on it, hunted for connections and meanings. Something stirred: he'd drawn that face, more than once.

He rose up out of trance, pulled the flat notebook from its constant place in an inside pocket of his coat, opened it. Recent drawings—of Amery, mostly, with a few snowscapes and a sentinel at his watch on periphery guard—gave way to older ones, from his life before the drones came, and then to the front cover. The face in his memory appeared nowhere. He frowned, then found a pen and started sketching it.

The first line, following the hard angles of cheek and jaw, took minutes to draw. The next few lines came more easily, and then the face exploded into being in a flurry of penstrokes: taut line of her mouth, old bitter eyes, hard forms of bone beneath wrinkled skin and flesh, hair pulled back tightly to a knot behind her neck. As he finished she gazed up at him from the paper, bleak and unrelenting, expecting no compassion, offering none.

He knew her. That much was certain before he'd finished the drawing, as certain as anything could be. Strong emotions linked him to her: fear, respect, a whisper of unwilling and unanswered love. Her name? That was hidden from him, though a murmur of sound—three words, he guessed—darted through his awareness as he searched for it.

Another fragment of memory surfaced. She'd been speaking to him, saying something of the utmost importance. They were sitting together in a room with bare concrete walls, a little room lit by electric lamps. What had she been saying? Pain flared in his temples as he struggled with the memory, fell back in defeat.

Once again the sounds murmured through his mind. He began to brush them aside, stopped. There was a reason why he should not think of those sounds, above all else should not speak them aloud. He could find the reason nowhere in his memories, but the forbidding pressed on him with startling force.

He wondered then if he should go to Tamar and ask for her help, or go to the judgment circle and put himself in their hands. The idea appealed, but something warned him off. Panic surged again. Clarity, he reminded himself, and returned to the awareness drills until the space of clarity opened up at the center of his mind again. A moment later, the knowledge he'd been trying to escape surfaced irrevocably.

Shcha lyu ang chwem: the shrill terrified voice that shouted those words, there at the foraging camp, had been his own. For a long still moment the stark recognition of the fact stood alone in his mind. Then understanding came, and brought with it a cold sick horror.

The words, the face, the not-void in his mind all formed a single pattern, he knew that, and even as he drew back shivering from the realization he knew what that meaning had to be. Clarity, he repeated again. Clarity.

The words not to be spoken moved again through his mind, elusive but inescapable. He struggled back to clear awareness, guessed what they might be and where they might lead. Using the Halka trick of subtle prompting on anyone else would have been beyond him, but he understood it well enough to use it on himself. A quick gesture of his mind caught the words, pinned them to the speech centers, forced them outward.

"Jerome Patrick Emmer." The words came out by themselves, echoed against the bare concrete walls of the room. For a heartbeat, nothing happened. Then, with the slow inevitability of an opening door, the not-void dissolved. Within lay remembrance.

A scream that would have meant discovery and death nearly burst from him then. He fought it down, clenched himself in on himself, made himself face the knowledge that unfolded before him, memories that stayed shielded through Tamar's probing, unfamiliar architecture of a mind honed by years of discipline long before Halka training overlay it. Another memory rose with absolute certainty: he'd faced such a moment before, and broken. Somewhere in the deep reaches of his mind lay a place of oblivion, a place where memory and knowledge could not follow him, and he'd fled shrieking to that place not so long ago. That path lay open again, and despite all that had happened it took him time and effort to draw back from the precipice.

No: only one way led forward. *Options,* he said inwardly, triggering geometries of consciousness he still only half remembered. Choices and consequences unfolded from the innermind and listed themselves in his awareness: few, desperately few, and only one that offered any hope at all.

He got to his feet, started as the notebook fell from his lap and landed on the concrete floor with a sharp noise. Stooping, he recovered it, began to put it into his pocket, then stopped, opened it, set it on the workbench next to where he'd been sitting. *Potential risk,* the innermind warned him, and listed possible consequences. Still, he owed them that much, a message they might be able to read, and time was too short to permit a second-approximation analysis. He turned away and hurried across the room toward the door to the helicopter hangar.

9

first rising at Andarre came, nonetheless, as a shock to the upper levels of the Directorate hierarchy, and the decisive response masked ferocious disagreements at the highest levels of power. Stark and her subordinates in Security Command urged a massive campaign of repression, while the Office of Settlement insisted this would only make matters worse.

Not there, Stefan thought, and skipped down half a page. Next to him, a forgotten bowl of tebbe sat, stone cold.

A letter from Carl Emmer, then in his second year as Director of Settlement, to his daughter preserves most of the surviving details of these controversies.

Was that the passage? Stefan thought so. He scanned past the bulk of the letter, found the words he'd been seeking near the bottom of the facing page:

> The letter ends on a note of startling prescience. If the Secu-
> rity view of the situation was accepted by the Directorate
> as a whole, Emmer wrote, "we risk beginning a war that
> we cannot win. Weak as they appear, the Andarre fanat-
> ics have strengths we have not yet measured. What those
> are, I cannot yet say, but I fear—I fear in my bones—the
> whole Directorate will learn far too much about them if
> Stark has her way."

Stefan touched the page beside the passage, considered it for a long silent moment. Years ago, before he'd taken baya, he'd read an article on the history of the dwimmerroot in some Halvedna journal. The author noticed that passage in Kregeth's *History of the Insurgency*, and speculated that Emmer—himself a brilliant botanist and agronomist, the author of books on meadowmosses and meria cultivation still in use two centuries later—might have guessed the dwimmer-root's psychoactive effects, tested it on himself, gained some fragmentary glimpse of the future rising around him. It was a tempting speculation; certainly no one else in the Director-ate had shown the least awareness of the trap they made for themselves.

And yet that same Carl Emmer who glimpsed the coming of the Insurgency had risen through the Directorate hierarchy to its zenith, ruled Eridan during the last six years of the Insur-gency, and prosecuted the war without flinching as everything he'd foreseen came about. Had it been no vision at all, merely natural intuition or a lucky guess? Or had his vision offered him no way to change the future he saw so clearly?

For Stefan, such questions were anything but abstract.

He stared at the passage for a time, then glanced toward the door as subtle awareness alerted him to movement in the corridor outside. As the movement slowed and stopped at his door, he called out, "Please come in."

The door opened and Tamar looked in. "Are you busy?"

"No." Startled, he nonetheless motioned her in, gestured to a cushion. "I thought you'd left with the other noncombatants."

"I volunteered to help with the wounded here." She sat. "I had some medical training—long ago, admittedly, but I can still bandage a wound."

He gave her a long dismayed look. "The command circle thinks Mirien may be attacked with an atomic weapon."

She nodded. "I guessed as much. Your vision isn't hard to interpret." Then: "In fact, that's most of the reason I'm here."

He said nothing, watched her. In the near distance, the sound of a helicopter taking off sent staccato pulses of sound through the Shelter concrete. After silence returned, she said, "You'll be in the battle?"

"I'll be in the combat reserve. In an emergency even visionaries fight, and Amery's declared an emergency." Flicker of a smile: "I don't think anyone disagrees."

She nodded. "There's a theory that visionary states are an old genetic heritage from prehuman times, a way of detecting danger that the five senses don't reveal. Your vision may do unexpected things if you're in immediate danger. I don't know if knowing that will help, but …"

Another silence passed. Stefan broke it finally. "It might. But I don't think that's what you came to talk about, Tamar."

She glanced up at him. "No, it wasn't." She paused. "Partly I wanted to see you again before the fighting starts. Partly—" She paused, made herself go on. "I wanted to say something about—what's been between us these last thirty years. I feel I owe you that much."

Stefan considered her, sensed the struggle it had taken her to speak at all. "We said everything that could be said about that thirty years ago," he replied, not without gentleness.

"I thought that too." She laughed, shook her head. "Bright Earth, Stefan! We were so sure of ourselves in those days.

You made your decision, I made mine, both of us convinced that no other choice could possibly make sense for anyone, anywhere. But ..." A shrug. "Certainties change. I've become convinced these last few days that you made the right choice."

The words hung in the silent air between them. He stared at her, shaken. "I have never expected to hear you say those words."

"The right choice, for you," she went on. "For Amery—her talents would have been wasted in the Halvedna order, though I tried to convince myself otherwise four years ago. For Jerre, and for so many others. But it's not everyone's choice. Do you remember Bethan? The first patient you ever brought to me?"

Stefan nodded after a moment. "The child we rescued from outrunners."

"Yes. She's become an artist, probably the best alive today—possibly the best we've yet had on Eridan. I met her in Zara two years ago, and saw some of her work. The Halka order gave her her life back, and what she's made of the gift is something the Halka order couldn't have given our world themselves."

He thought about that. "And you're suggesting that the Halvedna ..."

A sudden wide smile. "The Halvedna are the same. The Halka make it possible for us to give something to the world, but it's not something the Halka themselves can give. Stefan, when you started bringing me patients, I knew you meant it as a challenge. You wanted to force me to look at the reality of violence and suffering, the things the Affirmation can only deal with at the level of root causes. But I answered the challenge with one of my own, and I'm not sure you saw that. Tell me this." The smile faded as her gaze met his, unfaltering. "If I'd made your choice, taken up the gun and not the Affirmation, what would have become of Bethan? What of Amery, Jerre, all the others? If all the old Halka of Mariel's time had donned black rather than our many-colored robe, how much would there be for you to defend? The Halka are a black wall around everything worth defending on this world, but if there's only the wall and nothing within it, what then?"

He did not answer.

"After the drone came to Istal Shelter …" Her gaze fell. "All I could see was that my dream of taking baya and becoming a sen Halka was a child's fantasy, that I had to take another path instead. I couldn't see that a different choice might be right for you, and because of that I did my part, and perhaps more than my part, to wreck what was between us then. I'm bitterly sorry for that."

Stefan found his voice. "You know I've never loved anyone else."

"I was fool enough to try."

Silence, again. Stefan considered her for a long moment, thinking of the young woman she'd been, the years since. "You're saying," he said at length, "that you and I should have done what the Halka and Halvedna did back at Zara."

She looked blank, then started to laugh. "Yes. Stefan, you are beyond price. Yes, we should have had a little Convention of our own, and agreed that the Halka are the Halka, the Halvedna are the Halvedna, and somehow we'd have to manage with that." The last of the laughter trickled away. "I'm not sure we could have done it back then, of course. Maybe we could do it now, except for the war."

Stefan tried to speak, fell silent, then slowly nodded. "Maybe we could." He held out his hands; she clasped them in hers, smiled up at him.

A moment later footfalls came pounding up the corridor outside. Someone rapped at the door, the sound urgent. Then, Carla's voice: "Stefan?"

He let go of Tamar's hands. "Come in."

Carla pulled the door open, started to say something; saw Tamar and stopped in surprise. To her: "I'm sorry, Tamar." To Stefan: "You need to come at once."

He was on his feet in a moment. "What is it?"

"Primary case."

Stefan blinked, startled. The phrase meant a deliberate violation of the Six Laws. He turned to Tamar, found nothing to say.

"Go," she told him, her voice surprisingly gentle. "If we both survive this ..."

He nodded, turned, followed Carla out the door.

Carla led him at just short of a run to the nearest main stair and up to the top level. Cold air heavy with the scent of snow flowed down the stair, foretaste of the winter outside. At the top, they hurried down an empty corridor to a door that had been forced open, and through into an echoing space Stefan recognized only after a minute as the helicopter hangar. The great metal doors in the ceiling gaped open to the morning sky. In an open space where one of the Shelter's three helicopters should have been, sen Halka stood. Stefan caught sight of Amery, pale and haggard, with Benamin a watchful shadow behind her. Carla led him forward.

"... two outside fuel tanks," a man in pilot's coveralls was saying. "Doren is checking our fuel supply but I imagine they're full."

"How far could he get with that much fuel?" Amery asked.

"With this much wind against him, I'd guess eight hundred kilometers, maybe a little more. He'll have about six hours of flying time."

"We're low," another voice called from the far side of the hangar. "Both tanks for sure. We're also missing cold weather gear."

She nodded. "My thanks." To the Halka present, in a burst of innerspeech Stefan could read: *Six hours, and the drones will be here in two. That gives us our time frame, then.*

Can we evacuate Mirien? Carla asked.

Amery shook her head. *Not without leaving the center of our line unsupported and breaking up the innerspeech net. Either of those could cost us the battle.*

Members of the command circle glanced at each other. *Then we go ahead*, said Tena.

We go ahead. Amery held her hand out at shoulder level, palm down; the others put their hands atop hers. "*Halka na*," she said aloud, and the others repeated the phrase. A moment later most of them hurried out the door, scattered to duty stations.

Stefan glanced at those who remained—Amery, Carla, Benamin, the helicopter pilot. "I gather," he said, "that we had a spy."

"Worse than that," Carla said. She turned to Benamin, who handed her a notebook. "A helicopter took off fifteen minutes ago, without the Shelter council's permission. When we investigated we found this in the helicopter shop." She opened it, found a page, gave it to Stefan. "Open to this drawing. You'll recognize the artist."

"Yes," he replied. The old woman's face gazed up at him from the paper, bleak eyes daring him to find a reason for hope. "Who is she?"

Construct the voice, Carla said in the innerspeech.

Stefan gave her a puzzled look but nodded. The act itself was simple enough. Patterns of facial tension shaped the voice, and the drawing had more than enough detail to let the innermind turn those into sound. The voice took shape in his awareness, precise, cold, instantly familiar.

He heard the radio message from the drones' controller, Carla went on. *He came here, he drew a face that corresponds to the voice within three per cent variation, and then he took a Shelter helicopter and flew north. What happened seems clear enough. The worst of it is that he knows much of our strategy. Not all of it, but enough.*

But—Stefan stared at her in dismay. *How could something like that have stayed hidden from us through training—or through baya?*

I have no idea, she replied. *Maybe their mind training is stronger than ours.*

To that he had no answer at all.

"And now?" he asked Amery.

"We go on as before," she answered. "We don't have another choice." Beneath the hard surface of Halka discipline, he could sense emotions harsh and raw as an open wound. "I've sent out instructions that Jerre's to be held and questioned if he's found. Beyond that ..." A shrug, precise and forced. "*Halka na*, Stefan."

He nodded slowly. "*Halka na.*"

Amery turned away and left the hangar, Benamin following close behind. Stefan glanced after her, then turned to Carla. "Well." Then: "I'll need a greatcoat, grenades, and bullets. Especially bullets. Where do I find those?"

Carla glanced at him, then suddenly grinned. "That's a question I can answer. Winter gear is on second level just north of Shelter core. Ammunition and grenades are just inside the main north doors. I'll be visiting both of those next. If you like—"

"Please." They went to the door as the hangar doors in the ceiling began to slide shut, closing out the pale morning light.

CHAPTER 6

THE FIRES OF SHALSHA

1

Define an abstract space of n dimensions, he told himself.

Posit two primary conditions for the space, and a continuum t of time. Each condition is defined by values along certain dimensions and may be changed by changes in those values. Each condition excludes the other. Each can change into the other.

Define potentials for changes over t. One condition—call it $c(one)$—is stable across large values of t, but can only change into the other. That other—call it $c(two)$—is stable only over much smaller values of t, but has far broader potential. It may change into $c(one)$. It may also change into a third, nonprimary condition—call it $c(three)$—defined by maximized values across an entire continuum of dimensions left at zero by $c(one)$ and $c(two)$ alike. Finally, it may change into a fourth condition—$c(null)$—defined by zero values along all dimensions.

Given this situation, can a transition to $c(two)$ be justified?

Define an abstract space of n dimensions, he repeated.

Establish a prior sequence of events in that space, defined by changes over t. Both primary conditions have a part in that sequence. Further transition from either condition to the other involves reduction of values along a significant part of the total

217

range of dimensions. That reduction carries over into the new condition, and in the case of c(two) influences further transitions in the direction of c(null).

Given this situation, can a transition to c(two) be justified?

Define an abstract space of n dimensions, he repeated.

One subset of these dimensions—label it h—takes values which are partly dependent on current values of other dimensions, partly dependent on effects from prior values of t, partly free. Any transition from one primary condition to the other involves reducing the value of some of h to zero. Given the prior sequence of events over t, however, nearly all of h will respond homeostatically to resist a transition from c(one) to c(two). Completing such a transition may thus require reducing a majority of h to zero.

Given this situation, can a transition to c(two) be justified?

Define an abstract space of n dimensions, he repeated.

The situation as defined represents a specific reality. The space n corresponds to the colony world Epsilon Eridani II, the primary conditions to sociopolitical structures among its human population. The subset h corresponds to human beings, human lives. A role for moral factors cannot be ruled out, and yet the applicable moral calculus is far from clear.

Given this situation, can a transition to c(two) be justified?

Define an abstract space of n dimensions, he repeated.

The value of one dimension determines the outcome.

Outside the helicopter cabin, the winter sky rushed past in a torrent.

2

Visual contact. Imagery danced in the innermind: distant angular shapes moving among trees. *Location, six point two kilometers due north of Mirien, just west of the old highway. Speed, ninety kilometers per hour. Direction, due south.* The innervoice paused. *Straight down our barrel. Good hunting.*

The message ended. A different innervoice followed: *Any response?*

None, Amery replied. *Thank you.*

On the low table before her, a map of the countryside around Mirien traced out terrain, forces, movements. Each of the Shelters anchoring the defensive line had been marked in white, the line itself in yellow, the combat reserve just behind it in green. Purple marks down from the north showed where drones had been sighted. As she watched, the young sen Halka assigned to map duty made another mark. Not much longer, then.

For the fifth time in as many minutes, Amery reviewed her plan, the instructions she'd sent out, the responses she'd received. Everything was in place. Only one task remained, the most difficult of all: waiting. At least she would not have to wait long.

She glanced up. The windows in front of her showed high thin clouds over forest and snow. In less dangerous times, the common room around her had been a favorite spot for the Shelter folk, but windows facing north and a single short corridor between it and the radio room suited it for combat command. Outside, Mirien's prepared defenses stood empty, waiting their role as a fallback position in case the line two kilometers north had to retreat.

Visual contact. Innerspeech whispered through the net. *Location, four point six kilometers north of Mirien, on the old highway. Speed, ninety kilometers per hour. Direction, due south.* Another innervoice followed: a moment passed before Amery recognized it as Carla's. *That's been passed to the line. We're ready. Anything more?*

Yes, Amery sent. *Number and formation?*

A moment later, Carla's innervoice answered. *About twelve hundred in column—standard traveling formation in Mariel's time. Apparently they've forgotten Chandor Hal. We'll have to remind them.*

Amery allowed a taut smile. She'd speculated that the drones' controllers might fall back on old programming if their plans went awry. The Halka of Insurgency times had learned to exploit every weakness those programs had. *Alert the combat reserve*, she sent. *If the drones maintain formation we'll need to back up the center.*

Done. An instant later: *Visual contact. Coming up the valley along the old highway. They'll be among the sen davannat in minutes.* Carla paused. *Halka na.*

Halka na, Amery replied.

The map in front of her and the world outside the windows defined her world. Stiffly—she'd been in *ten ielindat* for close to two hours—she got to her feet, walked around the map and went to the window. Two kilometers away, thousands of sen Halka and tens of thousands of Shelter folk braced to meet the drones. She'd wanted, desperately, to stand among them.

And somewhere beyond the battle line and the drones—

Combat mode numbed the reaction, but even so her mind veered away from the thought. Still, the portion of herself she'd set aside to calculate probabilities, as Allan Berelat had taught her, seized the thought and carried it out remorselessly into a wilderness of numbers and times:

The likelihood that Jerre Amadan had personal contacts within the enemy command, eighty-five per cent;

The time remaining before the helicopter reached the end of its fuel supplies, four hours;

The likelihood that the enemy command would be able to react to news of Halka intentions before the end of the battle, ninety-two per cent;

The time needed for a drone carrying an atomic weapon to reach Mirien from the drones' current position, three minutes;

The likelihood that the enemy command would respond to news of Amery's strategy with an atomic attack on Mirien, ninety-nine per cent.

And the likelihood that any of this reflected Jerre's intentions? Even in the enforced clarity of combat mode, she could find no probability for that at all.

Carla's innervoice cut through her thoughts. *Entering combat.*

A sudden blue-white flash lit the sky to the north. Another followed, and another, reflecting off the clouds from below. A moment later half the northern sky was ablaze.

"Bright Earth," Benamin murmured behind her. "That will be the hermits."

Amery's mind barely registered the words. Trained responses cut through momentary shock and linked her with the groupmind. *What's happening? Report and relay.*

Carla responded. *So far, everything we'd hoped.* Images came back, relayed from the front line. Suddenly she found herself watching from a low hill beneath meria trees as figures in winter gear crouched in trenches dug in snow and frozen soil. Out beyond them, faint marks in the snow showed where the sen davannat had hidden themselves, and further out the long column of drones came into sight.

Amery considered them as they crossed the snow that separated them from the hermits. Any one of them might have been the one she'd fought and destroyed north of Talin: Type Twelve drones, their sloping alloy armor striped in the blue and gray of Directorate camouflage, violet flare of lifter fields lighting the snow beneath them. Cruising speed brought them over the sen davannat in a matter of moments. Though she knew well enough what would happen, she found herself tensing as the drones sped toward the forward line.

Close to a quarter of the column was over the hermits when the first explosion came. Sudden and blinding, it flared from well back in the column. Two more drones flashed into incandescence as the burning wreck of the first plowed into the snow. A moment later the column was in chaos, explosion followed explosion, drones scattered in all directions, and into the confusion the Halka and Shelter folk in the front line opened fire.

The imagery ended as suddenly as it began, five minutes of subjective time compressed into an eyeblink. The northern sky still blazed with blue-white glare. The mutter of distant explosions came faintly through the glass. *I estimate we've destroyed sixty of the drones*, Carla went on. *Now to take care of the rest.*

For a moment Amery allowed herself to hope that the drones' assault might collapse in the face of a sustained defense. Still, she knew better, and before the drones started to regroup she'd begun trying to anticipate their response.

Before long, though, she had no need of guesswork. Another flurry of messages came through the innerspeech net: drones already over the killing zone were struggling to draw up into combat formations, while the rest of the column spread out, formed wedges, and began advancing to either side of the old highway. Some of both groups blew apart as drone spears stabbed upwards from the snow, others slid out of control or went inert as bullets or grenades found their targets, but too many more kept driving forward, raking the line with gunfire.

A gesture of awareness sent prepared orders out over the innerspeech net, drawing in strength from the far ends of the line. *First third of the combat reserve*, she sent, *forward to reinforce the center. Be ready for hard fighting.* Then: *Carla? You'll have a third of the reserve shortly. What's the situation?*

We're taking casualties but holding. Estimate eighty drones destroyed and another twenty damaged. We can win this, Amery.

That I believe. A wordless flicker of innerspeech went out, encouraging.

The link closed down. To the north, blue-white flashes lit the morning sky. Amery stared at them for a moment, not really seeing, and then turned her attention back to the battle.

3

Pale light through clouds showed almost nothing in front of him: unbroken snow and the great looming mass of the nameless mountain blotting out the eastern sky. The kilometer or so from the helicopter had been hard enough, floundering through shoulder-deep drifts toward a landmark he only half remembered. Cold stabbed into his bones. He paused, then forced his way onward through another drift. He had little enough time left as it was.

At the far side of the drift he glanced up, blinked, allowed a smile. The black crag above him pointed the way. He started up the slope toward it.

At the foot of the crag, some trick of the wind had swept away most of the snow, allowed him to clamber in through a narrow opening into a bare little cave. In the still air, his breath burst in white clouds before him. He went to the back of the cave, faced what looked like a blank face of stone, and said aloud, "Jerome Patrick Emmer. *Dal threy am kreng, do thal.*"

Prickle of the sensor field swept over him, assessing. A moment later, a concealed loudspeaker answered him. "Jerome? Is that really you? We thought we lost you in the raid."

Baird, he remembered, fitting voice to name in his still-fragmentary memories: Baird Thompson, one of the Security staff. "Baird? You nearly did, twice: once to the drones, once to the Halka. I wasn't able to get free until the war started. I'll give a full report later today."

"Fair enough. Any news of the war?"

"Yes, and it's not good. The Halka have anticipated our strategy. Our drones are headed into a trap. I need to talk to the Director now."

Silence. "Just a moment." Air hissed, and the stone face slid away. He stepped forward into the narrow space inside, waited while the outer door slid shut and the inner door moved ponderously aside. Baird stood inside, wearing green New Directorate coveralls: older than he remembered, the last fringe of his hair gone white. Behind him, a stark gray tunnel lit by bare electric lamps led into distance.

"I'll take you to the Director," Baird said. "She won't be happy." Then: "But it's good to have you back." He turned.

A moment later the butt of Jerre's pistol smashed into the back of his head, and he slumped to the floor without a sound. Jerre knelt beside him, delivered a second blow to the atlas vertebra. Baird stiffened and went limp. A moment to let subtle awareness check for a pulse Jerre knew he wouldn't find, another to draw in a ragged breath and quell the nausea that surged in him as he considered what he'd done: then he was on his feet, gun in hand, making sure no one else from Security was nearby.

Nothing moved in the tunnel. Jerre hid the corpse in a utility closet next to the door, moved deeper into New Shalsha.

4

Stefan sprinted across open snow to the boulders, skidded to a halt behind them. To either side, he could see sen Halka and Shelter folk moving forward in the pale afternoon light as the last of the combat reserve advanced. Rattle of gunfire, shrill whine of lifter fields, and rolling thunder of explosions punctuated the air. Just past the meria wood ahead of him, he guessed, the center of the defensive line still held its position against the main force of drones.

Sight and subtle awareness searched the landscape before him for threats, found none, located the next bit of protective cover ahead of him. He paused, then dashed forward, dove behind a clump of merias. Though a heavy pack pulled at his shoulders, though his own death was all but certain before day's end, he felt light as wind. For the first time since the vision burst into existence behind his eyes, he could set aside worries about an imponderable future and turn to a task he knew better than anything else on Eridan. Grenades and spare magazines at his belt, gun in his hand, and drones nearby: for the moment, those were the things that mattered.

Those, and one other. He could feel it rushing toward him, somewhere ahead of him in the north, bearing the fulfillment of his vision with it in a blur of possibilities: darkness, light, sound, shadow. He thought of Tamar's words about visions and the presence of danger, wondered if he should have said something then. Would it have helped her to know that the thing had already happened, the vision leaping into polyphase patterns that gave him, at long last, the chance to meet it with actions of his own?

Nothing moved in the meria wood except others of the combat reserve, moving toward the battle. He ran forward again, weaving among the trees. Inner senses keyed to highest pitch swept the wood before him, caught echoes of the fighting just past it. Snow sprayed around him as he plunged through a drift at the far edge of the wood, crouched behind a last clump of trees, looked downslope.

For a moment he saw only confusion: drones weaving and turning, their guns spitting fire; figures crouched in trenches dug in across the slope, firing back with rifles and grenade launchers; sudden *whump* as a drone exploded into blue-white flame; smoke from hundreds of wrecked and burning machines hanging over all. All at once a gesture of the innermind gave meaning to chaos. The defensive line still held, and wreckage scattered along the forward trenches told Stefan that drone spears had been part of the reason why. The drones had broken formation and shifted into hunter-killer mode. Maybe half of them had been destroyed or disabled; sprawled shapes and blood on the snow showed the cost to the defenders.

He left the shelter of the trees and ran down the slope. Bullets whizzed over his head; the nearest drones had noticed the reinforcements. Cries and the sound of weight hitting snow behind him warned that some of the bullets had found targets. A moment later he scrambled down into the rearmost trench, out of immediate danger.

"Sen Halka!" Shelter folk pressed around him. "The reserve—"

"Here. Sen Lundra's committed all of it to the center." He unslung the heavy pack from his shoulders. "It's early for Winternight, but we've brought presents." Eager hands opened it, found dozens of grenades and two stubby grenade launchers of Halka pattern.

To either side, more of the reserve came skidding down into the trench, carrying burdens of their own. Grenades, ammunition, the last of the heavy weapons brought up from the south weeks and months before passed from hand to hand. The Shelter folk around Stefan handed out one of the grenade launchers, stopped at the other. "Will you want this, sen Halka?"

Stefan broke into a grin. "No. I've hunted drones with this—" He motioned toward his gun. "—for thirty years, and I don't plan on changing now."

The last grenade launcher and a bandolier of grenades went to a stocky brown-haired woman Stefan thought he remembered from Mirien Shelter. As the weapons went forward, he followed them. "Are there other Halka on this part of the line?" he asked.

"They went to the forward trenches, sen Halka," the woman with the grenade launcher answered. "I don't know how many are still alive."

Stefan nodded, followed the zigzag trench forward to the main trench, ducking as bullets whined overhead. A grenade exploded, close. A moment later the louder *thump* of a drone being blown apart told him that the grenade had gotten under the armor skirting and fused the lifter elements. A ragged cheer went up further along the trench.

"How do I reach the forward trenches?"

The woman pointed. "Down there. You'll be in among the drones, sen Halka."

"I know." A quick smile. "Good hunting."

He found the access trench, hurried along it, crouched low to stay clear of drone sensors. Where it met the forward trench, two sprawled corpses in Halka black all but barred the way.

He pushed them aside, searched the bodies for ammunition, found some on each: a gift they would have wanted him to take. "*Halka na,*" he said under his breath, and went into the trench.

More corpses and the smoldering wreckage of a dozen drones barred the trench on his left, but the right was open. He scrambled along the trench, found a place where the hulk of a single inert drone half-tipped into the trench offered protection and a chance to size up the battlefield. Off to his left, maybe fifty meters away from the sound, someone was still shooting: Halka from the crack of handgun fire. He risked a glance, saw two drones heading that way. If the nearer one turned another ten degrees …

It turned, and Stefan's gun fired three times: a first shot to test windage, a second at the three-centimeter-wide target, a third in case the second missed. One ricocheted off the drone's armor, but the other two vanished into the cooling port he'd targeted. A moment later black fluid spouted out of it, the drone lurched, and then fell to the snow as its power core burnt out.

By then Stefan was already aiming at the other. A first burst missed the sensor housing as the drone veered unexpectedly. Stefan muttered a curse, cleared his mind and let subtle awareness take over. Two more shots thudded into a carefully chosen weak spot in the drone's armor. Light flashed a moment later as one of its ammunition bins exploded, flipping the drone onto its side. Before Stefan could react the other sen Halka sent a shot into the exposed lifter elements and blew the drone to fragments.

A glance both ways across the battlefield showed no other drones nearby, though angular shapes moved through the smoke off to his right, assaulting another part of the line. Stefan's face creased in a smile. For thirty years he'd studied the art of hunting drones, learned every vulnerable spot on the killing machines, put that knowledge to the test in combat. A final test waited, and he was ready for it.

He scrambled up over the edge of the trench, sprinted across open ground, crouching low. Hulk of a wrecked drone gave him shelter after ten meters. Another dash, and he scrambled down into a crater blasted in the ground when some well-aimed shot hit a drone's vulnerabilities. The drones off to his right didn't seem to have noticed him. A third dash over the snow, and then he was on the first killing ground of the battle, half-hidden among dozens of shattered drones. Ahead, a looming presence in his inner eye, the drone bearing his vision drew closer. And the others flanking it? Polyphase vision blurred as he tried to shift his perceptions outwards from the center: drones, but how many he could not tell. He moved forward across the killing ground, inner senses wide open, gun in his hand.

Howl of lifter fields in the distance ahead, far off but growing closer, warned him as he neared the far edge of the wreckage. He could see nothing ahead through the drifting smoke, but subtle awareness reached outward and gauged the sound: at least another hundred drones, probably twice that. That made no sense if their only purpose was to guard one drone with an atomic weapon. Had the drones' controllers planned something else?

A glance back into the battle brought sudden insight. The drones already fighting had begun to draw inward from the edges of the line, shifting out of hunter-killer mode into battle formations. A common Directorate strategy during the Insurgency, that: spread out the insurgents, then concentrate on a single portion of the line and attempt to punch through. Two hundred fresh drones might achieve that, were probably meant to achieve that. And if they did ...

Darkness, light, sound, shadow: too-familiar images waited behind his eyes. Mirien was less than two minutes away at cruising speed.

He turned, faced back toward the line, let subtle awareness reach toward it. Somewhere in the chaos sen Halka still might have contact with the innerspeech net. If he could contact them, the center might be able to dig in and hold while the ends of the line drew in to reinforce it. The chances of making contact weren't good but that hardly mattered.

This is Stefan Jatanni sen Halka, he sent. *I'm north of the battle zone. There are more drones approaching; I estimate two hundred. They may intend to push through the center of the line. One probably carries an atomic weapon.* He paused, phrased the rest as clearly as possible. *I'll attempt to stop it but may not succeed. Anything not identifiable as a Type Twelve drone must be destroyed at all costs. Please relay to Mirien.*

That was all. He waited for a moment, listened for a response he didn't expect to hear, and then turned away from the battle, toward the north.

The distant whine of lifter fields drew closer. He thought of the foraging camp north of Talin then. The people there would have heard the same sound rising out of the north in the minutes before they died. A private nightmare thirty years old moved through the thought. This time would be different, he told himself. This time the hunters would become the hunted.

He moved ahead, past the last of the wreckage. With the smoke behind him he could see further down the slope, across untrodden snow. Trees at its foot hid the drones' approach, but he knew the route they would be taking: the old Shalshan highway south to Werelin. Were the drones' controllers still using maps from the time of the Directorate? It seemed likely.

He turned his awareness to his vision, plunged into the shifting patterns of possibility that framed it. Somewhere among the dance of maybes lay a pattern that would bring him up against the one drone he needed to kill. He'd already guessed at the nature of that pattern, but he needed more than guesswork, needed one piece of knowledge only the vision could give him.

All at once, clarity. He moved forward, down the slope, pushing through waist-deep snowdrifts, following the vision to its end.

Subtle awareness took the glimpse he'd been given, spun it out into a web of events. The new force of drones would come up *this* way, following the line of the highway, and climb the slope at *this* angle. The drone at the heart of his vision would be in the heart of the formation as well, not quite halfway back, larger than a Type Twelve and more heavily armored as well. The Directorate had used aircraft to launch its atomics during the Insurgency, never drones, so the enemy would have had to design and build a new type, with weaknesses and strengths Stefan's experience and the banned-tech manual could not gauge. That left only one certainty.

Partway down the slope the unseen ground dropped away suddenly, leaving him more than shoulder-deep in snow. That would be enough. He crouched down, slid his gun back into its holster for a moment, dug his way forward into the snowbank two meters or so and used his weight to push snow out to all sides until he'd made an open space large enough to hold him if he sat in *ten ielindat*. He settled, drew his gun, filled the magazine. Pure habit, that; he'd have time for two shots at most. That would be more than enough.

A glimpse into the innermind showed possibilities collapsing toward him, falling in on the path he'd hoped to shape. Subtle awareness went still, waiting. He braced his gun in both hands, pointing upwards. In Mariel's time he would have held a drone spear, but Mariel's time was gone forever, and nothing the drone's controllers could do would bring it back, not now.

Snow muffled the sounds of the fighting half a kilometer behind him, made the howl of the approaching drones a dim murmur. Stefan murmured a triggering phrase, let himself sink into the first level of trance. Unexpectedly, Tamar's words about the Halka surfaced in his mind. A black wall, she'd said, around everything worth defending: he'd been part of that wall for thirty years, since the drone came to Istal Shelter and drove him from the life he'd thought to lead. Drone after drone had fallen to his gun since then—thirty-eight of them now, from the first clumsy successes he'd had in his first years among Halka to the precise kills of the last decade—each of them an answer to what had happened at Istal.

One final answer, he thought then, to pay for all.

He cleared his awareness, merged with the innermind, waited. His thumb snapped off the safety on his gun. Snow-muffled, the howl of the drones grew louder.

5

Hurried footfalls on bare concrete gave way to a sudden hiss as the blast door slid aside. The old woman in green coveralls came into New Shalsha's command center, stopped. Five figures slumped in chairs at control stations, blue screens full of brightly lit maps and complex multifactorial graphs above them, blood pooling on the floor beneath. Harsh electric light showed a single bullet hole in the back of each head.

"Move away from the door," said a too familiar voice.

She turned, found him standing just to one side of the door. Bleak angry eyes took in his face, the gun in his hand. After a moment, she asked simply, "Why?"

"You should never have sent me into Convention territory." Jerre's voice was little more than a whisper. "If you raise some-one on lies, it's bad strategy to put him in a position where he can find his own answers."

The old eyes narrowed. "And the redemption of Earth means nothing to you?"

"Not enough that I'll risk killing this world for its sake."

She regarded him for another moment, turned away, and then suddenly spun around with a pistol in her own hand. Subtle awareness warned him of the motion while it was still no more than a thought, and his gun spoke in answer. The first bullet tore through her gun arm and sent the pistol spinning away. The second and third caught her in the chest. She staggered back, tried to say something, failed and toppled to the floor.

Jerre stared at her for a time that seemed to stretch on past measuring. Then, blind and awkward as a machine, he put his gun in its holster and turned to the nearest of the control stations. He pushed the corpse there out of the way, started punching buttons. Air hissed as the blast doors slid shut behind him. Bolts thudded into place, sealed with security codes no one else alive knew how to override. More buttons raised command and response frequencies on the screens before him, told him the one thing he most needed to know. The knowledge should have meant something to him, he knew, but it seemed abstract, distant as Old Earth.

He chose a command frequency, pressed buttons, began to speak.

6

Amery. Carla's innervoice showed strain even through the relay. *A message from Stefan. If he's right we're in trouble.*

Go ahead, Amery told her, facing out the window into the gray winter sky.

It's very indistinct. This is what we got. Then, blurred and fragmentary but shot through with Stefan's distinctive innervoice: *This is Stefan ... north of the battle ... drones approaching; I estimate two hundred ... through the center of the line ... an atomic weapon. I will attempt ... may not succeed ... not identifiable as a Type Twelve ... all costs ... Mirien.* Carla's voice again: *I haven't been able to confirm but the drones are concentrating on our center.*

Bring in anyone you can spare from the flanks, Amery told her.

I've already ordered The message cut off in midsentence.

Carla?

We have visual contact. He's right—our scouts report about two hundred drones coming along the old highway, headed right for our center. They're just over two kilometers north of us.

Can you hold them?

A long silence. *We'll do our best.*

The link cut off, leaving Amery staring north, fighting for clarity. There was nothing she could do, she knew that, nothing but—

"It might have been useful," said Allan Berelat's voice behind her, "if you had informed me about Jerre Amadan."

She turned. The old man had come into the command center without a sound, stood a few paces behind her, not far from Benamin Haller.

"Probably so," she admitted, turning to face him. "There are—personal issues involved."

Allan's pale eyes regarded her from beneath half-lowered eyelids. "All the more reason to discuss the matter," he said. "You are allowing your feelings to cloud your thinking."

She nodded, suddenly weary of the conversation and the issues that swirled around it. In a few more minutes, she knew, she and Allan and Mirien Shelter would most likely have ceased to exist. It seemed an utter waste of time to spend those last minutes on words.

"You have given up hope?" said Allan. "Think, Amery. Don't react."

It was the first time he'd ever used her first name. Startled, she wondered what he meant, tried to make sense of it, failed. "I don't know …"

Footfalls in the corridor, fast, and a shout: "Sen Lundra!" One of the technicians from the radio room came to the door of the control center at a run. "Another message over longwave. Command language, sen Lundra. It's—"

A glance at his face told her all she needed to know. A quick gesture of awareness to the innerspeech net, and she pushed past the technician, dashed down the corridor to the radio room. She reached the door and stopped as the world around her went utterly still.

"Shol fang dal shrae. Shol dau mrin shrae. Shol aeth chwem shrae."

She'd expected the old woman's voice, until the technician's face told her otherwise, and hoped all the way down the corridor that he'd been wrong. After a moment, she went in and crossed to the longwave receiver. The technician came in behind her, stood watching. Behind him, a moment later, Benamin followed.

"*Shol mrem thun shrae. Shol kau bel shrae. Shol dau krang shrae.*"

Utterly familiar, utterly unmistakeable, Jerre's voice sounded through static. She could hear appalling strains on the voice and unfamiliar patterns structuring it, but silenced her emotions before they could begin to react. The strains and patterns meant something. What?

"*Aol ban shrae fang, dal ae, num kral. Zal, shol, threng.*" A pause. "*Dau mrem bom thrai.*" Another. "*Thon.*" Silence, then. The dials in front of the receiver went all but still. The technician went to the receiver, put on the headphones, starting working dials. "That's all, sen Lundra," he said after a moment. "If there's any more I'll let you know at once."

"My thanks," she told him, the courtesy little more than an automatism. She glanced at Benamin's face, saw only the stark clarity of judgment mode, and went to the door.

At that instant light flared through the windows of the combat command room, bright enough to cast shadows down the corridor.

Amery froze, knowing no possible action could matter if the light was the atomic blast she expected. No one else moved. The light rose and fell, though, and after a moment a low rumble like thunder sent echoes scurrying through the Shelter ventilation ducts. She flung her awareness into the innerspeech net. *Carla? Are you there?*

Yes. The older sen Halka sounded stunned. *And completely at a loss. The drones appear to be destroying themselves.*

The words seemed so improbable Amery wondered if she'd heard them correctly. *What? Can you relay?*

Readily. A moment of stillness, and then images came back. She found herself standing on the low hill topped by meria trees she'd seen at the start of the battle. In place of the smooth

snow she remembered beyond the trenches, though, a cra-
tered waste of snow and soil scattered with wrecked drones
and corpses stretched out before her, half-veiled in smoke and
afternoon light. Drones in combat wedges pushed upslope
toward the rear trenches; the forward and main trenches had
been overrun. Shelter folk and sen Halka hurried in from the
sides, shooting at the drones from both flanks, but not enough
of them to matter. In the middle distance, at the bottom of the
slope, a column of drones came out from under the trees and
surged toward the line.

Then, as though something had happened to the innerspeech net, the drones stopped firing and moving. Only flashes
of gunfire from the rear trench and half-seen figures running in
from the flanks told Amery the image still came through intact.
A long moment, and the drones in combat withdrew down the
slope; the column emerging from the trees stayed motionless.
Another long moment, and then blinding flashes of light burst
from drone after drone, shattering hulls and sending great gouts
of smoke and flame billowing up through the troubled air.

The image ended as abruptly as it began. *Confirmed from one
end to another of the line*, Carla said, *and our scouts say the new
column is gone. Maybe you can explain what happened.*

Only then did Amery let herself accept the reality of it. *I can*,
she sent. *Or I think I can. Just before the drones stopped, we picked
up another longwave message in command language. Not the old
woman's voice. Jerre's.*

A long silence followed. *Well*, Carla said finally. Then,
after another long moment: *I've just had a report from scouts on
the eastern flank, near Dabeth Shelter. They saw explosions on the
lakeshore, investigated, and found drone fragments and craters in the
mud. It looks as though several buried drones also destroyed themselves. If that's Jerre's doing he was thorough.* Then: *What are your
instructions?*

*Keep all available Halka in place until we're certain there are no
more drones*, Amery told her. *Get your wounded and all the Shelter*

folk back here, or to whatever Shelter's closest. I'll have helicopters on their way at once.

I'll pass word along, Carla sent. She still sounded stunned.

The link cut off. Amery drew in a deep breath, turned her attention to another part of the innnerspeech net, sent messengers to Mirien's helicopter hangar and across the snow to three other Shelters. Another burst of innerspeech alerted medical staff at Mirien and elsewhere. Shaking herself out of the net, she turned to the lone shift operator who'd volunteered to keep the radio message net in place. Messages would have to be sent at once—

"Sen Lundra." The technician at the longwave receiver turned to her. "Another transmission. It's—it's not command language." He turned a switch.

"... relay." Jerre's voice again, flat with weariness, empty. "Mirien Shelter, please copy and relay. This is Jerre Amadan sen Halka. I am reporting a primary case." He stumbled a little over the legal term. "Specifically the First, Third, Fourth, and Fifth Laws. Eighty-four people were participants at the time of formal discovery. Eighty-three of those are dead as of this report. The eighty-fourth is myself." A moment of silence, then: "The helicopter I took from Mirien Shelter is at the following location—" He read off a string of numbers. "It's out of fuel but otherwise in flyable condition and should be safe until weather allows recovery." Then: "I'll be returning to Con—to settled territory as soon as circumstances allow, which probably means spring. Mirien Shelter, please copy and relay."

A burst of static followed, and then loudspeaker hiss, broken only by the scratching of the shift operator's pen on the other side of the radio room. "I've got that, sen Halka," she said a moment later. "Should it be relayed at once?"

"No," Amery told her, trying not to think about Jerre. "I'll need to draft and send two other messages first." She faced the door, knowing who would be waiting there.

Allan Berelat considered her, a slight smile twisting the corners of his mouth. "Your war is over," he said. "You've called your forces back to Shelters, of course."

"All but the Halka," she told him.

"That is probably wise. They may as well savor their guardian's role while it lasts. Our world will not be the same after this." A moment's pause, then: "You may wish to consider a new specialty. There will be a shortage of strategic problems for some time to come." He turned to go. "I will be in my room if I am needed."

"Allan?"

He stopped, glanced back at her.

"My thanks."

A fractional nod was his only answer. His footfalls, slow and measured, whispered down the corridor to the main stairs.

7

Once the last messages went out and the pounding rotors of the helicopters broke the evening silence on their way to and from the battlefield, Amery left the radio room and went down to the main northern doors, with Benamin Haller close behind her. Halka tradition made her duties as combat commander last until the combat force returned. Worries and griefs pressed her closely enough that waiting for a message from the doors was more than she wanted to bear.

She reached the doors just as the first of the Halka reached Mirien Shelter. She'd already been briefed on the dead and the wounded who probably wouldn't live out the night, and expected missing faces to add bitterness to the burden she already carried. Instead, a sudden bright pride flared up in her as she watched them. The Halka had made a promise to all Eridan two centuries back, a promise sealed at the Convention of Zara and confirmed in blood. The men and women who stumbled in from the cold night, shaking snow off their boots and unfastening greatcoats, had fulfilled that promise to the letter. Whatever the aftermath might be, that much remained.

Sen Halka poured through the doors. The handful she knew by name greeted her with quick bright flickers of innerspeech. Others simply nodded, the quiet gesture of respect welcome despite the tangle of her emotions. Near the end of the long line came Carla Dubrenden, her head bandaged, hood thrown back and iron-gray hair blown all anyhow by the wind. She spotted Amery and wove through sen Halka to reach her. *Amery, that was splendidly done.*

My thanks, Amery replied, feeling anything but splendid. *What happened to you?*

Fragments from a drone. I wasn't able to hit it until it was nearly over us.

A sudden cold thought. *The sen davannat. Did any of them survive?*

Maybe a hundred. Some of them dug themselves in to defend the rear trench or the track back here, and the drones never reached them. We sent them to Dabeth for food and medical care; some of them have frostbite. A whisper of rueful emotion. *I don't think I'll ever be able to think of myself as brave, not after watching them.* Then, cautiously: *I assume there's nothing more from Jerre.*

No. Emotions strained at Amery's shielding. *Nothing at all. I*—she stopped, seeing another face she'd hoped to see among the living.

Stefan glanced at her, and his face creased in a smile. *Amery. Well.*

One urgent question remained. *Your vision?*

Gone. About two minutes before the drones destroyed themselves, all of it went spinning away into nothing. When I search the innermind now, all I see is what any other sen Halka sees. I cannot say that distresses me.

I imagine not. Two minutes, she thought, remembering Jerre's voice, the hard syllables of command language through static.

Seemingly he sensed the thought, and his smile failed. *Carla told me about Jerre*, he said. *I wish I knew what to think about that.*

Amery nodded and began to say something else, but noticed Stefan suddenly looking past her, all his attention turned down the emptying corridor. She glanced that way, caught a glimpse of a Halvedna robe. Stefan sent a flicker of innerspeech, apologetic, and stepped past Amery as Tamar came toward the doors and stood facing him.

Amery turned to watch them. She couldn't see Stefan's expression, but Tamar's was a smile compounded of more emotions than Amery could count. The two of them stood facing each other for a long moment. Then Stefan offered his hands; Tamar took them in hers, and suddenly put her arms around him and buried her face in his shoulder. The soft sound of her weeping, muffled by the cloth of his greatcoat, became audible as the last murmur of Halka footfalls faded into silence.

That's something I've hoped to see for thirty years, said Carla.

Amery glanced at her, but said nothing.

"I believe," Benamin Haller said behind her, "that your last duty's complete, Amery."

She blinked, turned to face him. Judgment mode still closed off his thoughts to her, but she thought she could sense a vast relief behind the mental shields. Recalling her duties, she turned to Carla. "Everyone's back?"

"I made certain of it," Carla assured her.

"Then I'm terminating combat discipline, effective immediately," Benamin said. "Amery, you're relieved as combat commander." He handed her gun back to her. She took it, glanced at it with a bleak expression, returned it to its place at her side.

8

Crackle of sound from the radiation detector warned of power core fragments not yet decayed to safety. The sen Halka stepped back, let subtle awareness search. Spring meadowmoss and half-melted snow made footing treacherous and traces of the destroyed drone hard to locate, but after a moment the inner-mind found her a hand-sized shard of gray metal buried in snow. There would be fireflowers there next year, she thought. She took a thin wooden shaft topped with a flag from the basket on her back, planted it in the ground next to the shard, backed away.

As the radiation detector fell silent, subtle awareness pulsed again, warned her of the presence of watching eyes.

She looked up, let the innermind guide her. A gaunt figure in a winter greatcoat stood at the edge of the forest maybe fifteen meters away. After a moment she circled the radioactive shard and approached him, guessing who it had to be.

He came forward to meet her. Three month's growth of beard did nothing to hide marks of hunger and terrible uncer-tainty in his face. Boots of Halka style, stained with mud and melted snow, told her everything subtle awareness did not.

"Jerre Amadan sen Halka?" she asked.

"Yes."

"I must ask you—"

"Of course." He drew his gun from inside his coat, handed it to her grip first. "If it matters, where am I?"

If it mattered? The sen Halka wondered at that for a moment, then caught a flicker of his emotions, realized he half expected to be shot on sight. "This is Talin Shelter," she told him, indi-cating the half-wrecked wind turbine towers behind her with a minute motion of her head. "There's been no ruling on your case yet, sen Amadan."

"No?" He considered that for a moment. "I trust you'll summon a judgment circle for me, then. I'm not certain of the proper procedure."

A fractional nod. "If you're ready?"

"More than ready." They started across the melting snow toward the Shelter. "Talin Shelter. I didn't plan on returning here, but maybe it's for the best."

The sen Halka glanced at him, said nothing.

Half an hour later a messenger from the radio room hurried into the Halka quarters at Mirien Shelter. "Sen Lundra? A message from Talin."

Amery looked up from the final judgment she'd been writing: her last task as combat commander in the war, and nearly the last thing the Mirien command circle would act on before it formally disbanded. "What do they need?" she asked.

"It's not that. Jerre Amadan's arrived there."

Startled, she got to her feet, scattering papers in all directions. "Just now?"

"This afternoon, they said. A judgment circle's been summoned. If you'd like to see the whole message ..."

"Please." She took the paper the man handed her, read it, handed it back. "My thanks. I'll send a response shortly."

The messenger nodded and went back the way he'd came. Amery looked after him for a moment, then stooped and gathered up the papers from the floor. A few moments later she started down the same corridor, knowing that two others needed to hear the same news.

Jerre. She'd thrown herself into the hard work that remained at war's end, as much because that made it easier not to think of him as for any other reason. Each Shelter attacked by the drones needed food, medicine, supplies, volunteers, all of it in the brief intervals between winter storms. Though the Mirien command circle had no official part in the rescue effort, no one argued when Amery moved at once to help coordinate the response. Long hours in the radio room followed, broken only when the judgment circle called to assess the Mirien command's actions summoned her to describe, recount, explain. Then, after many days, their response:

"Your actions in this crisis were legally problematic." Sharra Macalley sen Halka, perhaps the most respected legalist living, brushed gray hair back from her eyes. "In a strict sense they violate Halka tradition in several important particulars.

However, this circle finds merit in the Mirien circle's suggestion that Halka tradition exists to serve the purposes of the
Convention of Zara and must not be treated as an end in itself.
Furthermore, several members of the circle point out that case
law justifies involving Shelter folk and Shelter properties in
Halka activities in some circumstances, and suggest that this
forms a precedent for your actions."

The others in the judgment circle, senior legalists from
across the continent, faced Amery with unreadable expres-
sions. She'd turned her gaze back to Sharra.

"Our judgment," said the legalist, "therefore finds your
actions appropriate, and proposes the establishment of a new
branch of Halka regulations to deal with circumstances in which
sen Halka may request help from Shelter folk on a local, regional,
or planetary basis. That proposal will have to be ratified by the
order more generally, of course, but our immediate judgment
need not be." Innerspeech flickered across the circle, and the
legalist next to Amery, an old man whose name she'd never
learned, handed her gun back to her with a nod and a smile.

That had been a surprise, though not totally so. She and
Benamin had discussed the possibility more than once, during long winter nights when storms brought the relief effort
to a halt for the moment and the radio net settled down into
routine traffic she felt no need to monitor. Halka tradition had
its flexibilities as well as its unbreachable limits, and the same
rules that made it legal to ask Shelters to set aside a few rooms
for Halka use offered a precedent she knew the circle might
choose to follow—so long as the Convention and its Six Laws
remained unaffected. Those were sacrosanct, and a swift death
waited for anyone who breached them.

A swift death, she thought, passing the door to the radio
room. She'd accepted that for herself often enough. Why did
the thought of Jerre meeting it seem so intolerable?

She'd thought more than once that he might already have
found it. As soon as weather allowed, a Halka force armed

with heavy weapons had flown north to the coordinates Jerre named and found the helicopter there, half buried in snow but able to fly home to Mirien once its tanks were filled. Nearby they spotted sheared rock where the side of a mountain had collapsed, and radiation detectors soared off the scale as they approached. It took scholars a week of digging in the historical library at Embran to find old accounts of atomic reactors and identify the signs of a core meltdown. Until the message came from Talin she'd wondered if Jerre died inside the mountain, vaporized by the explosion or crushed by tons of falling rock.

She reached one of the Shelter's main stairs, started down it. More than a thousand sen Halka and five times as many Shelter folk found their own quick deaths during the battle, and reports still coming in from the Shelters further north made for a final toll many times that. The winter had taken another sen Halka well after the fighting stopped, too: Allan Berelat's fragile health finally gave way, and he died in the Mirien Shelter medical rooms after a weeklong struggle with failing lungs. He'd said nothing at the end, simply closed his eyes and waited for death to take him. Amery expected nothing else, but she'd arranged for someone else to fill her duties and spent more than a day in silent meditation in the hallow room afterwards.

She left the stair and started down a corridor, passed windows looking over one of the Shelter's roof terraces. Most of the snow had already melted away, leaving pools of still water reflecting a sky full of billowing clouds. Memory twisted in her, cold as metal: she'd found Jerre on that same terrace the evening before the drones' assault, listening to the year's last sama on the samahane below. Words of remembered inner-speech burned: *And I knew that if I opened myself to you there would be no way back, ever.*

And if the way forward led only to a Halka bullet?

She forced her mind clear, let subtle awareness count eleven doors along the corridor, stopped at the twelfth. Before she could tap on it, Stefan's voice sounded from inside: "Please come in, Amery."

She'd expected to find him in Tamar's room, had learned to look there first when she wanted to find him. The door slid open to show him sitting calmly to one side, while Tamar tried to stuff too many things into a shapeless bag maybe half the necessary size.

"We just heard about Jerre," he said by way of explanation. "Tamar's certain we can find a helicopter to take the three of us north."

"You're both coming?" She managed a smile. "I think that will mean much to him."

"Maybe so, but there's another factor." Stefan's expression was bleak. "All three of us are informed persons." The term meant anyone with personal knowledge regarding a breach of the Six Laws. "If the circle knows its business, they'll send for each of us anyway."

Tamar gave up her struggle with the bag, found another for the excess. "I hope they do know their business. Do you think there's any hope they'll take circumstances into account?"

The two sen Halka in the room met her gaze in silence. After a moment, Tamar looked away. "I didn't think so, but ..." She left the rest of the sentence unsaid.

9

Murmurs and movement filled the samahane outside Talin Shelter by the time Amery reached it. The judgment circle held most of its meetings in the temporary Halka quarters two levels below ground—Talin's Halka rooms had been wrecked in the fighting—but the Speaker ruled that the final judgment would take place where it could be heard by all. Despite uncertain spring weather the samahane was the only place at Talin large enough to hold the crowd.

As she came down the stairs, Amery noted close to a hundred sen Halka there already. Over to one side sat a cluster of sen Halvedna in rainbow-colored robes, Tamar among them. The Convention gave the Halvedna order the right to observe Halka judgments, and though that right saw use maybe once in twenty years Amery felt no surprise to see it invoked here. Beside the two orders, well over a thousand Shelter folk and technicians sat on the packed soil of the samahane, facing the space at its center where the judgment circle already waited. Forest spread purple and blue in the near distance, just outside the metal of the protective circle; clouds scattered across blue sky soared over all.

Amery worked her way over to the other sen Halka, found a place between Stefan and Benamin Haller. Innerspeech passed wordless greetings. She settled into *ten ielindat*, glanced both ways. Benamin would have been a member of the judgment circle had he not been an informed person in the case, and he'd followed the legal issues closely, discussing them late into the night with other legalists who weren't part of the circle. Amery tried to follow some of the discussions but quickly found herself out of her depth. With Jerre in seclusion, Benamin busy with legal issues, Tamar closeted with the other sen Halvedna, and Stefan wrapped in a calmness she could not read at all, the slow pace of peacetime Shelter life left her feeling adrift.

She glanced at Stefan as he sat in meditative silence next to her. Something basic seemed to have changed in him between the time he'd left the helicopter hangar before the battle and his return to Mirien. He'd said little about his actions, though she heard enough from others to guess what he'd tried to do and how close he'd come to doing it. Had that finally laid the ghost of Istal Shelter to rest? Through the bitterness of her own feelings, she found room to hope so.

Murmurs through the crowd alerted her, and she glanced up. A figure in a green robe came out of the Shelter doors. He was most of the way down the stairs before she knew for sure it was Jerre. Halka patterns shaped his movements, but beneath them flowed mind training of another shape, different from Halka or Halvedna but intensive as either. Stillness in his face spoke of a self-possession he'd never had at Mirien. One thing more shouted across the space to her, though she wondered how many others could sense it: he expected to die before day's end.

He made his way inward to the judgment circle, nodded his thanks to the sen Halka who'd brought him, sat.

"Jerre Amadan sen Halka." The Speaker's voice cut through the sudden hush.

"Sharra Macalley sen Halka."

"I have been named Speaker for the circle. Is this acceptable to you?"

That called up an unexpected smile. "Of course."

"The traditions of our order instruct us that a sen Halka who kills or injures another person, who is accused of an offense against our traditions, who reports a violation of one of the Six Laws or who declares one of the high emergency codes without a judgment circle's approval shall submit to judgment. It is my understanding that you sent a message by radio four months ago reporting a primary case and naming yourself as a participant. It is also my understanding that you sent out a judgment three weeks ago formally accusing yourself of complicity in that case, and stating that you took a Shelter helicopter without leave, violated a declared state of combat discipline, and killed eighty-three persons. It this your understanding as well?"

"Yes."

"Knowing the alternatives, do you accept the judgment of this circle?"

The gun and the container of dwimmerwine waited, but he did not hesitate. "Yes."

Sharra considered him. "Before we begin the formal proceedings, I have one question. You're certainly aware that sen Halka facing judgment traditionally attend the circle in Halka black. I assume your failure to do that was deliberate. I would welcome an explanation."

"It was entirely deliberate," said Jerre. "I chose not to prejudice the decision in my own favor, because I'm facing trial here in two capacities, sen Macalley. One you're aware of. The other you're not. I'm here as Jerre Amadan sen Halka, but my other name, the only name I had until two years ago, is Jerome Emmer, and my other title is Deputy Director of the Planetary Directorate at New Shalsha."

For a moment nothing made sound except the wind in the meria trees out past the protective circle. Then Jerre spoke again. "I know those two details settle any doubts this circle may have had about my fate. I've accepted that. But ..." He fell silent for a moment. "I know there are procedures for this, sen Macalley, but I need to ask your indulgence and the circle's. I want to explain what happened and why, but the only way I know how to do that is to tell a story. It's a long, bitter story, and I need to tell it in my own way. I hope you'll permit that."

"The procedure at this point," said Sharra, "is simply for the Speaker to request a full explanation from the person under judgment." She brushed gray hair back from her eyes. "Consider the request made."

"Thank you." He fell silent again, folded his hands in his lap, began to speak. "It's a long story, as I said, and it didn't begin on this world. It began aboard *Journey Star*.

"I was taught that this planet was a rare discovery among the colony worlds. Most of the others were lifeless rock, but the unmanned probes to our system sent back news of a world full of life, with an atmosphere human beings could breathe. Where the other colony worlds got mostly engineers and technologists, *Journey Star* had on board some of Earth's best people in the life sciences—ecologists, agronomists, atmospheric chemists, and the like. The evacuation authorities wanted to be sure that what happened to Earth wouldn't be repeated here.

"They had good reason for that. By the time *Journey Star* left Earth orbit, the homeworld was already dying. After three hundred years of unrestricted atmospheric pollution, not even a total halt could keep temperatures from rising until the oceans boiled. So the scientists on *Journey Star* listened day after day to the radio as the last desperate measures failed and the world they'd left turned into a greenhouse planet with temperatures hot enough to melt metal.

"I—" He said nothing for a moment. "I can't imagine what it was like, sitting there in deep space and listening as Earth died. The people on *Journey Star* had plenty of time to think, and what happened to Earth must have been on their minds nearly every hour. No one told me who first decided to find a solution, or who finally worked out the method. All I was taught was that before *Journey Star* reached our world the thing had been accomplished."

A murmur spread outward through the crowd. "I was told that your histories claim that's a lie, a scrap of Directorate propaganda," said Jerre. "I don't doubt the Directorate used the claim, but the fact itself is real. I know the full atmospheric reengineering protocol and I've run small-scale experimental tests myself that confirmed it. By the time our ancestors came here they knew how to restore Earth to life.

"And the Directorate, the factory camps, all of that happened because the leaders of the colony couldn't see our world as anything but a staging ground for the redemption of Earth. They wanted to build a planetary industrial society as fast as possible, use *Journey Star* as an orbital base, launch new starships full of engineered microorganisms to tip the balance of Earth's atmosphere and bring the homeworld back to life. And when they demanded too much for too long and the Insurgency began, all they could see was a betrayal of their deepest dream and an obstacle that had to be removed at any cost.

"Even when Shalsha died, the hope didn't die with it. Some of you may know of Melissa Emmer as an agronomist, the daughter of the last Planetary Director, who stayed out of politics and survived the Insurgency. But she was also the founder of a network of Directorate survivors who kept the protocol safe, along with the principles of science and technology we needed to make it happen. I say 'we', for I was a member of it.

"The network had several names, but in my time we called it Bredin Shelter after an old hill country folktale. That served us well, since no one who stumbled on us could get others to believe them, and sen Halka who sensed our existence and claimed they'd found Bredin Shelter were shot when evidence couldn't be found. It never was found, because it was all inside our brains. We had our own system of mind training: mnemonics to store the knowledge that had to be preserved, shields to keep Halka and Halvedna from finding it there.

"Our hope was that as the memory of the Directorate faded, technological progress would lead to an industrial society that could support spaceflight. That didn't happen. No one in the Bredin Shelter network really understood what the dwimmerroot meant. No one realized that Loren Frederic's discovery made a mental technology more accessible than the industrial technology of Old Earth. All they saw was technological stagnation, the same helicopters and radios and wind turbines copied unchanged from one generation to the next, while the dream of Earth's redemption withered and the network's numbers shrank.

"Forty years ago things reached the breaking point, and Bredin Shelter split into factions. The largest wanted to abandon secrecy, make the hope and the protocol public, and gamble that we could win support from the Shelter folk and avoid extermination by the Halka. They worked out a modified protocol that allowed the whole project to be done with one large starship. The plan was to build chemical rockets, get a crew and the necessary supplies up to *Journey Star*, and sail it back to Earth. That might have happened, except for a woman named Laura Emmer.

"She had a different plan. She hated the Halka for what they'd done to Shalsha, and she argued that we could break them and take everything we needed for the full protocol.

250 THE FIRES OF SHALSHA

She played on fears and hatreds, used blackmail and assassination—and she had one strength beside those. The Emmer family knew about a hidden base the Directorate built in the far north in the last year of the Insurgency. It was only half complete when Shalsha fell, but she convinced most of the network that they could finish it and use it as a springboard to seize control of Eridan. Those who disagreed were killed. The rest went north and set the plan in motion.

"That's where I was born." A little helpless gesture, out of keeping with the calm self-possession of his voice. "I was the only child who lived to adulthood; we knew the theory of atomic engineering but we had to rediscover the practice, and too many mistakes were made. Nearly half the original group died of radiation poisoning or cancer, and most of the children with them. Others simply disappeared; I found out later that they tried to leave New Shalsha—that's what we called the base—and Security staff killed them.

"I didn't question." His voice wavered for an instant. "I believed in Earth's redemption. I believed that what we called Convention territory was full of people who would welcome progress and industrialism if not for Halka guns. My loyalty was absolute. So when the drones and the atomic weapon were ready, Laura Emmer sent me south to update our maps and get the last details we needed for the invasion.

"I rode a drone around the north end of the mountains and down the east slopes as far as Wind Gap, and went on foot from there to the plains around Werelin. I was supposed to go straight north, but I went south instead to the ruins of Shalsha and then north from there. I wanted to see what the Halka had done, and when I saw it I was—" A bleak laugh. "Afire with indignation. If I'd had a dozen atomic weapons just then I would have used them all. I hadn't yet started to think, or to notice what was around me.

"But I went north, going from Shelter to Shelter with other young people, and it dawned on me that I wasn't seeing what

I expected to see. I saw sen Halka now and then, but no one seemed frightened of them, and no one seemed especially desperate for more technology than they had already. I listened to people's hopes and dreams and kitchen talk. I danced sama for the first time, and made love for the first time. And finally ..." He stopped, made himself go on. "Finally I came here, to Talin Shelter.

"My instructions were to wait until the first foraging camp went north of the Shelter, send a coded message over the radio net with time and location, go to the camp, and meet the drone that would take me back to New Shalsha late at night. That's what I was told, but either the plans changed or they lied to me. I was still in the camp, helping to gather meria seeds and trying not to face my own doubts, when I heard lifter fields.

"I'm not proud of what happened next." His voice uneven, he forced himself on. "All I could think was that something had gone horribly wrong, but I couldn't warn anyone, couldn't reveal myself. If I'd shouted a warning then, people might have scattered and some might have survived, but—but I couldn't. Then a drone came up over the rise and started killing everyone. I panicked and shouted a command to the drone, telling it to break off the attack and return to base: *shcha lyu ang chwem* in command language. It—it ignored me. It kept firing until everyone else was dead. Someone ran into me in the middle of the killing and knocked me down, and I used autonomic control to lower my breathing to levels sensors can't detect. I was terrified, sure that the drone would kill me too."

He was silent for what seemed like a long time. "I think now that they never imagined I would react that way. Lives meant nothing to them. They probably ordered the drone to identify and spare me, and thought once the killing was over I'd ride it back to New Shalsha.

"But that's not what happened. I saw everyone lying dead around me, I knew that for all practical purposes I'd killed them, and I knew that I'd helped plan a war that would kill hundreds of thousands of people like them even if everything went the way we'd planned. I looked at the corpses and I remembered the kind words and friendship those people had given me, and I couldn't bear it. And I fled into the core of my mind and found a place where the memories and the horror weren't there any more."

He looked down at his hands. "I don't know if I can explain what happened after that. After a long time I awoke, but to this day I'm not sure if the person who awoke was the same as the one who fled. I remember both now, but then I didn't remember anything at all. You've doubtless been told about catamnetics by people who know much more about them than I do. But under the catamnetic I lost the keys to my own mental shielding. Jerome Emmer was gone, and all I remembered was the name and identity I'd taken on my mission, Jerre Amadan.

"As Jerre Amadan I listened to the people around me, heard about the drones and the threat of war, fit those together with the scraps of memory I could still reach. As Jerre Amadan I went to Stefan Jatanni sen Halka, asked for baya, and went through the Halka training. At the time all I knew was that I had to do something about the drones. After my memories returned I realized that what drove that was guilt. At some level I remembered the deaths at the foraging camp were my doing, and that was a debt I had to repay.

"When I took baya I remembered again, but only for a moment. Afterwards I recalled only that I gained and lost some memory that seemed important. But a few days later I was called to the Mirien Shelter radio room, and I heard Laura Emmer's voice. I don't think even catamnetics could make me forget her voice. After my duty shift was over I went to a private place, fought with my memories, and finally found the key to my mental shielding and remembered being Jerome Emmer.

"And—" His voice broke. He mastered himself, went on. "I knew enough of the war, enough of both sides' strategies, to know that our whole world stood on the edge of a knife. Laura Emmer's plan was to break the Halka with drones and an atomic weapon. Amery Lundra's plan was to use surprise and massed force to crush the invading drones. The two plans fit together too well, and both the drones and the Halka would likely have been destroyed. The first assault was the key to the entire plan—we knew that only the shock of total defeat would break the resistance—but Laura Emmer would never have stopped; she had the materials to build tens of thousands of drones, and New Shalsha was invulnerable to anything but atomic attack. With the Halka gone, the only future I could see was full of battle-drones flooding south until the last human being on Eridan was dead.

"I thought of the foraging camp. I'd failed to act then, failed to do anything, and everyone at the camp died because of it. Now the same thing was about to happen to our whole world, and I had precisely one chance to stop it.

"I think you know what happened after that. I took a helicopter, flew north, got into New Shalsha, and started killing people." He stared at nothing in particular. "People I knew, people I'd grown up with, whose dreams I'd once shared. I killed one with my hands, shot six more, and used New Shalsha's internal defense systems to kill the rest once I'd taken over the control center. One of those I shot was my mother, Laura Emmer." Looking up at the members of the circle: "After that I sent out a self-destruct command to the drones, disabled the cooling systems on the reactor, and got out as fast as I could. I hope no one's gone too close to what's left of New Shalsha. The whole mountainside will be fiercely radioactive for years."

"Our patrol had radiation detectors," said Sharra Macalley. "They noted the radiation and stayed clear of the contaminated zone."

"That's good to hear." Then: "But that's my story, or most of it. I sat out the winter in an emergency shelter we had about fifteen kilometers away, and started south as soon as I thought the weather would allow it. I thought more than once, when I was waiting, of simply walking out into a snowstorm and letting that take care of the matter. Still, I wanted someone else to know." A helpless gesture, palms out, and the last of his self-possession trickled away. "Simple egotism, maybe. The whole bitter story of Shalsha and Bredin Shelter ends with me, and I'm vain enough to want someone else to hear it before I die. And ..." He drew together the shreds of himself. "I've written out the full atmospheric reengineering protocol in layman's terms and in the technical language of systems ecology. You'll find it in my room. If that could be taken to Zara and kept there, I'd be grateful. It's just possible that someday we might be contacted by one of the other colony worlds, and if that happens the old dream might finally go forward despite all that's happened in its name."

The Speaker paused, then said, "These are the facts as you know them?" When Jerre nodded: "The circle has several questions to ask."

"Of course."

"When you left Mirien, had you already planned your actions at New Shalsha?"

His gaze fell. "I wish I could say yes. All I knew then was that I had one chance to do anything at all, and I had to take it. I spent the whole flight north trying to decide what to do. The other option was to tell the Directorate command staff everything I knew about the Halka deployment, and let them use their atomics on the Halka force rather than on Mirien. I rejected that, but I'd be lying if I told you I didn't consider it."

Sharra glanced across the circle to another of the legalists, and innerspeech moved between them. "Why did you reject it?" she asked.

He met her gaze. "The drone spears."

Sharra waited for him to continue, then said, "Please explain."

"I saw hundreds of people carrying them," he said, looking away again. "That told me I'd been lied to—that the Shelter folk would stand together with the Halka and would quite literally die before they'd submit to a new Directorate, and that all my mother's hopes added up to an empty dream. Beyond that, I knew what kind of death they faced if the war continued." In little more than a whisper: "I couldn't allow that."

The Speaker waited another moment, then said, "Another question. We've had more than two hundred reports of underground explosions, all from the same time the drones north of Mirien destroyed themselves. Those are still being investigated, but the ones we've inspected so far were buried drones. Perhaps you'll explain that."

Jerre glanced up, and for the first time since he'd begun talking of his own life, a smile showed through the troubled look on his face. "I used a set of self-destruct codes meant to wreck every drone on this continent, including the ones in standby mode. The old Directorate used longwave in the first place because it reaches underground and underwater. I wanted to be sure that what happened here would never happen again anywhere on this world." Then: "Thank you. It's something to know that that worked."

Sharra considered that briefly. "There's one more question," she said then, "of historical interest. I've been requested to ask it now, since our sentence will be immediate if the circle rules against you. You implied just now that Loren Frederic discovered the dwimmerroot. Is that correct?"

Jerre looked blank for a moment, then nodded. "Of course," he said, "you wouldn't know that. Yes. Loren Frederic was the chief botanist in the Department of Settlement in the early years of the Directorate, and he did quite a lot of work with medicinal plants." Another smile, almost unwilling. "He and Carl Emmer supposedly met when he was an old man and Emmer was a young agronomy student. The story is that they took dwimmerroot together, and that's when Emmer decided to enter politics. It was a joke at New Shalsha that the Halka and the Halvedna were still trying to catch up to him."

Quieter than the wind, a murmur moved through the sen Halvedna who watched. Sharra Macalley waited for silence to return, then said, "We have no further questions. Is there anything more you wish to say before we proceed?"

"No," Jerre replied. "Thank you, but no."

"Then we will determine our judgment." She closed her eyes, and her thoughts hid themselves behind a mental shield of unexpected power. The other members of the circle did likewise. Jerre glanced around the circle of faces, then drew his own awareness to its center. In the days before baya—it seemed long ago now—he'd found a space within himself where the pressures of emotion and memory fell away, though emotion and memory themselves did not: a place of remembrance instead of oblivion. Halka awareness drills still fit awkwardly with the Bredin Shelter disciplines he'd learned in childhood, but he managed to balance himself between the two, to find the bright space of clarity and remain there while the circle deliberated.

Ten meters away, seated among the Halka, Amery made herself review every word of Jerre's narrative and accepted the hard reality at last. By his own admission Jerre had taken part in the worst violations of the Six Laws Eridan had seen since the signing of the Convention. Circumstances, motives, all other considerations: Halka tradition and law made those irrelevant. The Convention mattered more than one person's life, more than …

In the core of her mind, a realization cold and bitter as ice unfolded, though she tried to draw back from it. More than how many lives? How many people had the Halka order killed over the two centuries since the fires of Shalsha gave them control over the destiny of a world?

We brought peace, she said to the cold place inside her. We kept a people who had known nothing but tyranny from falling back into it, and we kept ourselves from becoming tyrants at the point of our own guns. Nothing else would have done that. Surely that weighs against the cost.

And Jerre's New Directorate, the cold place answered her. Did they think otherwise, when they weighed the lives they planned to take against the purpose they hoped to achieve?

She wrenched her awareness back to the present moment: packed soil beneath her, blue sky and billowing white clouds above, black-clad Halka surrounding her, the judgment circle a silent presence in the innermind, and Jerre on the edge of it. They would announce their judgment soon, she guessed. It could not be much longer.

Within, the cold place and its questions waited with the patience of turning stars.

The silence went on, and on, and on. After what must have been a quarter hour, Amery glanced at Benamin. A flicker of subtle awareness made sure he was open to innerspeech. *I'm not sure what's taking so long*, she said.

The longer they take, the more hope there is for Jerre, he replied.

That got him a sudden sharp glance. *Hope? Please don't mock me, Benamin. There's no possible way the circle could acquit him.*

True. But I don't mean to mock you.

She tried to think of something to say in response, but no words came. Caught between the yes and the no, she drew her awareness into herself and waited.

Finally, after most of an hour, Sharra Macallay blinked and rose up out of rapport. The other members of the circle followed by ones and twos.

"We've arrived at a judgment," she said in a conversational tone. "Because it's complex, and because many of those present today are not of the Halka order, the circle has asked me to explain it in detail. I trust that will be acceptable to all.

"First, the three secondary charges. Jerre Amadan sen Halka, you stand accused by yourself of appropriating Shelter property without permission, breaking combat discipline, and killing eighty-three individuals. These are serious charges in Halka tradition.

"However, Halka tradition permits sen Halka to borrow Shelter property in emergencies so long as every effort is made to return the property undamaged or replace it thereafter. Halka tradition allows sen Halka who have not been assigned a battlefield duty station to violate combat discipline in response to an immediate threat. Halka tradition has never prohibited the killing of armed opponents, or of persons actively violating any of the Six Laws. These considerations apply in the present case, and the circle therefore finds your actions within the limits set by tradition."

Jerre nodded.

"There remain the primary charges. You stand accused by yourself of participating in defined deliberate violations of the First, Third, Fourth, and Fifth Laws. Your statements to this circle confirm those accusations, and the evidence and testimony we've reviewed supports them in detail. Until two years ago, if we understand correctly, you willingly participated in a hierarchy of superiors demanding obedience from inferiors, helped plan violence against hundreds of Shelters, assisted in constructing armed and armored vehicles, and had frequent contact with Directorate machines beyond that required to repel or destroy them."

"That's correct," said Jerre.

"Under existing case law we may acquit you or condemn you. Several senior legalists in this circle have argued that acquitting you would break with two hundred years of Halka legal tradition and conflict with central principles of the Convention. By your own admission you took part in violations of our most fundamental laws, and the penalty for violating those laws is death. Those have traditionally been the only facts that matter, and for the highest reasons.

"The Halka order has no right to judge the thoughts and purposes of the people we serve, and sometimes must kill.

Under the Convention we can only judge actions, and then only those actions that affect the Six Laws our order exists to defend. The people of Eridan may believe as they wish, think as they wish, speak as they wish. They may even act as they wish, so long as those actions don't violate the six simple rules the Convention established. If they do violate those rules, the same logic demands that their beliefs, thoughts, speech, and other actions cannot justify those violations. Since the facts of your case aren't in doubt, we cannot acquit you. So some of us have argued, and the circle finds their arguments compelling."

Jerre closed his eyes, nodded once.

But Sharra had not finished. "Several senior legalists among us argue for another view. They point out that while legal theory embraces absolutes, legal practice doesn't. Two of the standard hypothetical cases we use in legal training deal with this issue, and I trust the sen Halka present will bear with me if I repeat them for the benefit of the others here today.

"One hypothetical imagines a two-year-old child at play near a foraging camp, who finds some scrap of a destroyed battle-drone in the ground and uses it as a toy. That violates the Fifth Law, and if the child was told not to touch such things but found it too enticing to resist, it's a deliberate violation. Still, no sen Halka would claim the child should be shot.

"The other hypothetical imagines a starship from another world landing on ours. The crew, as *Journey Star*'s crew was, is organized into a hierarchy, and on board is a weapon with a fifteen hundred meter range. At the instant of landing, then, they're in violation of the First and Fourth Laws. Halka legalists have argued over the proper response for more than a century, but no one holds that sen Halka should kill the crew the moment they land.

"The present case, according to this view, is of the same kind. You were born outside the reach of the Convention. You grew to adulthood there, and participated in violations of the Six Laws initiated by those who raised and taught you.

As an adult, you came to what you've called Convention territory, and after your arrival you committed no new violations of the Six Laws. You gathered information for the invasion, but no law forbids gathering information. You had contact with a battle-drone, but only in an attempt to repel it. Thereafter, when the opportunity first presented itself, and at some personal cost, you yourself brought an end to the violations of the Six Laws in which you'd participated.

"The legalists holding this view argue that we cannot condemn you without affirming that the two-year-old and the starship crew of the hypotheticals should also be condemned. Like them, you had no way to understand the meaning of your actions under our laws at the time you did them, and condemning those actions would set a disastrous precedent. So some of us have argued, and the circle likewise finds their arguments compelling."

Jerre tried to say something, but Sharra held up one hand. "We cannot condone your actions, Jerre, and we cannot condemn them. A fine dilemma." She glanced over to the Halka outside the circle. "Or it would be, except for legal work done by Benamin Haller sen Halka. Before the war, as Speaker for the Mirien circle, he drafted a proposal for a new Halka procedure for dealing with our visionaries. Instead of judging them and shooting the ones who appear to be deluded, as we've done, he suggested that Halka judgment circles be permitted to declare such a case undecidable, and leave it until facts either confirm or deny the truth of the vision.

"We've heard compelling reasons today why his proposal should be taken up, and I trust he'll present it as a formal judgment in the near future. But his suggestion has other merits, and this case suggests one. The considered judgment of this circle is that this case is undecidable."

"I'm not sure I understand," Jerre said after a moment. "What does that mean?"

"For you?" Sharra's expression did not change, but judgment mode shaded her voice. "For the rest of your life, Jerre Amadan sen Halka, unless this judgment circle or another rules otherwise, you'll remain as you are now, bound by the laws and traditions of the Halka order but forbidden from taking part in its work except in emergencies. We don't ask that you remain in seclusion or stay at this one Shelter, and we free you from the rule that bars sen Halka from following other professions. You may go where you choose and do as you wish. We request, though, that when you arrive at any Shelter you inform at least one sen Halka of your presence there, and when you leave any shelter you inform at least one sen Halka of your destination."

Silence. After a time, pale and silent, Jerre nodded.

"One thing more." A gesture indicated his green robe. "The circle has noted your decision to set aside Halka garments today. We've considered your reasons, and while some members of the circle sympathize with them, there are serious issues involved. We've agreed that your decision should be its own judgment. You're forbidden from wearing Halka black for the remainder of your life. Of course your gun won't be returned to you."

"I'll ask one thing," Jerre said then. His voice stayed level, but those around him needed no subtle awareness to sense the strain in it. "Give the gun back to Tomas Mord, the gunsmith who made it, and have him give it to another sen Halka. Let it be just one more Halka weapon. I don't want the gun that killed Laura Emmer in a glass case at Zara."

Sharra Macalley considered him for a time. "That seems reasonable," she said. "Thaddas—" A quick glance across the circle. "—you'll see to that? Good."

"My thanks." He stood, his face composed but white as a ghost. "Unless there's something else?" A flicker of inner-speech answered him. He turned without another word and went back through the crowd to the stairs and the Shelter.

Sharra Macalley said something else then, but Amery couldn't make it out. From one side of the samahane to the other, now that the work of the judgment circle was done, stillness shattered into talk and movement. Amery got to her feet, wanting to follow Jerre into the Shelter but aware that he'd welcome no one's company yet. The crowd separating her from the Shelter doors settled the matter for her. She stood where she was instead, barely seeing the bright colors of the spring robes the Shelter folk wore or the clear pale sunlight that chose that moment to find a gap between clouds and flood the samahane. For the first time since messengers came running from the helicopter hangar at Mirien, the bond she'd made with Jerre promised something other than grief, and she let herself taste the reality of it for a long moment. The cold place and its questions still waited, she knew, but it could wait longer.

Benamin Haller's innervoice ended the moment. *That was the hope I mentioned*, he said. *A small hope but not, as it turned out, a forlorn one.*

I wasn't thinking clearly, she replied, embarrassed. *My apologies, Benamin. Jerre and I both owe you a great deal.* He nodded, and went to speak to another legalist.

A moment later Amery heard a familiar voice behind her: Tamar's. "Do you know," she said, "I don't think I've been half as impressed by any other act of the Halka."

She and Stefan both turned. "How so?" he asked Tamar.

"The Halka have finally admitted their own humanity," said the sen Halvedna. "In its own way, that takes just as much courage as facing drones."

That earned her a sharp look from Stefan, but Tamar met it squarely, and after a moment Stefan's gaze dropped. He said nothing but nodded, conceding the point.

Amery glanced from one to the other, and then the implications opened before her with blinding force. She stared at Tamar for a long moment, then suddenly turned away, looking for Benamin Haller in the crowd, sure at last that she had something at last to say to the cold place and its challenge.

10

Most of the tall windows around the courtyard still had boards over them. It would be months, they said, before enough glass reached Talin to make up for windows destroyed by the drones, and years before the war's traces could be wholly erased from the north country. At the center of the courtyard, though, the tree from Earth still raised its straggling limbs up into wind and sunlight. Two branches had been shattered by gunfire and the rough bark showed marks of flame here and there, but new green needles sprouted in tufts along the branches that remained. Amery looked at it for a long moment before she noticed the figure in a green robe sitting near it, motionless except for the hand that sent a pen dancing across one page of a notebook.

She came down the stairs from the roof terrace, Halka boots noiseless on the concrete, until she stood just behind him. He did not seem to notice. "*Shona*?" she asked then.

Jerre glanced up and saw her. "No." With an uncertain smile: "Not for you."

She sat on the bench next to him, looked at his drawing. Ink on paper turned the tree into a jagged shape like a reaching hand, frail but unyielding, straining toward sunlight past the dark masses of surrounding walls. A brittle energy moved through it unlike anything she remembered from his earlier work. She considered innerspeech, but subtle awareness brought her echoes of tangled emotions, a terrible ambivalence. Spoken language seemed less intrusive. "That's extraordinary, Jerre," she said aloud. Catching herself: "Or should I—"

"No." Whisper of unsteadiness in his voice told her the source of the ambivalence. "Jerome Emmer died at the foraging camp. That's the decision I finally reached. I'll carry the Emmer heritage until I die, but I'll do it as Jerre Amadan."

He added more lines, taut and elegant: the concrete bench, the stairs to the roof terrace. Amery watched him. Guessing: "You must have spent the winter drawing."

"Most of it." He finished the drawing with two wandering lines across the top of the page, spring clouds reduced to absolute simplicity. "On the way out of New Shalsha I went past my quarters and got some pens and notebooks. At the time I thought I was being a fool. If the reactor had gone supercritical ten minutes earlier than it did I would have been blown to bits. But—" A shrug. "It gave me something to do besides think. Lacking it, I might have walked out into a snowstorm just to silence my thoughts."

She looked at him, said nothing.

"For what it's worth," he told her then, "I'm sorry for hiding in my room for so long. I needed the solitude, but it can't have been easy for you. I kept wondering if you would come knock on the door."

"Did you want me to?"

"No." He slumped, face in hands. "Bright Earth, no. I needed find some way to deal with the judgment before I could face you, or anyone."

"You wanted to die so badly?" she asked.

His gaze snapped up to her, then fell away. "If the judgment circle had given me back my gun I'd have used it on myself. Between the foraging camp and New Shalsha I have more blood on my hands than anything will wash clean."

"And the lives you saved," said Amery. "What of those?"

"I try to remind myself of that."

"Stefan's is one of them, you know. During the battle he got past the drones somehow, and put himself where his vision said the drone with the atomic weapon would pass by.

He won't talk about it, but I'm pretty sure he hid himself in the snow and planned to shoot up into the lifter elements. He'd have died like the sen davannat."

Jerre considered that.

"And of course mine is another. We both know where the atomic weapon would have gone once Laura Emmer was sure the Halka response was based at Mirien."

"I know. If you'd died—" His voice broke. Innerspeech flickered between them as Amery risked a pulse of wordless comfort. He looked up finally, said, "This morning, when I came out, an old woman I knew slightly from last winter came up to me and thanked me for her life. I had no idea what to say to her. Should have I apologized because I spent years of my life endangering hers? I just don't know." Then, bursting out: "I belong to the Halka order and I don't. I belong to Bredin Shelter and I don't. I belong to Shalsha—" A gesture jabbed out, fell back defeated. "—and I don't. And I've been wondering for the last three days whether there's a place for me anywhere on Eridan." He stared at the concrete past his feet.

Amery watched him. He won't accept consolation, she thought, if he thinks the words are meant to console. She smiled inwardly, and thought: we're alike in that, perhaps. "Jerre, you need to know what's happened since you left Mirien, especially in the last three days. Allan Berelat said the world wouldn't be the same after the war. Of course he was right."

"The strategist?"

"Yes." She pieced her thoughts together. "You know that the circle's judgment three days ago was unprecedented. I don't think you know why it happened; I didn't know myself until I sat Benamin Haller down and had him explain it yesterday evening.

"The Halka order has had to face some very unpalatable facts. For two centuries we thought we could guarantee peace on Eridan, and when the test came we failed. Without Shelter folk and sen davannat we would have been overwhelmed. Without Stefan's vision and a few of us who were willing to listen to him, we'd have been taken totally by surprise.

"Worst of all, it turned out that we had plenty of warning if we'd only listened to it. The legalists have found seventeen cases of Halka visionaries who announced they'd found Bredin Shelter, and every one of them was shot by a judgment circle. All of that's been bitter medicine, especially the last. You're not the only one who's unsure of a place."

He looked up at her. "That could be dangerous."

"But it's desperately needed," Amery replied at once. "The Halka tried to be perfect, and we pursued that so far that it blinded us to our own fallibility. Now we've had to balance the perfection we tried to achieve against the reality that human affairs will always be messy and imperfect. I think of the first maxim we both learned in training, *tessat-ni-Halka shol ielindat*, and then I think of something Tamar said after the judgment circle finished. Maybe we need a second maxim, something like *kalat-ni-Halka beyel al'immanat*—the test of the Halka is the recognition of our own humanity."

She drew in a breath. "That's why I've decided to take up law. Allan said I ought to find a new specialty, and as usual he was right. I want to help reshape our law code into something more human. I want to find ways that we can act with clarity and compassion at the same time. Benamin Haller's agreed to teach me, and after everything's settled here we'll be going to Zara to begin my apprenticeship." Tentatively: "I hope you'll be willing to come south with me."

"To Zara." He looked away. She could sense his emotions, thinking of himself at Zara, among the relics of the Convention, the wellspring of everything he'd almost destroyed and then saved. "Anywhere else I'd say yes at once; if I have a place anywhere on this world it's where you are. But Zara—Amery, I'll have to think about that."

Flicker of innerspeech: *I understand.* She wanted to continue in the same way, but the moment hadn't arrived yet, she could feel that. Aloud: "But there's something else you need to know. I went to the radio room here yesterday." A sudden smile. "Pure habit. I spent so much time in Mirien's that I hardly know what to do without a loudspeaker hissing at me. But I read the message log and listened to radio traffic, and learned something I didn't know. It won't surprise you that what you told the circle has gone all over Eridan. It might surprise you what's been talked about the most." To the silent question in his eyes: "What you said about bringing Earth back to life."

"That does surprise me," said Jerre.

"You need to understand what the war meant to the Shelter folk, Jerre. For two hundred years drones have been their worst nightmare and the Halka have been their security—but when the Halka couldn't stand alone, the Shelter folk stood with them and faced the nightmare down. Tens of thousands of them fought massed drones and came through it alive. They're proud of what they did, and they know the old nightmare is gone forever. So what challenged us to the core gave them a confidence that won't be shaken any time soon. Do you remember a man named Dafed Serrema?"

"Dafed?" Jerre blinked. "Yes. If he's still alive, he's a technician who lives near here." A sudden smile. "We spent weeks rebuilding helicopter engines last winter."

"He's alive. He heard that I knew you, and came looking for me after the judgment circle finished. He wanted to ask whether I thought the Halka would object if he started working on chemical rocket engines."

He took that in. "What did you say?"

"That I'd ask Sharra Macalley for a formal opinion that evening. I did, too. She said that a rocket falls into the same category as a helicopter; as long as it doesn't carry guns or explosive charges it's not in violation of the Fourth Law. But she also told me she'd been asked the same question by six other people that day, including two members of Talin Shelter's council. Since then ..." A gesture out, away. "It's all over the radio net."

"Dafed might be able to do it," Jerre said then. He stared past her, at nothing. "He knows more about pumps and hydraulics than anyone else I've ever met, and that ought to help him with liquid-fueled rockets. But Talin's too far north to be a good launch site."

Amery gave him a startled look. "Jerre, how much do you know about rockets?"

"Quite a lot." Meeting her gaze: "Everyone at New Shalsha had multiple specialties. Mine were systems ecology, astronautical engineering, and interstellar navigation. They—" He stopped, looked away, went on after a moment in a quiet voice. "They trained me to be mission commander for *Journey Star* on the voyage back to Earth."

And you gave that up, she said in innerspeech, shaken. *Jerre—*
Emotions flared, brittle and harsh: *There wasn't another choice.*

But now there is. Aloud: "There's already a long line of people who want to talk to you. Tamar, of course, and Stefan. Halvedna masters—I think they've finished working with Stefan for the moment. His vision's gone now but they've learned quite a bit from him."

That startled him. "What about the barrier between the orders?"

"They think his vision happened because he tasted dwimmerroot before he took baya, so it's relevant to both orders. You taught us three days ago that the Halka need to know much more about visions, so certain old rules have bent where they haven't broken completely.

"But the Halvedna want to know all about the Bredin Shelter mind training, if you're willing to talk about that. Beyond them, Dafed Serrema wants to talk about rockets, and other people want to talk to you about what a mission to Earth would have to carry. Once people find out what you know, they'll be the first of many."

"And the Halka will allow that?"

"The Halka," said Amery, "have every reason to want Shelter folk distracted from weapons and war; Sharra told me as much. All this confidence and energy could mean disaster for everyone if it turns the wrong way—to quarrels between Shelter folk and the Halka, for example. Sharra said she's willing to give a space program her personal support and legal advice for that reason alone, if no other. And—Jerre, the Halka aren't immune to the hope of reviving Earth. Not at all, so long as the process doesn't violate the laws we're pledged to guard."

He was looking past her: at nothing, Amery thought at first, until subtle awareness caught a flicker of movement. She followed his gaze, spotted the jewelfly hovering near the tree from Earth, bright in a stray beam of sunlight.

Spoken language seemed intolerably blunt then. *Jerre*, she said in innerspeech, *you said if there's a place for you it's where I am. If there's a place for me, it's where you are; you know that. But you also said that Talin wasn't a good place for rockets. What would be a good place?*

Somewhere in the far south. His gaze did not leave the jewelfly. *The closer you are to the equator when you launch, the more of a boost you get from planetary rotation and the less fuel it takes to reach orbit. We planned to build a launch site south of the Morne delta, maybe even on Dal Island.*

Zara's not far from there, she reminded him.

The jewelfly lit on a branch, crouched there sparkling. Jerre turned toward her. She could see every detail of his emotions now, spread out before her in subtle awareness: guilt and grief and a terrible sense of failure, all the burdens of his past pressing down on him: then a first fragile stirring of hope beneath it, and all at once an image she didn't recognize at first, fluttering against hard limitations, possibilities opening along an unexpected path.

"Will you come?" she said simply.

He folded his wings and fell.

GLOSSARY

Affirmation, the: fundamental Halvedna statement of principles

Andarre: region in the southern foothills of the northern continent's one mountain range, famous for its hermits and mystics

Annan River: principal river of the north country and the Kaya Hills region

Annum Tal: site of a Directorate factory camp

banned-tech manual: Halka book describing surviving Directorate machines

battle-drone: computer-guided armored fighting vehicle of the Directorate

baya: first drinking of dwimmerwine by a Halka candidate, the initiation into the Halka order

Book of Circles: work of mystical philosophy partly written and partly compiled by Loren Frederic in the first decades of the Eridan colony; contains forty-eight glyphs expressing basic categories of human thought, which form the Sequence deck

Bredin Shelter: in hill country legend, a Shelter inhabited by survivors of the Directorate

catamnetic: drug used to suppress or erase memories

chemical catamnesis: Halvedna therapy using catamnetics to treat mental illnesses

combat discipline: Halka traditions governing action in a combat environment

combat mode: Halka mental discipline used to focus subtle awareness toward information relevant to survival in combat

command circle: Halka structure for planning and conducting combat operations

Convention of Zara: agreement establishing the Six Laws and setting out the responsibilities and limitations of the Halka and Halvedna orders, signed at Zara in 87

daula: sporophyte forest tree found on both of Eridan's continents, growing up to 200 meters tall

Directorate: see Planetary Directorate

drone: see battle-drone

drone spear: iron-tipped spear used to destroy battle-drones by fusing their lifter field lattices, a suicide weapon

drone trap: a mechanical device using a lifter field detector and a powerful spring to drive an iron spike into a battle-drone's lifter field lattices

dwimmerroot: rhizome of a shrub found on Eridan's northern continent, with powerful psychoactive effects on human beings; dwimmerroot intoxication weakens barriers between the conscious and unconscious minds

dwimmerwine: distilled preparation made from dwimmerroot; dwimmerwine intoxication erases barriers between conscious and unconscious minds with sometimes fatal results

Emmer, Carl: 26-84, agronomist and politician; Director of Settlement 63-72, Assistant Planetary Director 72-78, and Planetary Director 78-84; killed at the fall of Shalsha

Eridan: common name of the colony world Epsilon Eridani II

factory camps: slave labor camps established by the Directorate, in which some 4.5 million people died from malnutrition, disease, and overwork fireflower: a windflower that flourishes in soil tainted by atomic fallout

Frederic, Loren: –34-53, chief botanist in the Department of Settlement 21-38, discoverer of the dwimmerroot and author-compiler of the Book of Circles

Gathering: combined trade fair and social event held annually during the summer months; Eridan has dozens of small Gatherings but three primary ones, at Werelin near Wind Gap, Halleth in the central Morne valley, and Amris by the Morne delta

Halka: warrior mystic order derived from guerrilla soldiers of the Insurgency, charged with preserving the Six Laws by force

hallow room: Shelter space for meditation and ceremony, usually decorated with glyphs from the Book of Circles

Halvedna: pacifist mystic order derived from the hermits of the Andarre region in Insurgency times, committed to improvement of Eridan society but forbidden to use coercion or violence in any form

hill country: Eridan idiom for the Kaya Hills region north of the Morne valley

informed person: in Halka legal terminology, a person with direct knowledge of a violation of one of the Six Laws

induction probe: Halvedna neuroelectrical device that stimulates activity in specific portions of the brain; used for neurological and psychological testing

innermind: common Eridan idiom for the unconscious mind, understood as a mental continuum uniting individuals

innerspeech: Halka method of communication through subtle awareness

Insurgency: twenty-year guerrilla war that brought down the Directorate

jewelfly: native Eridan flying decapod, resembling Earth dragonflies

Journey Star: the colony starship that brought human beings to Eridan, still in equatorial orbit

judgment circle: Halka structure for assessing violations of the Six Laws or Halka tradition

judgment mode: Halka mental discipline used to direct subtle awareness toward information relevant to legal matters

Keltessat: site of a Directorate factory camp

Kendeval symbols: Halvedna eidetic language, derived from the Book of Circles, used for analysis of mental processes

Kregeth, Tamsen: 112-198, sen Halvedna and historian, author of the most widely read history of the Insurgency

kyrenna: nine-stringed electric instrument used to play sama music

lifter fields: levitation device used by battle-drones and other Directorate equipment, an offshoot of reactionless drives developed for starflight; lifter fields will not support weight when over an electrically conductive surface and fuse catastrophically if the field lattices are penetrated by an electrically conductive object

Mariel, Judith: 28-84, Directorate official until her resignation in 71, and leader of the Insurgency from 73 until her death at Shalsha in 84; claimed as founder by both the Halka and Halvedna orders

meadowmoss: lichenoid ground cover found throughout Eridan's land surface

meria: sporophyte forest tree on Eridan's northern continent, found mostly in the northern regions; its outer bark is a source of fiber and paper and a widely traded commodity

Morne River: principal watercourse on Eridan's northern continent; its broad valley forms the core of the human settlement

north country: Eridan idiom for the country north of the Morne's headwaters and the Kaya Hills

Orange Sky: Halka emergency code declaring a potential threat on a regional scale

Orange Sun: Halka emergency code declaring an existing threat on a regional scale outrunners: bands of nomadic brigands living on the edges of settled territory and obtaining protein through cannibalism

polyphase vision: a visionary state in which the visionary can see multiple futures radiating from specific choices, and choose actions based on their future consequences

Planetary Directorate: totalitarian government of Eridan's human colony, established in a coup in 16 and destroyed by nuclear attack in 84 after two decades of guerrilla war

primary case: in Halka legal terminology, a case involving violation of one of the Six Laws

primary scanning: Halvedna equivalent of subtle awareness

protective circle: ring of bare metal surrounding a Shelter to keep drones at bay

reactive withdrawal: Halvedna psychological diagnosis, roughly equivalent to acute catatonic schizophrenia

Red Sky: Halka emergency code declaring a potential threat on a planetary scale

Red Sun: Halka emergency code declaring an existing threat on a planetary scale

sama: ecstatic dance popular among Shelter folk

sama music: music designed to simulate the effects of mild doses of dwimmerroot

samahane: outdoor space set aside for sama

sea-scuttler: native Eridan seashore decapod, slightly resembling Earth crabs

Sequence deck: divinatory tool used by Halvedna and others, based on the Book of Circles

shaddat baya: formal request for Halka training by a potential candidate

Shalsha: capitol of the Planetary Directorate beginning in 28, destroyed and abandoned after atomic attack in 84

Sharru: site of a Directorate factory camp

Shelter: standard Eridan community form, concrete structure housing 5000 to 8000 people, generating electrical power with wind turbines and growing food in hydroponic vats

Shelter council: coordinating body for Shelter governance

Shelter folk: Halka idiom for members of the general population of Eridan

Shelter work: labor expected of each person living at a Shelter toward community needs

shona: "alone," but often used for "alone by intention" and "busy, occupied"

subtle awareness: Halka idiom for extended powers of perception made possible by the long term effects of dwimmer-wine use

technician: semi-hereditary class of technologically skilled people, the object of old prejudices among Shelter folk

tessat-ni-Halka shol ielindat: "the way of the Halka is clarity of awareness," one of the fundamental Halka maxims

ten ielindat: "posture of awareness," Halka seated meditation position

ten sedayat: "posture of contemplation," Halka seated meditation position

thilda: sporophyte forest tree common on Eridan's northern continent

Thomason, Marc: 39-83, Directorate military commander, killed at the fall of Werelin

Tol Edri: site of a Directorate factory camp

trade network: cooperative organization handling trade between regions

Werelin: city founded in 46 and depopulated after its capture by Insurgency forces in 83; from 107 on, the site of a regional Gathering

Wind Gap: principal pass through the mountain range on Eridan's northern continent, located just north of the headwaters of the Morne and south of the north country

Winternight: celebration of the winter solstice, a holiday on Eridan

windflowers: primitive wind-pollinated vascular plants of Eridan

Yellow Sky: Halka emergency code declaring a potential threat on a local scale

Yellow Sun: Halka emergency code declaring an existing threat on a local scale

Zara: Shelter and former city in the southern Morne valley, site of the Convention of Zara 84-87 and center of historical, legal, and scholarly activities on Eridan

Printed in the USA
CPSIA information can be obtained
at www.ICGtesting.com
JSHW031040231024
72178JS00007BA/62

9 781915 952165